ALSO BY JUDITH A. BARRETT

MAGGIE SLOAN THRILLER/MYSTERY SERIES

RILEY MALLOY MYSTERY SERIES

GRID DOWN SURVIVAL SERIES

DONUT LADY MYSTERY SERIES

DANGER IN THE FIELD

Grid Down Survival Series

Book 4

Judith A. Barrett

DANGER IN THE FIELD

GRID DOWN SURVIVAL SERIES, BOOK 4

Published in the United States of America by Wobbly Creek, LLC

2021 Georgia

wobblycreek.com

DANGER IN THE FIELD is a work of fiction. Names, characters, businesses, places, events, locales, and incidents either are the products of the author's imagination or used in a fictitious manner. Any resemblance to actual persons, living or dead, or actual events is purely coincidental.

Edited by Judith Euen Davis

Cover by Wobbly Creek, LLC

ISBN 978-1-953-87009-4

DEDICATION

DANGER IN THE FIELD is dedicated to the dark color that others see as black, navy blue, and other puzzling colors; and to all the kind souls who accept imperfection.

PREVIOUSLY. . .

Aimee Louise would tell you all this herself, but she's not much for talking except for technical stuff. We understand each other, so I help her out by talking about everything else. I'm Rosalie, but they call me Red because of my red hair, and they call Aimee Louise Angel because she's saved the life of more than one person. I'm eighteen, and Aimee Louise is nineteen. She's my best friend and sister; her grandfather, Pops, adopted me after Mom then Dad died.

The power grid went down a while ago; I was visiting Aimee Louise the first time it went down, and I'm glad that Pops wanted me to stay with them. The power is down now pretty much permanently, and the world has changed.

They say Aimee Louise is autistic. I don't know about that, but I know she doesn't see people's faces; instead she sees their clouds that tell her whether the person is happy, sad, angry, or dangerous. Deputy Stuart likes her a lot, and I know she likes him too, but she's not all that great at the social stuff like me. I have to coach her sometimes.

It's a long story, but the short version is that we picked up the team that was ambushed on the road after they left Pops' farm for the Newtons', Stuart's parents' farm. We had rescued the team's children earlier when we were on our way to help the Newtons and took the children along with us. We still don't know what happened to Henry's parents, though. Aimee Louise has taken him under her wing, and he calls her Mama Angel. He's so sweet, and smart too.

The best part about the Newtons' farm as far as I'm concerned is their nearest neighbors are the Websters. Their nephew, Andy Webster, is really cute, and he thinks I'm talented. Andy is a teacher and super smart. I already said he's cute, didn't I?

STUART

I'm breaking in with the real short version. After Aimee Louise figured out who was abducting children, we busted up the trafficking rings and permanently stopped the leaders. We stayed with my mom and dad on their farm, so we could help pull together the nearby farm families to set up roadblocks; Aimee Louise and I believe the attacks from other gangs will only escalate. What would you add, Aimee Louise?

AIMEE LOUISE

Time to get busy.

CHAPTER ONE

Stuart carried his boots as he crept down the stairs in the dark at his parents' farmhouse, so he wouldn't wake anyone. When he reached the first floor, he wasn't surprised to see the dim, flickering light of a candle coming from the kitchen.

"Good morning, care for a cup?" His mother, Sandra, smiled as she pointed to the cup on the kitchen table, and the three four-month-old puppies scrambled to greet him.

Stuart chuckled as he bent to scratch the collie and lab mix puppies before he picked up his cup and inhaled the welcoming aroma of hot coffee. "How did you know I was up? I thought I was quiet when I came down the stairs."

"You were," Aimee Louise said, and the puppies scrambled to her. "I heard you before you came down."

"I didn't see you in the shadows," Stuart said before he turned to peer at his dark-haired, favorite companion.

"I know." She opened the back door, and the puppies trooped outside behind her.

"We had another good night. Tracker, Brody, and Pixie were dry in their crates when I let them out this morning," Sandra said. "I was worried about three puppies at first, but Andy was right: Holly trained her babies to be house dogs."

"We were lucky the family who owned the puppies' father wanted one of them, or we'd have four, wouldn't we?" Stuart chuckled.

While Sandra fried eggs and checked on her biscuits in the oven, Aimee Louise and the puppies returned, and Scott hurried into the kitchen. "Your biscuits woke me up, Sandra."

She snorted. "You say that every morning."

After Stuart poured a cup of coffee for his dad, Scott sat at the table and sipped his coffee. "What's your plan for today, Stuart?"

"Breakfast is ready." Sandra handed plates to Aimee Louise and Stuart then carried Scott's and her own to the table.

After Stuart mopped up every trace of the dark orange egg yolk with his biscuit, he drained his cup. "We'll go to the Websters', so Aimee Louise can check the news on the ham radio then after we get back, Nate and I plan to see Mr. Mitchell to talk to him about his son's property."

"Rosalie and I will go too," Aimee Louise said.

"Of course, the Mitchell twins would be disappointed if Red didn't come to see them," Stuart said.

"You taking the truck?" Sandra asked.

While Aimee Louise refilled coffee cups, Stuart said, "No, we'll save gas and walk."

"Run." Aimee Louise cleared the plates on the table then slipped on her lightweight jacket before she threw on her backpack that held a change of clothes, a knife, a compass, and matches.

"Right." Stuart sighed as he picked up his backpack and rifle, and Scott chuckled.

"I'll be surprised if Andy doesn't go to the Mitchells' too," Sandra said before Stuart and Aimee Louise headed out the door.

When Stuart and Aimee Louise started their run to the Websters', the air temperature had dropped in the predawn. After they were in the woods, the sky lightened as the sun cleared the horizon, and Aimee Louise picked up the pace until they reached the clearing at the Smith barn that was on the property between the Newtons' and the Websters'. Aimee Louise removed her jacket and slowed the pace as they strolled past the barn.

"Dad told me he'd like for the barn to be his first project at the Smith place," Stuart said. "Even though Mr. Smith signed the deed over to him, Dad said if his old friend ever wanted his homestead back, he'd be more than willing to turn it over to him."

After they passed the burned remains of the house, Stuart said, "Thanks for the break, Aimee Louise. I'm ready to head out."

When Aimee Louise broke into a run, Stuart kept up the pace with her until they reached the Websters' farm. Stuart was breathing hard as they jogged down the Websters' driveway. When they turned the corner to the house, the Websters' collie, Holly, lay on the grass in the shade near the driveway; she lifted her head and grinned, and Leo's three farm dogs wagged their greeting before they flopped down in the shade of the barn.

"According to the dogs, we can expect a hot day today." Stuart paused to catch his breath, and Aimee Louise waited with him.

"Sun's getting higher." He shaded his eyes with his arm ash he scanned at the sky. "Okay, got my breath," he said, and they strolled toward the farmhouse with Holly trotting along behind them. "I keep thinking I can run as fast as you and Red, but I can't quite keep up. I blame Mom's cooking."

Red waited for them at the side door. "You better not say that in front of Mama Sandra if you value your next meal, Deputy Stuart Newton."

Stuart laughed. "You're right there. What's going on?"

"Uncle Leo is waiting for Angel in the computer room, and Andy wants to talk to you. He's down at the barn."

When Stuart and Holly reached the barn, Andy was stacking scraps of lumber in the corner. Andy's tattered Atlanta Braves ball cap and T-shirt were damp with sweat from exertion and the early morning humidity. He stopped stacking and sat on an old hay bale then grinned at Stuart. "Glad you're here; I was ready for a break. Rosalie send you?"

Stuart sat on another bale. "Yep, and I'm glad for a break too after the run here with Aimee Louise."

Andy nodded. "I don't even try to keep up with Red. So, one of Aunt Jennie's old friends stopped by last night. His home has been attacked three times, and the last time, they broke in and took all his guns that weren't locked in his gun safe. They beat him to try to force the man to open the safe until his wife shot one of them with her shotgun. She had birdshot in it, but I guess it was enough to chase them off. It's just him and his wife, so he decided to leave. They're going to Tennessee to live with their son and his family and offered their chickens and livestock to Aunt Jennie. They have twenty or so hens, a rooster, and two cows. One of the cows will be calving in the next couple of weeks. They're planning on taking four or five chickens with them, but that's all they can manage. Aunt Jennie wants some of the chickens but not the cows. We thought you could talk to your folks to see if they are interested in some chickens and maybe the cows. Be sure to let them know there's no pressure. He told Aunt Jennie he was giving us the first option before he offered them to his neighbors."

"I don't know anything about cows, but I'll ask Mom and Dad. How far away are they? Do the cows come with a trailer or something to haul them?"

Andy chuckled. "He lives five or six miles away and offered his horse trailer. He also offered any of his farm equipment that we could use."

"I'll talk to Dad. I hope he says no, but I'm afraid Mom will be interested in having milk with all the kids at our house."

When Stuart rose to leave, Andy said, "There's something else. Aunt Jennie and I would like for Red to stay when you and Angel leave for Florida. Aunt Jennie's suddenly become very security conscious. She quoted Red's rule that it isn't safe for anyone to be solo away from the house, but she's not comfortable leaving Uncle Leo alone. I'm selfish. I'd like for Red and me to stay together, and when I talked to Red, she told me the solution was simple because I'd go with you all to Florida. I can't leave Aunt Jennie and Uncle Leo alone, so Red and I are at an impasse. I think she might talk to Angel; I just hope the two of them don't gang up on me because I would lose."

Stuart snorted. "You're right about that. I'm worried about my folks too. Nate and his family are moving to the Mitchell house. It makes sense for everyone because they'll be more comfortable in their own home, and it frees up two bedrooms at our house. After David is here, I don't know what he and Peyton will do, but they may decide to leave or to move in with Nate and Charo. If I go to Florida, Mom and Dad would be alone, or Peyton might feel obligated to stay with them."

"No easy answers, are there?" Andy exhaled.

"Not that I can see. I'll talk to Aimee Louise and my dad."

Andy motioned toward his stack of wood. "I'm going to get started on Aunt Jennie's chicken coop. She hasn't decided yet where she wants it, but she told me she'd be out here soon, and we could pick a spot together."

When Stuart reached the barn doorway to go to the house, Jennie was hurrying to the barn. "Oh good. You're here too, Stuart. Do you have any ideas on where a chicken coop should go?"

"The chicken coop at Major's farm in Florida is fairly close to the house, which makes sense from a security standpoint. The coop is in the sun in the mornings but shaded in the afternoons."

"Let's take a walk around the house," Jennie said.

As they approached the house, Jennie said, "I think I'd like to be able to look out of my kitchen window and see the coop."

Andy nodded. "You wouldn't have to run outside to check the chickens. Makes sense. There aren't any trees close enough for shade, but we could add something before summer."

As he spoke, Rosalie joined them. "Angel and Leo are still on the radio. Leo sent me out to tell you that we have a bad storm headed this way. It'll probably hit around seven or eight this evening."

"Guess I won't start the coop today, after all," Andy said.

"Would it help if I worked with you?" Stuart asked.

"We could finish it in time, but I'd rather it had a chance to settle before a big wind hits it. I need to move the rest of my lumber into the barn."

"I'll help with that," Stuart said.

While they worked, Aimee Louise came into the barn.

"Are we going to be much longer?" Rosalie asked.

"Might take a little longer." Stuart wiped his damp forehead with his shirt sleeve.

Rosalie nodded. "Angel and I will run to tell Mr. Scott about the storm. We won't be long."

"Bye," Angel said as they sped away.

Andy stared at them. "I thought I ran fast with Red, but this is the first time I've seen the two of them run together at full speed."

Stuart nodded. "It's really sobering, isn't it? Anytime I think I'm hot stuff, I think about those two running and settle right back down to earth."

Andy snorted.

* * *

When Aimee Louise and Rosalie reached the Smith barn, Rosalie slowed their pace. "Andy wants me to stay here with him, and I'd like to, but I'm not sure I'd want to be here without you. I told Andy he should go with us to Florida, but he told me that he can't leave his aunt and uncle alone."

"Stuart's worried about leaving his dad and mom too."

"So, what do we do?"

"You stay with Andy. We will always be sisters. Stuart will talk to his dad."

They raced to the Newtons' homestead. When they bounded into the kitchen, Sandra said, "You two are sweaty. Did you run full speed the whole way? Where's Stuart?"

Rosalie giggled while Aimee Louise filled two glasses with water. "We raced. It's been a while since we've run together as fast as we can."

Scott and Nate came inside for water before Aimee Louise and Rosalie sat at the table. After Rosalie took a big gulp, she continued, "There's a big storm coming. It will be here around seven or eight."

"A big storm?" Nate asked. "We'll finish loading what we've packed so far then I'll take it to the Mitchell house and unload it."

"Need help at the other end?" Scott asked.

"Where's Stuart?" Sandra asked.

"He stayed to help Andy carry lumber to the barn," Rosalie said. "Maybe I should go back, so Stuart can come here to help."

"Yes, then Stuart and I can go with Nate," Aimee Louise said.

After the two young women drained their glasses then sped to the path back to the Websters' farm, Stuart returned to the Newton farm with Aimee Louise.

* * *

"You two are back sooner than we expected," Sandra said. "Nate carried the last box to Dad's truck and is checking the straps. He may be ready to go now. Dad, Peyton, the judge, and the kids are policing the yard to pick up any stray tools."

"Does Dad have anything for us, or do we help Nate unload?" Stuart asked.

"Help Nate. Peyton and the judge want to stay with Brandon and Dolly."

"Henry?" Aimee Louise asked.

"Henry plans to go with you, but I told him Brody is too little," Sandra said. "Nate told me Henry's waiting in the truck."

"Are you driving, Angel?" Henry was sitting on the backseat when they reached the truck.

"Good idea, Henry," Stuart said. "Jump up front, and you can sit next to her."

Henry rolled over the back of the seat and landed in the middle of the front seat. "Thank you, Deputy Stuart."

Stuart climbed into the passenger's seat. When Aimee Louise slid into the driver's seat, Henry leaned against her and smiled. "Are we going to Florida today?"

"No, we might not be going to Florida for a while. We need to make sure everyone here is safe before we leave."

"We always make sure everyone is safe," Henry said.

Stuart smiled. "Yes, we do." *Henry's amazing.*

Nate climbed into the seat behind Aimee Louise. "Everything's secure."

When they reached the open driveway gate near the house, Aimee Louise slowed then stopped the truck, and Henry slid into a crouch on the floorboard.

Stuart frowned as he whispered, "What's wrong?"

"Somebody's in the bushes," Henry said, and Aimee Louise nodded.

Stuart nodded. "I'm getting out. Cover me, Nate."

Nate slid over to the passenger's side, and when Stuart opened his door, he opened his back door and put one foot on the ground.

When Stuart stepped away from his door, a small voice whispered, "Is Red with you?"

"Sam?" Stuart asked.

The twins rushed out of the bushes. Their faces were stained with dirt and mud-streaked with tears as they wrapped their arms around Stuart's legs.

"Deputy Stuart, bad men hurt Grandma. She told us to run away and hide until Red came to get us," one of the sobbing girls said. "We were scared. I cried, but Sam said, 'No noise.'"

"Cami Sue's not a crybaby, but she forgot to hush; I cried too, but I kept my hand over my mouth, so I'd be quiet," Sam said.

Stuart bit his lip as he held onto the girls. *I hate that the girls had to go through this.*

"You're safe now."

After Aimee Louise jumped out of the truck, Sam released her hold on Stuart's pants leg and rushed to Aimee Louise.

"Go with Angel to the truck," Stuart said. "Where is your grandma?"

"She's at her house," Cami Sue said as she hurried to join her sister.

"I know the shortcut through the brush," Nate said.

"Let's take the truck instead," Stuart said. "I want us all to stay together."

As Aimee Louise drove back to the road to go to the Mitchells' house, Henry covered his ears while the girls chattered from the backseat with Nate.

Stuart leaned over and whispered to Henry, "Smart move. When the two of them talk at the same time like they are, I can't understand what they're saying."

When Aimee Louise cautiously eased down the dirt driveway, Nate asked, "Where is your grandma?"

"She was on the floor in the kitchen when we left," Sam said.

"Girls, sit on the truck floor and be very quiet. Stay very still when we get out of the truck," Stuart said. Henry slid down to his position on the floor at Stuart's feet.

After the girls settled, Stuart and Nate lowered their windows. When they reached the house, the front door was open, but there was no one in sight.

"Aimee Louise? Anything?" Stuart whispered.

"No. It's quiet, and I don't see any signs of anyone."

"Nate, I'll slip around back. Take cover in front. I'll return the same way from around the house. Ready?" When Nate nodded, Stuart eased his door open, and Aimee Louise ducked.

As Stuart stepped quietly toward the back of the house, he glanced inside the bedroom windows as he passed them. *Blinds and curtains are torn down. Looks ransacked.*

When Stuart reached the back door, he eased it open. A man lay face down near the doorway with a single gunshot wound in his back.

"Mrs. Mitchell?" Stuart asked in a hushed voice.

"Here."

Stuart stooped to check the man. *Dead.* He stepped over him then strode to the other side of the kitchen island, and Mrs. Mitchell raised on one elbow. Her face was swollen, and one eye was shut. Her glasses were on the floor several feet from her, and a rifle lay on the floor next to her.

"Is that you, Nate?" she asked. "Do you see my glasses?"

"No, it's Stuart Newton. We have the girls; they're safe." Stuart picked up her glasses and held them out. "Here are your glasses."

After she put them on, Stuart helped her as she sat up then leaned against the cabinet. "Is anyone else in the house?"

"As far as I know, they're all gone except for the guy that I shot. I'm quite certain he's dead."

"Will you be okay by yourself for a few minutes?"

After Mrs. Mitchell nodded, Stuart swept from room to room to clear the house. He returned to the kitchen then stepped over the dead man as he left.

"Be back soon."

When he neared the corner, he called out, "Nate, it's Stuart. House is clear."

"Okay," Nate said. "Coming your way."

When Nate joined him, Stuart caught him up on what he found. "Tell Angel then meet me in the kitchen."

Stuart returned to Mrs. Mitchell and knelt next to her. "Can you tell me what happened?"

She sighed. "It was a nightmare. Tom heard one of his friends who has a farm within an hour or so walking distance of us was having trouble with his cattle escaping and needed help repairing fences. He left before dawn yesterday and told me he'd be gone no more than two or three days. Four men showed up in a truck early this morning, and I thought maybe Tom had gotten a ride home. Dumb mistake on my part. When I opened the door, the man pushed past me and knocked me down, and I yelled for Cami Sue and Sam to run and hide. They have what we call a hideout that Tom put together for them after you found them. A second man came into the house and wanted to know where my husband was. When I told him I didn't know, he ordered another man to beat it out of me. The man pushed me around and knocked me into the dining table. After he hit me in the face a second time, I dropped and feigned unconsciousness. I hoped he'd leave me, and he did."

When she swallowed hard, Stuart asked, "Would you like a drink of water?"

She nodded, and Stuart found a glass in a cabinet and poured water from a pitcher that was on the counter.

She took a long drink. "I was dry. Thank you. While they tore up the house, I managed to crawl to the kitchen where I keep my deer rifle in a hidden drawer that Tom built for me. I stayed next to the island because I hoped to be less obvious. When one man shouted he was going after the girls, I crawled to the corner of the island and shot him before he reached the back door. I don't know why, but the rest of the men ran to their truck and sped away."

"They must have thought reinforcements had shown up," Stuart said as Nate came into the kitchen from the front door and emitted a long, low whistle.

"After Mrs. Mitchell shot the intruder who was going to look for the girls, the rest of the gang took off," Stuart said.

"From the looks of the house, they were looking for money and liquor. Maybe they left before they got to the kitchen because I would have expected them to have taken any food they could have found," Nate said.

"Do you think you can stand if I help you up?" Stuart asked.

"I need help getting up even on my best days." She snickered. "Can we put a bandage or something on my face before the girls see me? I don't want to scare them. I have a first aid box on top of the refrigerator."

Stuart grabbed the first aid box and set it on the island before he helped her to her feet.

"I'll talk to the girls and tell them you have a boo-boo on your face," Nate said.

"Thanks," Mrs. Mitchell said.

After Nate left, Stuart examined her face before he opened the kit. "If we put a bandage under your eye, we can cover most of the swelling, and you won't look quite so beat up."

"Let's try it," she said. "The girls are going to critique it no matter what we do, you know."

Stuart snorted. "I learned that from the kids at Major's farm in Florida. Not much gets by them, does it?"

Stuart put the bandage on then examined his handiwork. "Good enough. We'll take you and the girls to my folks' farm. Do you want to leave a note for Mr. Mitchell?"

"Good idea. I'll grab a plastic bag and a permanent marker, if you'll find me a sheet of paper."

When Stuart returned from the office with a blank sheet of paper, she wrote, "House is a mess. We're fine and at the Newtons."

Stuart chuckled when he read the note. "He'll sure know it's from you and not some forgery, won't he?"

Mrs. Mitchell smiled as she placed the note inside the one-gallon, clear plastic, freezer bag. "There's some packing tape in the drawer by the back door. Would you tape it to the front door?"

Stuart taped the plastic bag to the front door then closed and locked it.

When Stuart returned to the kitchen, Mrs. Mitchell said, "Nate dragged the body out. He said he'd be back in a bit."

Stuart narrowed his eyes at the amount of blood streaked across the kitchen floor to the back door. "Is it okay if I clean the floor before we leave?"

Mrs. Mitchell raised her non-swollen eyebrow. "Must have been quite an exit wound. That's a lot of blood. There's a roll of paper towels on the counter and trash sacks under the sink."

Stuart put on the rubber cleaning gloves that he found under the sink before he wiped up the blood then sprayed the floor with disinfectant. When he finished, the floor gleamed.

"You can pitch those gloves. I don't need any mementos." Mrs. Mitchell shuddered.

After he tied the trash sack and cleaned his hands with sanitizer, he said, "We should take your rifle. Are there any other guns in the house that we should take?"

"There's a twenty-two pistol at the back of the drawer where the packing tape was. All the other rifles are locked up in the gun safe."

Stuart found the holstered gun and stuck it into his belt. Mrs. Mitchell winced as she limped on her way to the door, and Stuart furrowed his brow. "Did he injure your ankle?"

"No, I'm just stiff from lying still on the floor all morning. I need to walk it out. I'll be fine after the swelling in my eye goes down."

"By then you'll have a shiner," Stuart said.

Mrs. Mitchell snickered. "My ladies' church group always said if any of us ever got a black eye, we'd all swear she got the last beer."

Stuart burst out laughing as she held onto his arm to walk across the uneven yard. "You can sure claim it."

When they reached the truck, the girls squealed, and Henry covered his ears.

When Stuart opened the back door, Mrs. Mitchell said, "Jump out, Cami Sue, and I can sit between you two."

Stuart helped her into the backseat of the truck then Cami Sue scrambled to sit next to her.

Stuart stepped to Aimee Louise's door. "Can we go for a short walk?"

They strolled along the driveway while Stuart told her about Mrs. Mitchell and the men then explained the joke about the last beer.

Nate strode to meet them. "Mrs. Mitchell told me you went for a walk. I dragged the body as far as I could. I didn't have the tools to bury him. If we want to come back later today, we can, but I didn't think we'd have time with an upcoming storm. Do I need to clean the kitchen floor before we go?"

"I cleaned the kitchen floor. We should take Mrs. Mitchell and the girls to Dad's farm then see what our time looks like. I'm hoping we'll still have time to return and unload your things at your new house. Let's go."

Henry kept his ears covered during the trip back. *Henry needs ear protection.* Stuart smiled. *I need ear protection.*

After they reached the Newton farm, Stuart hopped out of the truck then while Nate helped Mrs. Mitchell and the girls out of the truck, Stuart rushed to talk to Scott who waited for them at the back door of the farmhouse.

"You're back quicker than I expected," Scott said.

Stuart gave him a quick rundown of the events at the Mitchells'. "We still need to take Nate's boxes to his new place. Is it okay if I hand off Mrs. Mitchell and the girls to you?"

"That's fine," Scott said. "We'll take it from here."

Scott hurried to help Mrs. Mitchell to the house while the girls raced inside and squealed.

As Aimee Louise drove away from the farmstead, Nate said, "The twins were excited to see Dolly."

"I was wondering what all the commotion was about," Stuart said. "Did I just sound old?"

"Old like Henry and me." Nate snorted, and Henry nodded.

When they reached the Cabellos' new home to unload the boxes, Nate said, "I'll go inside to check the house first. I should have thought of it earlier; I won't be long."

While Nate was gone, Stuart checked the greenhouse and the other outbuildings.

"House is fine. Let's unload. We can put all the boxes in the living room against the far wall."

* * *

While Nate and Stuart unloaded the truck, Aimee Louise and Henry explored the yard.

"This is a nice garden," Henry said. "Mama Sandra would like this."

When they came to a pink swing set, Henry said, "I didn't even know they made girl swings."

After they returned to the truck, there were only a few boxes left to unload. Aimee Louise picked up one, and Henry peered into a sack. "Mama Sandra sneaked in snacks for them. She's awesome."

"Yes, she is. Can you carry the sack?" Aimee Louise asked.

After they were inside, Aimee Louise set down her box then she and Henry went to the kitchen with the sack.

Henry put the sack on the counter near the sink before they wandered through the house and looked at the rooms. "This is a big house," Henry said.

"Yes, it is. There's plenty of room for Mr. Nate, Ms. Charo, Judge Cabello, Dolly, and Pixie."

When they reached the living room, Nate and Stuart were sitting in the easy chairs near the fireplace.

"Ready?" Stuart asked.

After Aimee Louise parked at the Newtons', Nate jumped out and hurried to the house.

"Go on in, Henry," Aimee Louise said. "Mama Sandra probably has a treat waiting for you."

"We'll have one more trip to make today," Stuart said as they climbed out of the truck. "Nate's going to talk to Charo and his dad to see if they can pull enough things together so they can move today to clear their rooms for Mrs. Mitchell and the twins."

Aimee Louise nodded. "Henry and I noticed the beds had been stripped with clean, folded sheets on top of each bed."

Stuart pointed toward the house as the judge opened the back door then came out with a box in his arms. "Here they come."

"I'll move the truck closer to the house then jump into the back to slide the boxes inside," Aimee Louise said.

Stuart nodded then whistled to get the judge's attention. "Aimee Louise is bringing the truck closer."

Aimee Louise expertly backed the truck to within a few feet of the back door then climbed out.

"Thanks, Angel," the judge said. "Sandra's loading us down with groceries."

"You'll like the garden, Judge." Aimee Louise lowered the truck's tailgate then hopped into the back. As the judge, Stuart, and Nate carried out boxes, she organized the load.

"We've got four suitcases to come out then we're ready," Charo said.

Aimee Louise waited in the driver's seat while the judge, Charo, Nate, Dolly, and Pixie climbed into the backseat, and Henry jumped up front with Aimee Louise.

"Everybody in?" Stuart asked as he climbed into the passenger's seat.

"Wait." Sandra ran to the truck with a small box in her arms. "We almost forgot tonight's bath time snack."

"We'll have to call this the Cabellos' farm to keep from getting confused with the Mitchells' farm," Stuart said as Aimee Louise drove on the driveway to the Cabellos' new home.

While Nate and Stuart unloaded the truck, Charo went inside to make beds.

"Mr. Judge, would you and Dolly like to see the swing and the garden that Angel and I found?" Henry asked.

"That would be great," Judge said.

The judge and Henry walked, and Dolly skipped to the backyard; Pixie followed Dolly and scrambled to keep up.

While Dolly squealed and Pixie yipped, Aimee Louise stayed by the truck until she heard a sound in the woods between the Mitchells' and the Cabellos' farms.

CHAPTER TWO

She crept into the woods then ducked behind a tree as a man strode through the woods toward the Cabellos' new home. She hurried silently ahead of him then ran into the house and found Stuart.

"Mr. Mitchell will be here in just a few minutes. He's coming through the woods from his house."

"I'll go meet him, thanks," Stuart said.

Aimee Louise went out with Stuart but stayed near the truck while Stuart approached the woods. When Mr. Mitchell came out of the trees, he strode to Stuart, and the two men talked briefly.

As they walked toward the truck, Mr. Mitchell said, "We heard there was a big storm coming, so I left early this morning. They'll be able to finish up before the bad weather."

"Mrs. Mitchell will be glad to see you." Stuart told Mr. Mitchell about the attack.

"I read the note on the front door and was headed to the state road to go to Scott's farm until I heard a little girl squeal and thought it was Cami Sue or Sam. You know about the note my wife left? Nobody could have written it but her." Mr. Mitchell shook his head. "I went inside, and that gang definitely ransacked the house. Anybody else would have said the hooligans had demolished everything, but Lela saw a mess that we can clean up."

Nate came out of the house and shook hands with Mr. Mitchell. "Thank you again, sir, for offering your son's home to us. If this is a house that needs laughing, chaos, and noise, we're the right family." Nate chuckled. "We've almost finished emptying the truck. We packed quickly, so we could move here before the big storm blows in tonight."

He hurried to the truck then carried two large boxes into the house. Aimee Louise peeked inside the back of the truck before she hopped in and scooted the rest of the boxes within easy reach for Nate and Stuart to unload.

After Nate and Stuart emptied the back of the truck, Aimee Louise closed the tailgate, and Henry rushed to climb into the truck with her.

When he sat next to Aimee Louise, Henry said, "Dolly liked the pink swing. I only let her push me because she said it was fair for her to push me after I pushed her."

"It's fun to take turns," Aimee Louise said.

"I had fun," Henry said. "Dolly called me stinky boy, and I called her bossy girl."

On the way to the Newtons', Mr. Mitchell said, "I gave Nate the keys to the old truck my son stored in his equipment barn. It's not pretty, but Nate and the judge should be able to get it going with a little work. It ran the last time we started it, but that's been three or four months ago. It was a project my son and I worked on together and was a great excuse to get out of the house."

After Aimee Louise parked, Mr. Mitchell said, "Thanks again. Lela has always been a warrior, and she scares me to death."

Scott strode to the truck, "Glad to see you, Tom. The girls are helping Peyton and Brandon pick vegetables before the storm. Lela and Sandra are in the kitchen. They sent me out to check the grounds, but I think they wanted privacy while they gossiped and cooked."

"What do you need us to do, Dad?" Stuart asked.

"I haven't set up the girls bedroom yet, and I could use some help setting up Charo's old bedroom for the Mitchells."

As Stuart and Mr. Mitchell headed to the house, Henry asked, "What do we do?"

"Aimee Louise may want to put the truck in the barn," Scott said before he headed to the house.

After they reached the barn, Aimee Louise and Henry put away tools and cleared an area large enough to park the truck. Aimee Louise backed into the barn, and Henry stood at the back wall and guided her in.

"How did I do?" he asked when she turned off the engine and stepped out of the truck.

Aimee Louise walked around the truck to see how close it was. "Perfect."

As they headed toward the house, a strong blast of cold wind almost knocked Henry down, and large raindrops pelted them. Aimee Louise snatched up Henry, and he wrapped his arms around her neck as she held onto him and ran to the house while pea-sized hail bombarded them. Before they reached the house, the hail increased in intensity and size, and Henry cried out. Aimee Louise protected his head with her arm then pounded the back door with her fist when she was blinded by the blasts of gusting wind, driving rain, and pelting hail and couldn't find the doorknob.

Stuart jerked open the door and grabbed her before she fell over the threshold.

"Couldn't see," she said through her jagged breaths. "Hail came up fast."

"Mama Angel ran faster," Henry sobbed as Brody scrambled across the kitchen floor to him..

"I couldn't find you. Where were you?" Stuart held the two of them tight in his arms.

"We put the truck in the barn." Henry sniffled.

Aimee Louise leaned her head on Stuart's chest.

"Are you okay, babe?" Stuart asked.

"Yes. I was worried Henry would be hurt, and I couldn't find the doorknob."

"I'm okay." Henry wiggled, and Aimee Louise let him slide down to his feet. When he stood on his own, his puppy leaned against him, and he covered his ears and leaned against Aimee Louise while Stuart continued to hold her.

Aimee Louise patted Stuart's arm. "You can let go now."

"No, I can't." Stuart gave her an extra squeeze before he released her.

She cocked her head and gazed at his cloud. *Strong, sweet cloud. What is that?*

"What does my cloud say?" Stuart asked.

"I'm not sure, but I like it a lot." Aimee Louise gave him a quick hug then touched Henry's shirt. "Your shirt is soaked." She pulled away her damp shirt that was stuck to her skin. "Mine is too. Maybe after we change, Mama Sandra will have a storm snack for us."

"I sure will, honey," Sandra said. "You can gather the rest of them after you change to dry clothes, Henry."

* * *

After Aimee Louise and Henry left the kitchen, Sandra said, "I made a fresh pot of coffee. I poured you a cup."

"Thanks, Mom." Stuart inhaled the smoky, bitter aroma before he sipped the hot liquid. "I thought Aimee Louise was upstairs. She scared me when I opened the door."

"She scared both of us," Sandra said. "You certainly gave her fair warning that you're never going to let her go. I think she's just as serious as you are, in case you're interested in a mama's biased opinion."

Stuart sighed. "I hope you're right. I'm not seeing it."

"Seeing what?" Scott strode into the kitchen. "I smelled coffee. Are we having a storm party?"

"Working on it," Sandra said. "Aimee Louise and Henry got caught in the hailstorm. To quote Henry, 'Mama Angel ran faster.'"

"Seeing what?" Scott sipped the coffee that Sandra had handed to him.

"I said that Aimee Louise is just as serious about him as he is about her."

"Who is that news to?" Scott chuckled.

"Why do I feel ganged up on?" Stuart snatched a cookie as Sandra pulled out her first batch from the oven.

He snickered and stuffed the cookie into his mouth when Sandra smacked his hand with a potholder.

"Wait for the rest of them," she said.

While Henry and Brandon thundered down the stairs, Brandon shouted, "Storm snack in the kitchen. All hands on deck."

The boys raced to their seats, and Sam and Cami Sue hurried to join them. After the children were seated, Sandra served them cookies while Stuart poured cups of hot chocolate then dropped a homemade marshmallow into each cup.

When Peyton came into the kitchen, she said, "I decided I was one of the hands here. Good choice on my part, I see."

Scott handed her a cup of coffee then Sandra offered her the plate of cookies.

"This is great," Peyton said. "I heard there was a storm party in the works."

Aimee Louise slipped into the room and stood close to Stuart. As he put his arm around her shoulders, Henry rose from his chair and handed her a cookie.

"Saved one for you." His cheeks reddened, and he ducked his head.

"Thank you, Henry."

Henry beamed and returned to his seat as Sandra gave each child a second cookie.

As Aimee Louise gazed over Stuart's head, he whispered, "Same cloud?"

"Yes. It's so beautiful."

Stuart smiled then felt his face warm when his dad winked at him.

Mrs. Mitchell leaned on Mr. Mitchell's arm as she shuffled into the kitchen.

"Lela," Sandra said, "I would have brought you a cookie."

"Don't fuss over me; I need to walk off this stiffness."

"Oh lordy, woman. Is that what we're calling a broken leg now?" Sandra asked, and Tom chuckled.

Scott moved a chair to the table for her, so that she would be seated next to the empty seat for Tom. "Sit here."

"Tea kettle's hot if you want tea instead of coffee," Sandra said.

"Tea for me," Lela said.

Tom pointed to the coffee pot as Scott poured refills, and Scott poured coffee into an empty cup then handed it to his old friend.

"How'd you hear about the storm coming?" Scott asked.

"A ham operator who lives close to where we were working heard it on his radio and hurried to the farm because he knew there were a few of us from out of town there. We headed for home after we finished up a few things. There was one guy who had farther to go than me, but he left a little earlier. How about you?"

"Same. Aimee Louise is a ham operator; she and Stuart go to the Websters' farm every morning. When she and Leo have one of their radio discussions, I can't understand a word. After Aimee Louise and Red ran here to tell us about the upcoming storm, Nate decided to move their packed boxes before the bad weather hit."

Stuart added, "We were near your son's house when Henry and Aimee Louise spotted the girls hiding in the bushes, and the girls told us about Mrs. Mitchell."

"You all are an amazing team," Tom said.

"They are, aren't they?" Scott smiled.

"Party's over," Sandra said. "If you all would get Charo and Nate's room ready for the Mitchells, change the bedsheets in the judge's room for Peyton, and set up Dolly's old room for the two girls, Aimee Louise and I will pull together our supper."

"Henry, Brandon, and I will move Red's bed to Dolly's room then check the attic for another twin bed in case Red decides to return from the Websters'. Might as well leave the twin bed in Charo's room. It's easier to bring down a bed from the attic than it would be to haul a bed up the stairs." Stuart and the boys strode out of the kitchen, and Scott followed them.

* * *

After they left, Aimee Louise asked, "Will they find another mattress in the attic?"

"Probably. When people moved away to go to the city where they heard it would be safer right after the grid went down, they gave me lots of stuff. One of my friends told me that what her husband didn't know wouldn't give him fits." Sandra snickered. "Not a philosophy that I personally embrace, but thank goodness I had the sense to insist my donors put the bulky items in the attic for me."

Mrs. Mitchell nodded. "I am fond of contingencies."

"What do we do, Grandma?" Cami Sue asked.

"Show me your room. Maybe we can help by making your beds after the boys get them set up then you can help me make my bed. Grandpa will help me up the stairs."

After the Mitchells left, Peyton said, "David still hasn't shown up. He's got Vanessa's car, right? It shouldn't have taken more than two days for him to get here. I'm sick with worry."

"He's safe," Aimee Louise said.

Peyton slammed her hand on the table. "I don't need to hear crap like that when I'm worried, Aimee Louise." Peyton stormed out of the kitchen and slammed the door when she reached what had been the judge's bedroom.

"Peyton's scared, but David is safe," Aimee Louise said.

"How do you know?" Sandra glanced up from the stove.

"It's David," Aimee Louise said. "He walked from Orlando to Plainview and kept going even after a poisonous snake bit him—he has Peyton and Brandon radar."

Sandra smiled. "You're amazing, Angel. You definitely see things in a way that others don't understand."

"Rosalie and Stuart understand," she said.

"They love you, honey. Of course, they understand you." Sandra placed biscuits in the oven. "Don't you understand them?"

"Not always. Do you always understand Papa Scott?"

Sandra laughed. "Touché, Angel. He's a maddening enigma sometimes."

* * *

After supper, Stuart, Scott, and Tom sat at the table with their coffee while Peyton gathered the children in the living room for a game as the storm raged on.

"You cooked; I do the dishes." Lela shooed Sandra away from the sink. When Sandra relented and dropped into her chair at the table, Aimee Louise filled her empty cup with hot water.

While her tea steeped, Sandra said, "Peyton and the children picked vegetables before the storm hit. My first priority in the morning is to check the garden."

"That reminds me," Stuart said, "Andy told me that one of their neighbors is moving away and leaving behind fifteen or so chickens and two cows. One of the cows will be calving in the next couple of weeks. Mr. Leo raised his farm dogs to guard livestock, but Ms. Jennie wasn't interested in the cows. She wanted about half the chickens, but no cows. and asked if you'd like the rest of the chickens and maybe the cows."

"I wouldn't mind the chickens," Sandra said, "but I don't know anything about cows."

"I do," Lela said. "I grew up on a dairy farm."

"We're too old to take care of cows," Tom grumbled.

"Maybe so, but I'm not too old to teach someone if Nate and Charo are interested. We'll need to go to our house tomorrow anyway, so I can clean it up. We can talk to them then."

"I'll go along to help with the house if Peyton doesn't mind taking care of the girls," Sandra said.

"I almost feel that I should run ahead to tell Nate that you two are going to gang up on him. Would you folks give me a couple days' head start?" Tom chuckled.

Henry and Brandon came into the kitchen and shuffled their feet.

Brandon cleared his throat. "Excuse me, Mama Sandra, but isn't it time for our baths?"

"It certainly is." Sandra jumped up from the table. "Let's go tell your mom."

Henry and Brandon smiled as she hurried to the living room.

"We wanted a snack," Henry said.

Brandon elbowed Henry. "The little girls are tired."

After the boys left to follow Sandra, Scott chuckled. "The routine here is bath, snack, bed. Brandon didn't coordinate his motivation with Henry—he was only looking after the tired girls who obviously are ready for bed."

"I thought there might be something up when the two boys asked for baths." Tom snorted.

"It didn't take long for the kids to embrace the routine as a rule," Stuart said.

When the children were settled, and the Mitchells and Peyton had wandered off to bed, Stuart, Aimee Louise, Scott, and Sandra sat at the kitchen table. The glow of the candles that Sandra had set on the stove gave the room a warm, comforting feel as the rain continued to pelt the windows.

"Andy told me that the farmer who offered the chickens and cows is leaving because his home has been attacked three times, and the last time, they invaded the house and beat the farmer. Andy didn't have any details, but I'm afraid the attackers are unrelated, roving marauders."

"I'll talk to Tom tomorrow," Scott said. "He may want to coordinate their security more closely with Nate."

* * *

After he rose the next morning while it was still dark, Stuart was not surprised when he tiptoed to the kitchen and found fresh coffee on the stove and his mother standing at the counter while she mixed a large batch of pancake batter by candlelight.

"Good morning, Mom." Stuart poured himself a cup of coffee then opened the back door. "Rain's just sprinkles."

"That's good; it was still raining pretty hard when I got up earlier. I'll have pancakes ready for you and Angel in just a few minutes."

"Where did she go?" Stuart realized Aimee Louise's jacket was missing when he checked the row of jackets that hung on the pegs near the back door.

"She told me she needed to check the barn and would be right back. I assumed she ran to check on the truck."

"Dang it," Stuart groaned. "I need to hang a bell on her; I can't keep track." He jerked his rain jacket from its peg and stormed out of the house.

When he reached the barn, the truck was there, but Aimee Louise wasn't.

She is officially scaring me. Again. Maybe the Smith barn?

Stuart raced toward the Smith barn; when he met Aimee Louise on the path, he sighed in relief then grumbled, "You scare me when you disappear like that, especially when it's still dark. I didn't even see you on the path until I almost crashed into you."

"You knew where I'd go." She slipped her hand into his on their stroll back to the house.

Not the point, but not worth a fight that I'll lose.

"I need to sleep outside your bedroom, so I'll know when you get up."

"Okay, but it doesn't sound very comfortable to me."

Stuart shook his head. *That's exactly why I'd lose.*

"I'll think of something," he said. "Everything okay?"

"I stepped into puddles on the floors of both barns, but I couldn't see well enough in the dark to tell where the leaks might be coming from."

"We'll check later when it's daylight," Stuart said. "So, why did you really go to the Smith barn?"

"To see if David was there, but it was too dark, and I didn't hear anything, so I was on my way back to the house."

"Does Peyton know that?" Stuart asked as they went inside and hung up their jackets.

"No, Peyton's mad at me. I can't talk to her until after she's not mad."

"Very smart, Angel," Sandra said. "Your pancakes are ready."

As Stuart and Angel cut into their pancakes, Scott came into the kitchen, and Sandra handed him a cup of coffee. When Lela tiptoed into the kitchen, she said, "Y'all are early risers—my kind of people. I've been hiding in my room. How can I help?"

"Sit." Sandra pointed with her spatula. "After I pull Scott's two pancakes from the griddle, I'll make ours, so we can have breakfast together."

"That sounds nice. I always eat breakfast alone every morning because Tom dashes out the door for his latest project."

"Same for me." Sandra chuckled. "This group will clear out, and we'll have a little time to relax before the next wave hits."

When Aimee Louise finished her pancakes, Stuart collected their dishes and set them on the counter. After Aimee Louise threw on her jacket and backpack then bounced on her toes, Stuart grabbed his rifle, backpack, and jacket. "We're going to the Websters'."

Sandra waved, and Scott followed them out the back door.

Scott strode across the yard then stopped to gaze at the sky. "The clear early mornings are beautiful at sunrise after a big storm, aren't they?"

"I love sunrise," Aimee Louise said.

Scott continued to his truck, Aimee Louise headed up the driveway, and Stuart strolled alongside her.

"Are we going the long way to the Websters'?" Stuart asked.

"Yes, I want to check the driveway first to see if there are any branches across it before your dad tries to leave."

When they came to a large tree that had fallen across the driveway, the two of them tried to lift then roll it out of the way. Finally, Stuart raised his hand. "We'll tell Dad about this one, and he can bring his chainsaw to take care of it. Let's continue to the road."

Aimee Louise nodded.

When they came to a branch across the driveway, they dragged it to the side. After they reached the road, Stuart scanned the road and the surrounding fields before they turned back.

Stuart said, "It was smart to check the driveway. Dad can take care of the tree before the goes to the Mitchells' house."

Stuart strode to Scott's truck. "We walked the driveway—Angel's idea, of course. A large tree fell across it. If you can take your chainsaw to it, I'll help move the pieces when we get back from the Websters'."

"I'll get on it right now. Thanks."

When they headed toward the woods that led to the Smith farm, their pace was slower than usual as they checked the path for any downed limbs.

"It's extra work to go so slow, isn't it?" Stuart asked as they approached the Smith barn.

Aimee Louise dashed ahead and veered into the barn.

"Are you okay?" she asked.

Stuart raced to the barn. Aimee Louise knelt next to David, who sat on the ground in the last stall with his back against the stall wall. A large backpack, his rifle, and a thick branch were on the ground next to him; his backpack was wet, and his jeans were soaked with blood around a tear below one knee.

David frowned at his knee. "Dang, I tore my jeans." He sighed. "That was one rough night. I think I went one driveway too far then got turned around when the hail hit."

He scanned the roof and walls. "This barn has real possibilities, doesn't it? I couldn't tell how well-built the barn was, but I didn't care—I was out of the storm. I collapsed as soon as I was inside then dragged my soaked gear away from the door. After I hunkered down in this stall, I guess I was as exhausted as I felt because the next thing I knew, it was morning."

"Aimee Louise knew you'd be in the barn," Stuart said.

"Not surprised. I can sneak up on criminals but not on Angel." David chuckled.

"Peyton's been expecting you for quite a while. Didn't you have Vanessa's car?"

"Up until I weighted down the accelerator with a heavy rock and sent it speeding into a roadblock. Might not have been the smartest diversion, but I could see that the men who were heavily armed outnumbered me. I was in the woods when the car crashed into them."

"Can you walk?" Stuart asked.

"I can when I lean on my stick. I fell yesterday morning. I wish I could blame the storm, but I stepped wrong and fell into a ravine. Nothing's broken, but I whacked my leg hard enough on the rocks to make walking painful." He showed Stuart his palms with deep cuts on them. "I tried to grab onto the rocks as I slid down, but all I did was wreck my hands. My rifle slid farther than I did, but I managed to make my way to it."

Aimee Louise pulled out two rolls of gauze from her first aid kit in her backpack and wrapped his hands. After she was finished, Stuart handed David a pair of leather gloves from his backpack.

"I don't know if you'll be able to put them on over the wrap, but maybe they can cushion your hands so you can use your stick. If not, we'll help you walk. I'll help you up whenever you're ready."

David wasn't able to put on the gloves, so after Stuart helped him to his feet, David leaned on Stuart as they walked to the Newtons'.

"Peyton's going to be mad. Do you think if I tell her I wrestled a grizzly that she'll feel sorry for me?" David asked as he hobbled along the path.

"No," Aimee Louise said.

David had to stop for a break every few feet.

"When did you last eat or drink?" Aimee Louise asked.

"I lost my food pack when I fell, so I think it was the day before yesterday."

She handed him the water from her backpack before she raced away then returned with a utility wagon.

"You can't pull me over rough terrain," David said. "I'm too heavy."

"Sit in the wagon," Stuart said. "I'll pull, and Angel will push."

"Okay, but I don't think this will work," David sat in the wagon facing forward. After Stuart put a backpack under his injured leg, David tentatively positioned his leg across it. "Maybe it will work," he said.

"Hang on." Stuart pulled, and Aimee Louise pushed.

When they reached the Newtons' yard, David said, "Remind me never to doubt Aimee Louise."

"No kidding." Stuart snickered as he stopped. "Want to go the rest of the way on your own power?"

"Thanks."

Stuart and Aimee Louise helped David out of the wagon then Aimee Louise handed him his stick. While she returned the wagon to the barn, Stuart helped David until they reached the corner near the side door.

As they rounded the corner, Brandon shouted, "Daddy!" and raced from the garden to his father. His puppy, Tracker, ran with him, and Peyton threw down her garden rake and caught up with them.

Stuart positioned himself behind David to keep him steady when Brandon headed their way. David dropped his stick and held out his arms in preparation as Brandon barreled into him. When Peyton reached him, David grabbed her with one arm and hugged his family until Brandon mumbled, "Oof."

David laughed and released Brandon but held onto Peyton tightly while she sobbed on his chest.

Peyton's stream of tears slowed. "Let's get you into the house."

She sniffed back tears as they headed to the house together. Stuart carried David's backpack while David leaned on Peyton and held Brandon's hand.

"Mama Sandra will make you pancakes," Brandon said.

"Miracle food," David said as they made their way to the door.

As David and his family stepped inside the kitchen, Stuart dropped David's backpack near the door.

"Angel found David," Stuart said.

"Oh my goodness, she told Peyton yesterday that David was safe," Sandra said. "Sit down, David. We'll give you coffee and pancakes then after you eat, we'll clean up that leg wound. What's wrong with your hands?"

Peyton helped David to the chair that Brandon held for his dad, and Stuart smiled. "You're in the best of care, David. Aimee Louise wants to get to the radio at our neighbor's farm."

When Stuart stepped outside, Aimee Louise waited for him.

"Let's go." Stuart began running, and Aimee Louise passed him.

Aimee Louise ran ahead then waited for him at the Smith barn.

"I knew you needed to run," Stuart said.

She nodded and dashed toward the Websters' then waited for Stuart near the opening to their yard.

As they walked together to the house, Stuart said, "We've had a busy morning. I'm almost ready for breakfast again."

When Aimee Louise laughed, Stuart said, "You got my joke."

"It won't happen again," she said, and Stuart laughed.

"I thought maybe that might be funny to you," she said.

He hugged her. "You were right."

When they reached the house, Rosalie jerked open the door. "Where have you been? Uncle Leo's been waiting."

As Aimee Louise and Rosalie hurried to the radio room, Jennie said, "Coffee? I have two sausage biscuits left, and lunch will be ready soon."

"Coffee and sausage biscuit sounds great," Stuart said.

"How's everything?" Andy asked. "Any storm damage?"

"Aimee Louise found a leak in the barn roof, but that's all we've found so far." Stuart caught them up on the previous day's events and Aimee Louise finding David. "What about here?"

"Nothing obvious. We'll do a good assessment after lunch."

"I talked to Mom and Dad about the chickens and cows. Dad will talk to Nate Cabello today to see if he's interested in the cows. He and his family moved into the empty Mitchell house, and Mrs. Mitchell has offered to teach them about caring for cows. She said she grew up on a dairy farm."

"That sounds great." Jennie served Stuart his sausage biscuit. "Andy and I thought we might be able to begin on the chicken coop this afternoon and finish up tomorrow."

Rosalie came out of the radio room. "Aimee Louise is talking to Pops now, but earlier the hams talked about the gangs who are attacking farms; an organization that operates on the east coast and wants to expand across Georgia is recruiting the more ruthless gangs." She hurried back to the radio room. "I want to hear what Pops has to say."

"What are we going to do?" Andy asked.

"Exactly what we planned—fortify this road with the farms from the state road to the county line," Stuart said.

"Good plan," Jennie said. "Any details to that?"

"No, but we know we have four farms of people who won't be chased off."

"That's a start," she said. "We need to get ideas from our idea folks. Who is that?"

"Good question. Off the top of my head, I'd say you, Aimee Louise, David, my dad, and Nate for starters. I'll talk to Dad and get back to you. Dad's farm is in the center."

Leo, Aimee Louise, and Red came out of the radio room.

"I need some coffee," Leo said. "We've got news."

After everyone sat at the table, Red said, "The organization that we heard about that's expanding across Georgia is also expanding into Florida, according to Pops. This is not a small-time operation, and there has to be something profitable to drive them. Aimee Louise thinks it's drugs. Pops thinks it's a power grab."

"What do you think, Rosalie?" Leo asked.

"I think it may not matter what the motivation is, but whatever it is, the organization seems to be getting stronger. Pastor John and his family are thinking about moving in with the deputies, and Pastor John's brother and his family, along with Doc Jody, might move in with Pops. Pops said we should stay here. Aimee Louise told him that David made it here, and Pops was glad to hear it."

"Tell your folks we'll be at their house tomorrow for lunch. I'll bring a few things, so tell Sandra not to plan to feed a crowd by herself," Jennie said as she served their lunch of sweet potato soup and fresh biscuits.

"Yes, ma'am," Stuart said.

After everyone ate, Stuart asked, "Ready to go, Angel?"

"Yes."

They ran in silence to the Newtons' farm. When they reached the farm, Scott's truck was gone.

"Let's talk to David then go to the Mitchells'," Stuart said.

When they walked into the kitchen, Peyton was humming as she scrubbed vegetables at the sink, and David sat at the table with a cup of coffee. He had changed clothes, and fresh gauze on his palms replaced the hastily-applied gauze wraps.

Stuart said, "We need to talk to you." When Peyton joined David at the table, Stuart told them about the gangs, the organization, and what Major said about staying. "Ms. Jennie said they'd be here tomorrow for lunch so we can all talk. Angel and I will go to the Mitchells to talk to Dad, Mom, the Mitchells, and Nate."

"Are you taking the truck?" Peyton asked.

"Yes," Stuart said.

"No," Aimee Louise said.

Peyton smiled, "Angel, Stuart can't run as fast as you can, and we can't afford for him to be worn out the rest of the day. We have too much work to do."

"You're right, Peyton," Aimee Louise said.

When Stuart raised his eyebrows, David chuckled.

"Let's go." Stuart smiled at Peyton and mouthed, "Thanks."

As Aimee Louise drove to the Mitchells', she asked, "Why did you thank Peyton?"

"She reminded us that I'd be worn out the rest of the day if I tried to run."

"It was true. Sometimes I forget."

Aimee Louise gave two taps to the horn as she headed down the Mitchells' driveway. When she parked at the house, Nate came through the pathway and Scott waited for them in the yard.

When they stepped out of the truck, Stuart said, "We need to talk, and we need to include Mom and Mrs. Mitchell."

"Let's go inside the house," Scott said.

After they gathered in the living room, Stuart told them about David's arrival and repeated what he had told David and Peyton.

"So, we all get together for lunch tomorrow at Scott's farm, right?" Nate said.

"Yes," Stuart said.

"You have the advantage of two homes that are very close together. You might want to consider how to include a third family," Aimee Louise said.

"She's right," Nate said. "We have the potential for a third family with David's arrival."

"Let's go over to your house, so we can all discuss this," Lela said. "I like Aimee Louise's idea, but we need to talk about how it would work best for all of us."

"Shall I wait? Do we want to continue cleaning up?" Sandra asked.

"Let's stop for now; there's no reason for you to wait while we discuss options," Lela said. "We finished cleaning up the kitchen, so that much is done."

"I agree. I'll talk to Peyton and David then we'll all get together at our house for lunch tomorrow. I was thinking we could bring the twins here in the morning, but you could take them home with you," Sandra said.

"I'll bring a little something too," Lela said. "I'm looking forward to coming up with a good defense plan."

"Did you have time to discuss the cows?" Stuart asked.

"We talked about it," Nate said. "Ms. Lela and Charo are excited. Tom and I are skeptical, but we know we'll lose."

Stuart nodded then smirked. "Just wondered because I think the farmer already delivered the cows to the Websters' farm today."

Tom laughed. "I'll pick up the cows from Leo after lunch tomorrow."

"Ms. Jennie will be happy," Stuart smiled.

Aimee Louise and Stuart returned to their truck, and as Aimee Louise drove back to the Newtons' farm, Stuart said, "What do you think about staying? Are you okay?"

"It surprised me because it wasn't what I expected Pops to say, but I agree it's wise for us to stay here under the circumstances and not try to travel."

"You know I want to be with you always, right?"

"Yes."

Stuart waited. *I'm smart enough to give her time to process.*

CHAPTER THREE

After Aimee Louise parked at the Newtons' farm and climbed out of the truck, she stopped Stuart and slipped her hand into his as she gazed at his cloud. "I want to be with you always too."

When Stuart hugged her, she wrapped her arms around him and held him as tightly as he held her. When Stuart released her, she stepped back, and he smiled then lightly kissed her.

She touched her mouth where he had kissed her. "That was nice."

Wow, she said it was nice. Stuart smiled and hugged her again as his dad parked his truck.

Sandra waved as she hurried to the house. "Lela appreciated being included. I'll talk to Peyton and David about options for them, so they can have a little time to think too."

"I'll check for damage in the house if you'll check the barn." Scott followed Sandra to the house.

"I'll find the ladder then climb up to inspect the roof." Stuart smiled. "Just like old times when we put up Mr. Young's antenna on Major's house."

"That was a long time ago, but I'll brace the ladder for you— just like old times."

After Stuart climbed up and inspected the roof, he came down the ladder. "Good news. The wind caught a tip of one corner and bent it back. I think I can pound it flat then screw it down. I'll check with Dad for a second opinion."

"I'll gather the tools you'll need and put them into the pockets of a work apron. Metal screws, right?"

"That's right."

Stuart hurried to the house. "Where's Dad?" he asked as he went into the kitchen.

"In the attic checking for leaks," Sandra said.

After Stuart climbed the ladder to the attic, he asked, "Finding anything, Dad?"

"Not a thing, and I'm relieved. What about you?"

Stuart told him about the bent corner and his repair plan.

"Sounds good to me. You could apply a little sealant if you like. I checked that puddle, and, considering how much rain we had, not all that much leaked inside. I still think it's worth tacking down that corner, though, because the wind would just keep pulling it back, and we'd have a big problem later."

"That's what I thought. Thanks, Dad," Stuart said.

When he returned to the barn, Aimee Louise asked, "How's your dad doing?"

"What makes you think I was checking on Dad?" Stuart asked.

"If you'd wanted a second opinion, you would have asked me. Here's your work apron. I added sealant, in case you decided you needed it."

Stuart snorted as he climbed the ladder. *She knows me inside and out.*

After Stuart repaired the roof, he glanced at the clear sky then toward the road. "Is a car coming this way down the road?"

"Yes, I heard it. Don't fall." Aimee Louise raced to the driveway.

"Wait. Wait until I can get down." Stuart scrambled to gather his tools.

As he went down the ladder as fast as he dared, he fumed. *She drives me crazy when she runs off like that.*

Stuart left the ladder against the side of the barn and the apron on the ground before he grabbed his rifle and ran up the driveway toward the road. As he neared the road, he paused to listen then frowned.

I don't hear it now.

After Aimee Louise joined him, and they walked back to the house, Stuart said, "It drives me crazy when you run to a road to check a passing car."

"I knew you wouldn't fall," she said.

Stuart sighed as he turned away. "You're probably going to scare me the rest of our lives."

Aimee Louise tugged at his shirt. "Let's tell Mama Sandra what I saw."

When they went inside, the house was quiet, and the kitchen was empty.

"The garden." Aimee Louise abruptly turned and crashed into Stuart who stood behind her.

He caught her, so that she wouldn't fall over his feet, and held her before he soundly kissed her and gazed at her face.

"I'm sorry I can't see your cloud, but your face is beautiful." Stuart stroked her cheek with his fingertips.

Aimee Louise traced his face with her fingertips. "I can't see your face, but I can feel your cheekbone, jaw, chin, and your mouth and imagine your face, and it's beautiful too."

"Can I be handsome instead of beautiful?"

Aimee Louise laughed. "How about manly?"

"Even better." Stuart laughed with her as they turned to the door.

Scott stood in the doorway. "What's better?"

"Stuart's manly, not beautiful," Aimee Louise said.

"Good to know." Scott raised his eyebrows. "What's up?"

"Aimee Louise saw a family drive their car past the farm," Stuart said.

"It was loaded down," Aimee Louise added. "We were on our way to tell Mama Sandra."

"She's down at the garden," Scott said.

"I'll go talk to her," Aimee Louise said.

After Aimee Louise left, Scott asked, "How are you and Angel doing?"

Stuart grinned. "I'm manly."

Scott poured himself a glass of water as Stuart continued, "I always knew that Aimee Louise saw clouds not facial expressions, but I never put it together and realized that she can't see facial expressions because she doesn't see facial features. I don't understand that except I know if I asked her, she'd tell me she's wired differently."

"She's right, and the rest of us are too, just maybe in less obvious ways." Scott drained his glass. "I'd better inspect our old chicken coop. It might need a few minor repairs. I'll bet David could supervise Brandon and me. Peyton insisted that David go with her and Brandon to the garden. I think she wanted to keep an eye on him."

They strolled to the garden together.

"Do you think Henry will miss Brandon?" Scott asked.

"I'm sure he will, but we can always invite Brandon for an overnight," Stuart said.

While Peyton weeded a section of the garden, she repeatedly glanced at David who sat on the judge's bench and played with the puppies as he watched Brandon and Henry smash bad bugs and inspect good bugs.

"There they are." Scott pointed to Aimee Louise and Sandra who were huddled in the far corner of the garden in conversation. When Sandra threw back her head and laughed, Scott added, "They're talking about one of us."

"Must be you, Dad," Stuart said. "I'm not quite that funny."

When Scott snorted, Sandra turned then spoke quietly to Aimee Louise.

"Wish I had Aimee Louise's hearing sometimes," Stuart said.

"Scott," Sandra said, "We were just talking about you."

Stuart elbowed his dad as they joined Sandra and Aimee Louise.

"Aimee Louise saw a family drive by, and that reminded us that our chickens may be showing up soon. I told her you'd want to get busy on the coop."

I'll bet Mom said more than that.

"You're right." Scott strode to David. "Our chickens may have arrived sooner than we expected. Want to supervise Brandon and me tomorrow morning while we repair the old coop?"

"Sure do." He glanced at Peyton who frowned. "Brandon, ready to fix up a chicken coop tomorrow? Let's go see what we'll need to do."

Brandon rushed to David's side, and David picked up his makeshift cane then the three of them headed to the coop.

* * *

After supper, Brandon, Henry, and David took Tracker and Brody outside for a stroll.

When they returned, Sandra said, "You're walking a lot better, David."

"I think your poor body has to heal really fast before you injure it again." Peyton dried the last pan, and Sandra put it away.

David chuckled. "Can't argue with that. So, I understand the rule around here is bath, snack, bed. Did I get it right?"

"You sure did, Dad," Brandon said before he and Henry raced to the bathroom with the two dogs behind them.

"We won't be long," Peyton said. "Have you ever seen two dirty boys run so fast to take a bath?"

"That's why Mama Sandra made that rule ages ago," Scott said.

Later, while everyone else was getting ready for bed, Stuart and Aimee Louise strolled to the road and back in the moonlight then around the house for their last perimeter check of the evening.

"Sometimes I worry about Henry," Stuart said. "He's only six years old. He should be playing with Brandon, and running with Brody, not be security conscious and worried about being kidnapped or hurt."

Aimee Louise took Stuart's hand. "Remember we found him in a field after he'd been kidnapped and survived a tornado, by himself and out in the open; then that little guy told you to wave twice, so he'd know it was you and not another kidnapper."

Stuart chuckled. "Wasn't that something? I'm still in awe of Brandon taking Henry under his wing."

"Henry doesn't have a worried cloud. He's brave and trusts us."

"I didn't know that. Did you know you're brilliant?"

"And you are strong and kindhearted," she said as they continued their patrol.

Stuart smiled. *I'm a lucky man.*

When they returned to the house, Stuart locked up then took Aimee Louise into his arms and kissed her, and she returned his kiss. He released her then kissed her lightly and touched her cheek. "Good night, babe."

She squeezed his hand before she headed up the stairs. "Good night, honey."

* * *

When Stuart tiptoed down the stairs before dawn the next morning, his mother and Aimee Louise were already in the kitchen. Sandra handed him a hot cup of coffee.

"Want to watch the sun come up with me?" Aimee Louise asked.

"Sure do," Henry replied as he tiptoed down the staircase.

Stuart snickered. "It's a little chilly; let's grab our jackets and go."

After they greeted the sun and returned to the house, Sandra had their breakfast ready.

While they ate, Aimee Louise asked, "Henry, would you like to go with us to the Websters'?"

"I can't run fast," he said.

"That's okay, neither can I," Stuart said. "Angel can run if she wants, and we can walk if we want."

Henry grinned and brushed his hands on his pants. "I'm ready."

"Let's pull together a go-bag for you," Aimee Louise said.

"Sure. What's a go-bag?" Henry asked.

"It's a backpack with a few important things in it in case we can't make it back to Mama Sandra's house as soon as we expected."

"I'll need my dinosaur and my sword," Henry said.

Stuart nodded. *That's it. Sometimes I need my dinosaur and sword too.*

"We'll add a small flashlight and a space blanket," Aimee Louise said.

Henry ran upstairs then returned with his backpack. "I already put my dinosaur and sword in. What's a space blanket?"

"It's an emergency blanket, but it's not thick. I'll show you," Aimee Louise left to gather supplies.

Stuart said, "Here's a flashlight and a whistle. You can wear your ballcap or put it in your backpack."

"I'll wear it." Henry put on his cap.

Aimee Louise returned with a folded emergency blanket and showed it to Henry.

"It looks like aluminum foil," Henry said.

"It does. If we're caught outside in the rain, it will help keep you dry, or if it's cold, it will help keep you warm," Aimee Louise said.

While Aimee Louise and Stuart grabbed their backpacks, Henry slipped on his and said, "You're too little to go, Brody. Stay with Mama Sandra."

When Stuart picked up his rifle on the way out, he said, "This is my sword." He stopped in the side yard and frowned. "Is that a truck on the road?"

Angel raced up the driveway.

"She runs so fast that sometimes I think she's flying," Henry said. "Do you ever think that?"

"You may be right. Sure explains why I can never catch her. Would you mind waiting inside while I check too?"

"I'll do that." Henry went inside the house, and Stuart ran up the driveway then stopped before he reached the road and listened.

Is the truck making a second pass?

After he heard the truck pass the Newton farm and continue on toward the Websters', Aimee Louise came down the driveway from the road.

"It was a truck with a man driving and a woman in the passenger's seat. The truck was pulling a horse trailer, and a dog crate in the truck bed had a bunch of chickens inside it. I think it was the farmer who has cows and chickens. He must be looking for the Websters' driveway. It is easier to see going this way. They'll find it."

"I sent Henry into the house. Let's tell Mom and Dad what you saw then we can leave."

They ran together to the house and found Scott and Henry in the kitchen with Sandra.

Stuart said, "Aimee Louise saw a truck headed to the Websters' with chickens in a dog kennel in the back of the truck."

"And it was pulling a horse trailer," Aimee Louise added.

"That's exciting news. I'm glad David, Brandon, and I checked the chicken coop yesterday. The chickens can go into it anytime. We've still got a little more to do on the coop, but we could work around chickens," Scott said.

"I'm glad I reminded you," Sandra said.

Scott winked at Stuart, and Stuart nodded.

"We've got another reason to go to the Websters' farm this morning; we'll see you later," Stuart said.

After they reached the path to the Smith farm, Aimee Louise raced ahead then returned. "Thanks."

"Mama Angel likes to run," Henry said.

"She sure does. We need to find you a walking stick, Henry. I like to have one when I'm hiking." Stuart examined the small trees as they passed them.

Henry furrowed his brow. "We need a name for you, Deputy Stuart."

"You're right. We'll have to think about it." Stuart smiled. *Maybe Angel will come up with something.*

When they came to the Smith barn, Henry stopped and raised his head as he stared up at the roof. "Wow, that's a big barn. Is that where you found Brandon's dad, Mama Angel? Is it safe?"

"Let's go inside, and you can see that it's safe," she said.

This is amazing to see the world through Henry's eyes.

After they were inside, Henry inspected the barn then pointed to a pile of straw. "Where did the straw come from?"

"Check the stalls," Aimee Louise said.

Henry went to each stall and peered inside. "There's straw in the stalls. Brandon's dad must have pulled some out so he wouldn't have to sleep on the cold ground."

"I'll bet you're right," Stuart said. "I don't remember seeing the straw the other times we were here. You're very perceptive, Henry."

"Thank you. What is perskeptive?"

"Per-cep-tive means that you see things other people miss," Aimee Louise said.

"I'm per-cep-tive." Henry beamed.

As they walked out of the barn, the sound of gunshots rang out, and they froze.

"Webster farm?" Stuart asked.

"Or just beyond it on the road; I'm not sure," Aimee Louise said. "Henry, pick a stall and hide. We'll come get you as soon as we can. Will you be okay alone?"

"Yes," Henry said.

Aimee Louise raced off to the Websters'.

"Show me where you're going to hide. We'll come back to get you later," Stuart said.

Henry hurried to the last stall. After he sat in the corner, he covered his ears at the sound of more gunshots. "I'll be here."

"Perfect."

Stuart raced out of the barn toward the Websters'. He slowed then stood behind the trees while he scanned the farmhouse and the yard. Jennie's truck was in the yard and an empty horse trailer stood next to the barn; he heard chickens clucking inside the barn. Stuart shifted positions until he saw the cows inside the fenced yard that Jennie had built for goats. One of the dogs watched the cows from the gate, and the other two dogs patrolled the fence.

Haven't heard any gunfire since the Smith barn.

Aimee Louise sprinted down the driveway from the road toward the path to the Smith farmstead.

"I'm here," Stuart said quietly, and she raced to his side.

"Rosalie, Andy, and Ms. Jennie are near the road a little west of the driveway. I used our barred owl call, and Rosalie answered me. I ran back to get you," Aimee Louise said.

She turned and raced up the driveway; Stuart ran as fast as he could behind her and managed to stay close. When they reached the road, Aimee Louise hooted the barred owl call again, and Rosalie answered.

Stuart shook his head as they strode down the road. *She's not even winded, and I can barely walk.*

Rosalie raced to meet them. "The farmer and his wife brought the chickens and cows to the farm because they were anxious to leave. When we heard the gunshots after they left, Andy, Aunt Jennie, and I ran to the road. I ran ahead and saw a truck across the road in front of the farmer's truck. The robbers were shooting at the farmer's truck, and the farmer and his wife were shooting back. I shot one robber then shifted positions to shoot the second one when Aunt Jennie came up next to me and shot him before I could. Andy shot the third robber, who had kept advancing toward the farmer's truck. Aunt Jennie checked the farmer and his wife. She said the farmer's okay, but his wife has an upper arm wound."

"I'm going back," Aimee Louise said.

"Good idea," Stuart said.

Stuart and Rosalie continued to the trucks in the road.

"Where did Aimee Louise go?" Rosalie asked.

"We left Henry in the Smith barn."

"He's a brave little guy."

Stuart narrowed his eyes as they neared the trucks. When they reached the farmer's truck, Stuart asked, "Will the farmer's truck run?"

"I think so," said Andy.

"Turn it around and take the injured woman and Jennie back to the Websters'. Rosalie, do you think you could ride in the truck bed?"

"Good idea." Rosalie rushed to the back of the truck and jumped in.

"I'll walk with the farmer to the house," Stuart said, and Andy hurried to the truck.

Stuart stood next to the farmer, and when Andy started the engine, Jennie stepped into the truck with the woman and closed the passenger door.

As Andy backed up and turned around, Stuart said, "I'm Stuart Newton. They'll take your wife to Jennie's."

"Good." The farmer swayed on his feet before he collapsed.

"Hold up!" Stuart shouted as he caught the man and eased him to the pavement. Andy slammed on the brakes, and Rosalie jumped out of the truck bed and raced to Stuart.

Blood had soaked into the front of the man's torn shirt, and Stuart ripped it open.

"Chest wound," he said when Rosalie reached him. "Grab his feet, and we'll carry him to the truck bed. Swap seats with Jennie. I want her to ride in the back with me."

Andy jumped out and dropped the truck tailgate then rushed to replace Rosalie at Stuart's side. Rosalie raced to the truck and sat in the passenger's seat as Jennie hurried to the back of the truck. After the farmer, Stuart, and Jennie were in the truck bed, Andy lifted the tailgate into place.

Stuart said, "Go to Dad's farm." Andy nodded then headed to the Newtons'.

"Color's not great, but he's breathing. I should have checked him more closely," Jennie said. "Glad you showed up, Stuart. I would have left him to walk to my farm, and he wouldn't have made it."

"We didn't leave him. That's all that counts."

"You're right." Jennie sighed before she turned her focus to the injured man and placed two fingers in his palm, "Cal? Squeeze my fingers."

He closed his fingers around hers.

"Excellent. Take it easy, Cal," Jennie said. "We'll be at Scott's farm in a few minutes."

"Let's roll him to check his back before we get to the driveway," Stuart said, and Jennie made her way to the same side of the truck bed as Stuart.

"Ready?" After Jennie knelt alongside Stuart and nodded, Stuart continued, "One-two-three. Roll."

Jennie pointed to Cal's bloodstained ripped shirt, and the blood on the truck bed. Stuart held Cal steady against his knees as he ripped the shirt open. When he saw the gaping hole, he tore off a large section of the shirt and rolled it into a bandage and placed it on the wound.

"Back on three," he said. "One-two-three." They eased Cal onto his back. Jennie positioned herself at Cal's head with her hands under his head for support and her legs alongside his torso to steady him as the truck rolled with the ruts.

When they reached the farm, Aimee Louise and Henry stood near the driveway, and Scott and Sandra hurried to the truck.

"Whatcha got?" Scott asked.

"Gunshot wound to the chest with an exit wound in back. Wife, in front, has a graze wound on her upper arm," Stuart said.

Henry ran to the back door to hold it open while Aimee Louise helped Rosalie take the farmer's wife inside. Sandra rushed to join them.

"Henry, after they go inside, can you unlock the front door and ask Angel to come back to help me?" Scott asked.

"Yes, sir," Henry said.

"Stuart needs a blanket or quilt, Angel," Scott said when Aimee Louise returned.

She raced back into the house and returned with an old, frayed quilt. After Stuart positioned the quilt next to the farmer, he said, "We'll roll him toward me. Can you help, Jennie?"

Jennie joined Stuart, and they logrolled Cal then placed him on the quilt.

Stuart rose to his feet and moved from Cal's side to his head. "I'll lift his head, Jennie; you lift his feet, and we'll hand him off."

Jennie pushed herself to her feet then took her position at the foot end of the quilt.

"Ready? Lift on three." Stuart counted, and they lifted Cal.

As Jennie shuffled backward, Stuart said, "Dad, let Jennie know when she's close to the edge."

"Okay, stop," Scott said. "Angel, take over from Jennie; Andy, you and I will take over from Stuart when he reaches the end of the truck bed."

Angel took the foot end of the quilt from Jennie. After Stuart handed off the quilt to Scott and Andy, he hopped down to help Aimee Louise as they led the way to the house. Henry opened the front door then the group carried Cal to the living room.

Scott said, "Stuart, Jennie, and Angel, I'll need your help. Rosalie and Andy, go help Sandra. Henry, lock the front door then close the truck doors and ask Ms. Peyton to come here."

After Scott and Jennie examined the wound, Jennie said, "I need my field medic bag. Leo knows where it is."

Scott asked, "Angel, are you up to running?"

Stuart said, "Not—"

"Yes." She held up her hand and interrupted Stuart before he could finish his objection. "I need Rosalie."

"You're right, honey." Stuart sighed. "The two of you are our fastest runners."

"Anything else besides your field medic bag?" Aimee Louise asked.

"Antibiotics and disinfectant," Jennie said.

"I'll grab Rosalie."

After the two young women raced out of the house, Scott asked, "What else do you want to do before they return?"

"Is it possible we could put him on a bed?" Jennie asked.

Henry returned with Peyton. "On it." Peyton said.

Henry followed her to her room then almost immediately returned. "Big Bear, Ms. Peyton needs you."

Stuart rose and hurried to Peyton's room.

"I need plastic or something to put over this twin bed, so we won't stain the mattress with blood," she said.

Stuart strode to the bathroom with Henry on his heels.

"Hey, Henry," Stuart said as he removed the shower curtain. "I just realized you called me 'Big Bear,' and I immediately jumped up. How did you come up with that?"

"Ms. Peyton said, 'Go get Big Bear,' and I did."

Stuart chuckled. "Let's take her this shower curtain, Little Bear."

Stuart folded the shower curtain then Henry carried it as they hurried back to Peyton's room.

"Brilliant," she said when Henry handed her the plastic curtain.

"Henry, stay with Ms. Peyton in case she needs anything else. I'm going to check with Papa Scott, and we'll be coming to the bedroom soon with our patient."

Henry saluted, and Peyton smiled as Stuart returned the salute before he left.

When Stuart reached his dad, he said, "Peyton is fixing up the twin bed in her bedroom. We can move whenever you're ready."

"No time like the present," Scott said.

After everyone was in position, Stuart said, "You call it, Andy."

"On three." Andy counted then Andy and Stuart lifted Cal's head while Scott and Jennie lifted his legs.

"Jennie and I will lead the way," Scott said.

After they positioned Cal on the twin bed, Andy and Scott stepped back.

"Anything else for us?"

Jennie surveyed the room. "I need a pair of scissors then that's it."

Henry and Brody disappeared down the hallway then walked slowly back as Henry carried a pair of scissors that he held pointed at the floor.

"Well done, Henry," Jennie said. "You all are excused. Scott and I will go from here until the girls return."

As Stuart and Andy strode to the kitchen, Aimee Louise and Rosalie burst into the house, and the two young men stepped back to keep from being run over.

"Peyton's bedroom," Stuart said.

The young women dashed to the bedroom then returned to the kitchen.

"Did anyone check the three assailants?" Stuart asked.

"I did," Andy said. "They are dead."

"We need to move their bodies and the truck," Stuart said.

"I'll tell Aunt Jennie and Mr. Scott," Andy said, and Rosalie followed him.

"We're cleared to go. Ready?" Andy asked when he returned.

"Grab some water," Aimee Louise said. "Rosalie and I have ours."

"Is she always right?" Andy whispered to Stuart as they stuck two containers of water into Stuart's backpack.

Stuart snorted. "Pretty much."

"We'll run slow this time," Aimee Louise said as she and Rosalie sped away.

"This isn't slow," Andy said as they chased after the young women.

When they reached the Websters' farmhouse, Aimee Louise and Rosalie waited for them in the driveway.

"We checked in with Uncle Leo. He had walked to the road earlier, and the truck was still in the middle of the road," Rosalie said. "He planned to move the truck, but I told him we were taking care of it."

"Can we walk to the road from here?" Andy asked. "You know, so we'll be quiet in case anyone's waiting to ambush someone like us."

"No," Rosalie said. "Let's go."

Aimee Louise sped away, and Rosalie quickly caught up with her while Stuart and Andy pushed themselves to stay close behind them.

When the four of them reached the road, Aimee Louise said, "I'll check."

"Okay," Stuart said. When Rosalie and Andy stared at him, he pretended not to notice.

Aimee Louise returned. "Three bodies where we left them. Guns are still on the road, and the truck hasn't moved."

"Do we travel on the road?" Stuart asked.

"Yes, on the shoulder, so we can dive across the ditch into a field if we hear anything."

Stuart led the way, and Aimee Louise stayed close behind him. Rosalie then Andy followed Aimee Louise.

When they were close to the heavy-duty truck, Stuart narrowed his eyes at the truck bed with the sides built up by boards. He faced the others and whispered, "Andy, you and I will check the truck before we approach the bodies to move them to the far ditch. Aimee Louise, watch our backs. Red, you're our shooter. We'll set our rifles in the truck before we approach the bodies."

Aimee Louise touched Stuart's arm. "They are dead."

Stuart sighed in relief. "Thanks. Change in plans, Andy. It's okay if we carry our rifles with us to the bodies."

When Stuart climbed up on the trailer hitch to check the truck bed, he let out a long, low whistle. "There are extra rifles and a downright storehouse of ammunition back here."

Andy peered inside the truck cab. "Keys are still in the ignition. They were feeling confident, weren't they?"

"There's the smell of money here. This is not a run-of-the-mill gang of roving thugs," Stuart said as he and Andy approached the bodies splayed on the ground.

Stuart examined each man then pointed. "This is Red's shot."

"How can you tell?" Andy asked then glanced at the others. "Never mind, it's a precision shot in the middle of the forehead and is exactly where she wanted it, right?"

"Yep."

"She's only eighteen years old," Andy shook his head as they dragged the bodies to the ditch. "Where'd she learn that?"

Stuart chuckled. "Ever heard of Major Dave Elliott? He's retired now from the Florida State Police. He's her grandfather."

"Of course, I've heard of Major. He's a legend. So, he taught her to shoot?"

"Yep, but she picked it up right away and surpassed all of us who had been training, practicing, and shooting for years."

"She told me she was adopted by her grandfather. I didn't realize it was Major because she always calls him Pops. When was that?"

Stuart snorted. "Ready to feel totally incompetent? Because the rest of us did. She was sixteen."

"What?" Andy shook his head as he straightened up after he pushed the body into the ditch. "Rest in peace, fella. Your life of crime is over."

As they walked back to the third body, Andy asked, "Are you sure? Sixteen? That was only two years ago."

Stuart nodded. After the last body slid into the ditch, he said, "Red was a natural—she just needed the right instructor, and Major is the best."

"Why doesn't Angel shoot? She's not afraid of guns, but she doesn't shoot."

"I'm not sure, but I think it's because her hearing is so sensitive. She can't hold her hands over her ears and shoot—probably her only shortcoming. Major told me she was a good shot, but I've never seen her shoot."

As Aimee Louise and Rosalie raced to the truck, Andy asked "I've noticed Angel sees things. What's that all about?"

"Ask Red. She'll tell you." Stuart waited at the truck bed for Angel as Rosalie rushed past him to jump into the passenger's seat.

Stuart and Aimee Louise climbed into the truck bed. Before Andy turned the truck around, he asked, "Where do we go?"

"Your place," Stuart said. "We'll walk to Dad's from there. You and Red may want to spend some time with Leo. I'm afraid we've left him out."

After Andy parked the truck near the Websters' farmhouse, Stuart and Aimee Louise headed to the shortcut that led to the Newtons' farm.

"We can walk," Aimee Louise said.

When they came to the Smith barn, Aimee Louise said, "Rosalie told me she's staying with Andy."

"Did that bother you?"

"No, but I didn't understand why she thought it would be a surprise to anyone."

"We didn't even think to tell her that we already moved her bed to Dolly's old room. Wonder if we should have asked," Stuart said.

"No. She told me she's going to marry Andy, but he doesn't know it yet."

Stuart smiled. "He might. A man can read his woman, just like a woman can read her man."

"That sounds like something Mama Sandra would say—very philosophical."

"I must get it from Mom. Want to run the rest of the way?"

Aimee Louise took off, and Stuart sped up to run alongside her.

When they reached the house, Aimee Louise said, "Good walk, good talk, and a good run." She hugged Stuart, and he grinned as he returned her hug before they walked inside the house with their arms around each other.

"I'm glad you're back. I was worried about you," Sandra said. "I'm worried about the Mitchells and Cabellos coming here. Don't you think we should consider sending Peyton, David, and Brandon to the Mitchells now before the next attack? I wanted to talk to you before I brought it up to Scott, Peyton, and David."

"I'm right here," Peyton said. "We're leaving now."

"The Cabellos and Mitchells may already be on their way," Stuart said. "The Cabellos will keep everyone safe."

"You may be right, but that's not the point," Peyton said. "I think we need to get there now while we can. Ms. Jennie said we can take her old car. David, Brandon, and Tracker are on their way to pick it up, and I'm leaving to join them."

"I don't agree, but I know you'll keep your family safe." Stuart shrugged.

"Just for the record, your dad agrees with you, and I understand, but we have to go now." Peyton grabbed her rifle and backpack and hurried out the back door.

"I've spent the morning being anxious about everything." Sandra said. "Cal and Blanche being shot shook me up."

"How are they doing?" Stuart asked.

"Blanche's resting. She'll be fine. I'm worried about Cal."

"I'll see if Dad and Ms. Jennie need any help," Stuart said.

"Would it help if I washed and cut up the potatoes?" Aimee Louise asked.

"Sure would, and it'll be nice to have some company in the kitchen."

CHAPTER FOUR

Stuart stood in the bedroom doorway and watched his dad and Jennie. Jennie pursed her lips then adjusted her stethoscope in her ears before she briefly listened to Cal's chest then pulled up the top sheet to cover his bandaged chest wound.

Scott glanced up. "I'll be right back, Jennie. I need to talk to Stuart."

When Jennie turned to look at Stuart, her tight face was pale, and she bit her lip. "Don't be long."

Scott nodded and led his son to the living room. "Cal's breathing is ragged, his pulse is rapid and weak, and his skin is gray. I'm worried he may be bleeding internally, but Jennie is adamant he's going to be better, but she doesn't seem comfortable in what she's doing. I think she's over her head; he needs medical help beyond Jennie's skills. You have any ideas?"

"I'll talk to Aimee Louise." Stuart strode to the kitchen.

"Aimee Louise, can you help me with the truck a minute?" Stuart picked up his rifle.

"Sure can." Aimee Louise put down her paring knife and the potatoes, and they went outside. While they walked to the truck, Stuart said, "Cal's not doing well. We need a doctor."

"Okay." She turned to run, and he grabbed onto her arm.

"Don't go without me. I need to tell Mom we're going to— where are we going?"

"Websters'. Leo will have some ideas, and we'll have the radio."

As they hurried to the house, Stuart said, "Grab our backpacks."

"Mom, we're going to the Websters' to see if we can find a nearby doctor for Cal. Don't wait on us for lunch or for the defense discussion. I trust Dad to speak for us," Stuart said.

"Sorry I'm running out on the potatoes," Aimee Louise added.

"Don't worry about it, Angel. Here's a sack with some sandwiches and cookies. I know you have water," Sandra said.

Stuart stuck the large lunch sack into his backpack before they ran to the Websters'; Andy met them at the house. "What's going on?" he asked.

"We need to talk to Mr. Leo," Aimee Louise said. "Mr. Cal needs a doctor."

Stuart and Andy followed her as she rushed into the radio room.

Leo's eyes widened when he saw Aimee Louise and Stuart. "What's wrong?" he asked.

"Mr. Cal has a gunshot wound in the chest with a large exit wound in his back," Stuart said. "Dad is afraid he's bleeding internally. His pulse increased, and his color is bad."

"Jennie's with him, right?"

"Yes, but Dad's afraid Cal's condition is more serious than it appears."

"I understand. There's a retired surgeon near the county line. Let me see if I can raise him on the radio. If I can't, Andy can take me there, and we'll pick him up."

When Rosalie came in from outside, Andy and Stuart explained the situation and the plan to find a doctor.

"If we go to the doctor's place, I'd like to take the ambushers' truck and have extra ammunition on hand," Stuart said.

"We didn't unload the ammunition yet," Andy said. "We'll check it to make sure the ammo we use is included."

After five minutes, Leo said, "Let's go. Nobody's on the radio this time of day."

"We're taking the ambushers' truck. Angel, you drive," Stuart said.

"Red and I will ride in the truck bed," Andy said. "Ammo's fine for us, Stuart."

"Everybody's going?" Leo asked.

"Yes, let's go," Stuart said. "You and I will ride in front with Angel."

Leo picked up his shotgun and followed Stuart to the truck.

On the way to the surgeon's house, Stuart looked in the lunch sack. "There's enough here for all of us. Want to eat on the way?"

Aimee Louise nodded, and Stuart handed her a sandwich.

"Can you slide open that small window behind you and pass back two sandwiches?" he asked Leo.

"I'll give it a try." Leo struggled with the latch then with the window that wouldn't slide at first. When he opened it enough to hand off the sandwiches, Stuart gave him two, and Leo waved the sandwiches behind his head.

Andy took the sandwiches then Leo closed the window. Stuart gave Leo a sandwich, and Leo said, "It's been a while since anyone has opened that window. We'll need to attack it with a little grease."

After Leo ate his sandwich, he said, "If he isn't there, I heard a nurse practitioner and his family left Tallahassee and moved in with his folks on their farm about twenty miles south of us."

"A possibility, but from what Dad said, I'm not sure Cal has that much time," Stuart said.

Leo sighed. "I guess Doc Larkin just better be there."

"Hope so," Stuart said. "Just as well that you didn't reach him on the radio because he'll be safer riding with us."

"Men up ahead, and they're moving a car to block the road. I need a ball cap," Aimee Louise said.

Stuart handed her his deputy cap, and Aimee Louise crammed it on her head.

"When we get close, tell them to move it or we will," Aimee Louise said.

Aimee Louise slowed, and Stuart lowered his window and leaned out as he shouted, "Hey, you thick-headed morons. Get that piece of junk off the road, or we'll do it for you."

The two men stared at Stuart. One of the men raised his fist and yelled, "Oh, yeah?"

Aimee Louise stomped on the accelerator and barreled down the middle of the road toward the men. They jumped away from the car and into the ditch on the side of the road as she swerved to the far shoulder and tapped the car lightly as she sped past it. The car spun into the ditch and landed near the men.

"Holy moly," Leo said. "That was phenomenal driving, Angel. Why did you want a ballcap?"

"I didn't want Stuart to have it on when he leaned out the window." She handed the cap back to Stuart. Stuart rolled his eyes as he put on his cap while Leo laughed.

"Is that it for a while?" Leo asked.

"No," Aimee Louise said.

Stuart stared at her. "They were amateurs. We may still run across professionals."

Stuart scanned the road and the surrounding countryside as they sped toward the surgeon's home.

"All the fields are overcome with weeds," Leo said. "Looks like a lot of farmers have left."

"They may have quit mowing their fields that border the road," Stuart said. "No reason to advertise there's anyone around to rob."

Leo nodded. "We'll turn left at a dirt road about two miles ahead, Angel."

When she neared the road, she said, "Tell Red and Andy to hang on."

Stuart lowered his window and shouted, "Turn to left. Hang on."

Andy tapped on the cab to let Stuart know they'd heard him.

"Brace yourself," Aimee Louise said as she slammed on the brakes and swung onto the dirt road then accelerated. After she rounded a curve, she pulled over, turned off the engine, and jumped out of the truck without closing her door.

"What's she doing?" Leo asked.

"Listening for any vehicles that might have been following us. Stay here." Stuart stepped out but didn't close his door either. He glanced up as he passed the truck bed, and Red and Andy stood on ammo boxes for a better view of the road.

"Truck coming," Aimee Louise said. "Down."

Red and Andy ducked, and Stuart concentrated but heard nothing except birds then he heard the whining tires of the oncoming truck that was approaching their dirt road. He froze as the truck sped past them. Stuart stepped closer to Aimee Louise who continued to listen before she said, "We can continue down the road now."

After Aimee Louise started the truck and headed down the lane, Leo asked, "Why did we stop? They couldn't have seen us after we rounded that curve."

"The road's dusty, and they might have been able to see our dust plume," Stuart said.

Aimee Louise nodded.

"These houses look abandoned," Leo said. "I think most of the folks were retired. After one more house, we'll see Doc's driveway on the right. You can't see his house from the road."

Aimee Louise slowed then pulled into the driveway and stopped at the downed tree.

"Looks like he's not here," Leo said.

"Looks like he could be to me." Stuart smiled. "He dropped that tree. There's a clean cut on that stump."

"I'll walk down the driveway to the house and let him know it's me," Leo said.

"Good. I'll go with you," Stuart said.

"I'll back out and reposition. Let Red and Andy know what we're doing," Aimee Louise said.

After Stuart briefed Andy and Red, Leo walked down the driveway while Stuart stepped quietly through the woods in parallel with Leo.

When they neared the house, Leo stopped. "Hey, Doc. It's Leo."

Leo took another step and shouted, "It's Leo Webster."

"Hold it," a man called out. "What's your house dog's name?"

Stuart nodded. *Smart man.*

"Holly."

"Come to the yard then stop, so I can see it's you," the man said.

When Leo reached the yard, the man asked, "Are you alone?"

"No, Scott Newton's boy, Stuart, is with me."

"You two can come up to the house."

When they reached the house, Doc leaned on his cane as he came outside. "What brings you here?"

"Cal Henderson was ambushed and shot in the chest," Stuart said. "He's at Dad's farm and is not doing well. He has a gaping exit wound, and Dad is afraid he's bleeding internally."

"We came to get you, Doc," Leo said. "Jennie's with him, but Cal's in bad condition."

"I need to take a few things. Stuart, come in, and you can help me gather what I need."

When they went inside, an old black dog with a gray muzzle greeted Stuart.

"This is Ethel. I don't suppose she could go with us," Doc said.

"She sure can. We can lift her into the back of the truck."

The doctor chuckled as he cleared one pantry shelf of medications and medical equipment into an old, cracked leather medical bag, and two more shelves into a box. "I bought this valise years ago because I thought every country doctor should have one. Never used it before."

When it was full, Dr. Larkin said, "If you'll carry this, I'll grab my overnight bag."

After he returned with a small overnight suitcase, he said, "My neighbors gave me food and I've got a box of canned goods in the pantry, four fifty-pound sacks of dogfood in the closet, and a few boxes I keep packed in case I have to evacuate fast. Can we take all that and Ethel's bed and a couple of quilts she likes?"

The two older men and the old dog walked up the driveway to the truck while Stuart rushed ahead with the canned goods. After Stuart lowered the tailgate, Andy took the box from him.

"We'll have an old dog traveling with us and four fifty-pound sacks of dogfood along with some boxes. I saw a utility cart in the yard. If we load it, we can bring all four bags and her bed to the truck in one trip then the rest of the boxes in a second trip."

Andy jumped down, and they ran to the house. After they loaded the bags and Ethel's things into the wagon, they hurried to the truck then lifted Ethel into the back before they loaded the dogfood.

"I'll ride in the back with Ethel," Dr. Larkin said, and Andy and Stuart helped him up.

After Stuart and Andy hauled out the boxes from the house and loaded them into the truck, Andy climbed into the truck bed, and Stuart asked, "Everybody set?"

When Andy nodded, Stuart raised the tailgate then hurried to his seat. Aimee Louise started the engine then drove to the end of the driveway and waited a moment before she accelerated.

"That went faster than I expected," Leo said. "Kudos to you and your team, Stuart."

"Thanks, but now we have to get everyone to Dad's farm safely." Stuart focused on the road ahead and the fields and woods as the truck sped down the highway.

After they crossed the county line, Leo said, "Not much farther. I hope we're in time."

Aimee Louise slowed the truck. "Uncle Dan. Tell Red."

"Where?" Stuart asked, and she pointed to the field ahead on the left.

Stuart lowered his window and hung out as he shouted, "Uncle Dan ahead on the left, Red."

After he pulled himself inside the cab, he glanced back at Red and Andy who had moved the doctor and Ethel to the middle of the truck. Red was positioned at the left side of the truck, and Andy was at the rear.

"I expect them to throw something heavy onto the road. Be prepared for me to swerve," Aimee Louise said.

"Should we warn Red and Andy?" Leo asked.

"Red would know," Stuart said.

Aimee Louise accelerated as she continued toward the danger ahead of them. Aimee Louise veered toward the right before two men reached the roadside and rolled a fifty-five-gallon drum onto the road then veered left as the drum rolled across the road to the right shoulder. When more men popped up in the field and began shooting, Red and Andy returned their fire and four men dropped into the weeds. After the truck sped past them, the two men in the ditch rose with rifles. Red and Andy shot them, and Aimee Louise maintained her speed.

"We can't slow down?" Leo asked.

"No," she said. "How far are we from the next crossroad?"

"Maybe two miles," Leo said.

Aimee Louise pushed the accelerator to the floor. Stuart glanced at the speedometer.

One hundred miles per hour. She intends to outrun the jerks.

Stuart squinted out his side window at the blur of waving weeds and grass then blinked to refocus on the road ahead. "Leo, if I can raise up, can you slide over to my seat?" he asked.

"I think so."

After Stuart stood to place his hands on the back of his seat, he pushed his back against the windshield. Leo struggled to get past him, so Stuart stepped over Leo's legs before he dropped onto the seat next to Aimee Louise. Leo handed Stuart his rifle, and Aimee Louise leaned forward as Stuart held his rifle behind her and aimed out her window.

As Aimee Louise sped past the intersection, Stuart said, "I thought I saw a car pull onto the road down a ways, but I'm not sure."

Aimee Louise nodded but didn't ease off the accelerator.

Stuart moved his rifle away from Aimee Louise, and she leaned back. Stuart narrowed his eyes as he scanned the road, trees, and fields ahead.

"I see something in the road ahead," he said.

"Yes," Aimee Louise said. "Move to your window."

"Leo, we have to switch seats again. Ready?" Stuart asked.

"Go," Leo said.

The second that Stuart lifted himself off the seat, Leo slid next to Aimee Louise, and Stuart stepped over him and held onto the grab bar as he eased down to sit on the seat next to the window.

"I was a little more graceful that time." Stuart focused on the countryside on the right.

"Ahead," Aimee Louise said. "Concrete blocks across the road and men hiding in the fields on both sides of the road. Are there any side roads we could take before we get there?"

"Yes," Leo said. "Slow down. It's hard to see, but there's a dirt road on the right that looks like a driveway."

As Aimee Louise slowed her speed, Stuart said, "They must not know about it or they would have built their roadblock on this side of it."

"Unless they expected vehicles coming the other way," Leo said.

"Just ahead," Stuart said.

Aimee Louise swerved on the road to simulate loss of control then careened down into the ditch before she turned and slowed as she drove in the grass alongside the rutted dirt road.

"They're going to think we went into the ditch, aren't they?" Leo stretched to peer into the back of the truck. "Do you think everybody back there was braced for it?"

"That was the idea, and Red would have caught on when Aimee Louise swerved the first time," Stuart said. "It will take the attackers a while to catch up with us. Where will we come out?"

"We'll be on a back road that goes to another dirt road not too far east of Scott's house."

"Can we get to the state road?" Aimee Louise asked.

"The road dead ends, but there's a path that hunters have used for years."

Stuart lowered his window and stuck his head out to listen for any vehicles.

Red leaned over the side. "I call raincheck."

Stuart nodded and held out his hand for Red to see as he put up his thumb.

"What did she say?" Leo asked.

"Raincheck." Stuart chuckled, and Leo laughed.

"What does that mean?" Aimee Louise asked.

"It means that we have to get Doc to Mr. Cal and don't have time to waste on any more attacks, but we'll be happy to fight them later instead," Stuart said.

"All that in one word?" Aimee Louise asked. "Fascinating."

As they approached another dirt road on the left, Leo said, "This is our turn."

Stuart's eyes widened. "Is it wide enough for us?"

Leo shrugged. "This truck's pretty wide, isn't it? I hope so."

Aimee Louise slowed as she maneuvered the narrow, single track road. Low-hanging tree branches and bushes scraped the hood of the truck, and downed limbs across the road slowed their travel pace. When Aimee Louise came to a section of deep ruts, she dropped the truck into four-wheel drive and maintained a slow and steady speed while she gripped the steering wheel to maintain control.

When they were past the worst of the ruts, Leo exhaled. "You're a natural driver, Angel. I can't imagine anyone else getting through that section of road."

Stuart smiled when she nodded. "That's why I always ask her to drive," Stuart said.

"We just passed the back of my property," Leo said. "Our turn isn't that much farther away."

When the eight-foot-wide dirt road came up on their left, Stuart said, "That looks like a regular interstate highway after being on this road."

Aimee Louise turned left and increased her speed.

Stuart narrowed his eyes as he stared at the road ahead. "Looks like the road ends."

"We're almost there. Angel, watch for an opening on your side. It's the hunters' path and will be overrun with weeds."

Aimee Louise nodded as she slowed then drove into the brush.

Stuart frowned and clutched his armrest. *I don't see a path.*

As Aimee Louise maneuvered the truck through brush and weeds, Stuart examined both sides of the truck and peered at the front. *The trees are thick alongside us. How can she tell where there are no trees?*

"State road's coming up," Leo said.

Aimee Louise stopped and lowered her window, so Stuart lowered his to listen.

I hear birds and a few cars, but I can't tell if it's interstate noise or someone's coming this way.

When Aimee Louise continued to the state road and paused before she turned left, Stuart scanned the road to their right. *Must have been interstate.* "I'm clear."

After she turned at the Newtons' driveway, Leo exhaled. "That's about all the excitement I can take for a long time."

Sandra, Henry, and Brody waited in front of the house as Aimee Louise pulled in then parked. Stuart jumped out and rushed to the back of the truck and dropped the tailgate. Ethel wiggled to him.

"She's had enough travel and excitement," Doc said as Stuart lifted out the old dog. Stuart helped Doc out of the truck bed, and Andy handed the doctor his medical bag.

Doc hurried to the house then he and Sandra went inside. Henry and Brody rushed to Stuart, and Stuart knelt down, hugged Henry, and scratched Brody's ears. When he released Henry, the boy and his dog raced to Aimee Louise while Andy and Stuart moved dogfood to the edge of the tailgate.

Rosalie jumped down. "I'll grab a utility wagon."

"The dogfood needs to go in the house, but I don't know where." Stuart pulled the overloaded wagon, and Andy pushed.

"I'll ask." Rosalie ran into the house.

When she returned, Rosalie said, "Mama Sandra wants it near the bench at the back door."

As they carried the dogfood into the house, Sandra hurried into the kitchen. "Doc needs the box of medical supplies. He said you'd know which box." She filled a large pot with water and set it on the stove to boil.

Stuart ran to the truck and grabbed the medical box while Andy brought the wagon. Stuart handed the box to Andy. "Take this in, and I'll load the rest of the boxes into the wagon. If you have a chance, ask Mom where she wants Doc's things to go. We'll need to unload the ammunition. I think Dad will want it in the living room but ask him."

"Will do." Andy hurried to the house with the box.

Henry and Angel came to the back of the truck while Stuart loaded boxes into the wagon.

"Big Bear, do you think it would be okay for me and Brody to take the dog inside?"

"Sure. Her name is Ethel."

Henry gave Ethel and Brody dog treats then clapped his hands. "Come on, Ethel. Come on, girl. Let's go, Brody." Ethel followed him to the house while Brody pranced along and tried to catch her tail.

"Aimee Louise, after we take Doc's boxes inside, we'll have to unload the ammunition."

She strode to the driver's seat. "I'll back up the truck closer to the house."

Andy returned. "Your mom said to put Doc's things in the living room for now."

After Stuart and Andy placed the boxes in the living room, they headed out to the truck to unload the ammunition. "I suspect Mom's planning on putting a bed in the living room for the doctor, so he'll be on the first floor," Stuart said.

"Your house sure fills up quickly," Andy said as they began unloading the boxes of ammunition. "So, where are we putting the ammo?"

"I guess in the living room until Mom or Dad comes up with a better place. I think Mom's trying to keep the kitchen and family room available for people to gather."

"Or sleep." Andy snorted.

After they stacked the ammunition in the living room, Leo stood in the doorway. "I don't want to cause any extra work, and I don't see how I can help much here. I'm worried about Holly; she's not used to being apart from me this long."

Red came up behind Leo. "We'll walk back with you. It's an easy walk."

"I should have thought about this earlier, but you should take some ammo with you," Stuart said. "Let's see what's here that you can use, and you can load one of the utility wagons."

"That's a good idea," Andy said as Red surveyed their inventory.

"This one, this one, and this one." She pointed to three boxes.

Andy and Stuart each carried out a box then Stuart returned for the third.

"Your dad has my proxy," Rosalie said as they prepared to leave.

"Mine too," Andy added.

After they left, Aimee Louise met Stuart before he entered the house. "Your mom sterilized instruments for the doctor. He agreed with your dad and intends to find the source of the internal bleeding. I asked your mom if she'd heard any gunfire, and she told me she's been too busy to pay attention to anything else. Shouldn't the Cabellos and Mitchells have been here by now?"

"Yes. I'd forgotten all about them."

"I'll run to the road to see if they're in sight."

"Give me a minute to grab my rifle." He hugged her. "Don't leave."

"I can't unless you let go of me."

"That's not going to happen. Stay right here."

Stuart snickered as he picked up his rifle. *I got even. I went literal on her.*

After Stuart returned, Aimee Louise raced up the driveway, and he ran at his usual pace. *She'll let me know if there's any trouble.*

When he neared the end of the driveway, Aimee Louise was nowhere in sight. He stepped into the trees then crept through the woods in parallel with the state road until he was closer to the Cabellos'. He moved toward the state road, peered along the side of the road toward the Cabellos' and Mitchells', and spotted Aimee Louise's feet sticking out of a culvert. As she backed out of the culvert, he glanced up the road and saw the roadblock on the other side of the Mitchells' driveway. He stepped back into the trees and waited for her.

Aimee Louise crawled into the trees then joined Stuart, and they moved away from the road as they headed back to the Newtons' farm.

"What are you thinking?" Stuart asked.

"We probably need Andy and Rosalie. If this one is like the other roadblock, men are hiding in the cover alongside the road. Is there a way to walk to the Cabellos' a back way?"

"I'm sure there must be, but it's been a long time since I roamed these woods. I'd rather check with Dad, and you can see if Red and Andy will leave Leo by himself."

They ran back to the farmhouse together then Aimee Louise peeled off and raced to the Websters'.

When Stuart went inside the house, Henry was sitting on the kitchen floor and pulling a long string along the floor. Brody stalked the string then pounced on it while Ethel dozed nearby.

"Do you know where Papa Scott is?" Stuart asked.

"With the doctor," Henry said.

When Stuart neared the bedroom, Scott stood in the doorway.

"Can I talk to you a minute, Dad?"

The two men went out the front door.

"Angel and I want to check on the Cabellos and Mitchells." Stuart rested his rifle in the corner.

Scott frowned. "They should have been here by now. I think we've all lost track of time."

"I did too until Angel reminded me. We went to the state road and there's a roadblock just past the Mitchells' driveway. If it's anything like the one we saw on the road, there are men hiding in the fields. Do you know of any way that Angel and I could get to the Cabellos by foot?"

Scott sat on a rocker and gazed at the sky. "I'd like to say no because you and Angel scare me to death, but yes, there is. Let's go inside, and I'll draw you a rough map."

When they went into the office, Scott closed the door then pulled out a county map before he drew a crude map. "This is the state road, and this is our driveway. Here's the Cabellos' driveway then the Mitchells' driveway. Here are the overpass and the interstate."

He added an X at the far end of the Cabellos driveway then tapped the X. "That's the house." Scott pointed to the county map. "This gives you an idea of how bad my scale is, but you get the general idea."

He continued his sketch. "West of us, just past our property line, is a deer trail. Hunters have kept it open and, at least until two years ago or so, have put out deer corn."

He drew a straight line then curved it up then down to the X. "Right after this curve, the deer trail veers off to the left. There's no path between that point and the Cabellos, but you'll be close enough to find your way through the brush. Wear high boots and long-sleeved shirts. There are some patches of wild blackberries in there."

"Thanks, Dad. Angel's gone to the Websters to see if Red and Andy want to go with us."

"Whatever you do, be safe, but I know you will." Scott rose. "What's Henry doing?"

"Playing with Brody in the kitchen."

"I'm not serving any useful purpose by standing around; I might have an outside project for Henry and me. I'll talk to him after you leave."

Stuart smiled. "He'll like that. Thanks, Dad."

Scott went inside, and Stuart waited on the porch for Aimee Louise. When she returned with Red and Andy, Stuart asked, "Do you need a break before we head out? Dad said we'd need long-sleeved shirts and boots."

Andy and Red opened their backpacks and put on their shirts. "Uncle Leo always told me the same thing, so I carry a long-sleeved shirt in my backpack," Andy said.

"I need a shirt. Does everyone have water?" Aimee Louise asked.

"Probably only you," Rosalie said. "I'll get water for three while you get your shirt."

When Aimee Louise and Rosalie returned, Rosalie handed Andy and Stuart their water bottles.

"Here's the map Dad drew for us." Stuart explained the map.

"Sounds relatively straight forward," Andy said.

Stuart folded the hand drawn map and put it in his back pocket. "Let's go."

"What's our plan?" Rosalie asked.

"Don't go where the bad guys are," Andy said.

"Got it." Rosalie snickered. "Who leads?"

"Aimee Louise," Stuart and Andy said in unison.

Aimee Louise raced to the path to the Smith farm with Rosalie at her side.

"That was a mistake, wasn't it?" Andy asked as he and Stuart ran to catch up with the swift young women.

CHAPTER FIVE

When Stuart and Andy approached the Smith barn, Aimee Louise waved then she and Rosalie ran toward the Smith driveway.

"We'll wait for you at the state road," Rosalie said before they disappeared.

"We can either jog or take a break. There's no sense in running hard in this heat," Stuart said.

"Let's walk for just a bit to cool down then jog," Andy said, and Stuart chuckled.

When they reached the driveway, Stuart said, "Let's go."

As they neared the state road, Stuart said, "We're running faster than I expected, but it's a comfortable pace."

"It took the pressure off when we decided we didn't have to keep up with our star runners."

Aimee Louise and Rosalie waited at the end of the driveway.

"The roadblock goes across the pavement but not the shoulders. There was no one in sight," Rosalie said.

"What?" Andy's face reddened. "You might have been seen and shot."

Stuart sighed. "No, they wouldn't have spooked their prey. I know for a fact that Angel has the stealth of a hunting predator."

Andy stared at Stuart then exhaled. "Aimee Louise leads, right?"

Stuart aimed his rifle toward the roadblock, and Andy faced the opposite direction as Aimee Louise and Rosalie darted across the road. After they disappeared into the woods, Stuart said, "Go."

Andy dashed to the woods while Stuart maintained his stance. When Stuart didn't see any movement, he joined Andy in the woods, and they crept along the hunters' old trail with Andy in the lead and Stuart five yards behind him. As they approached the curve in the path that headed to the left, Andy turned back and shrugged, and Stuart held up his hand for Andy to stay where he was.

While they stood motionless, Stuart scanned the area until Rosalie peered at them from behind a tree in the brush then waved for them to follow her. Andy rolled his eyes at Stuart before he stepped into the brush. Stuart closed the distance between him and Andy to keep Rosalie in his sight. After Rosalie vanished into the brush, they paused until she reappeared. Stuart exhaled in relief when Aimee Louise moved silently toward them through the thick brush. *I knew she was waiting for us, but I still don't like it.*

"Follow me through the brush," Aimee Louise whispered. "We're almost at the house. We didn't see anyone, so we don't know if they are inside or if they are okay. Red's in place to your left. You and Andy cover the other side of me. If you take a few steps straight ahead, you'll see the house. Red will call for Nate, and I'm going to check the back."

Stuart growled, "I don't like it."

"Knew you wouldn't." Aimee Louise disappeared into the brush, and Stuart and Andy stepped forward quickly then stopped.

She was right. There's the house.

"Hey, Cabellos." Red shouted in her remarkably loud command voice. "Anybody home?"

"Who wants to know?" A man's voice shouted in response.

Stuart frowned. *Sounds like Nate, but I'm not sure.*

"Red, for starters," Rosalie said.

"Who else?"

"Red's Angel team," Red said.

Stuart smiled when he glanced at Andy who rolled his eyes.

"Better not be armed—I'll sic my killer dog on you."

Rosalie laughed. "Dang it, Nate. It's hard to be all scary serious when you threaten me with that little roly-poly puffball, Pixie."

Nate chuckled as he opened the front door. "Nobody laughs like you, Red. The Mitchells are here. We're all hunkered down; I guess you know about the roadblock and the ambush set up at the state road."

"Yep. Okay if I check the house?"

"Sure. I'll wait for Stuart and the rest of them out here."

Andy groaned. "I wish she wouldn't do that."

"Know what you mean." Stuart strode into the yard and waved at Nate.

When Rosalie returned to the front porch, she said, "All clear."

Andy hurried to Rosalie's side and hugged her as Aimee Louise walked toward the house from the back.

"Let's go inside," Aimee Louise said.

After they were inside, Lela said, "Why don't I challenge the kids to that ladder board game that Sam likes so much?"

Lela, Dolly, Cami Sue, Sam, and Brandon hurried to the family room to set up their game, and Pixie and her brother, Tracker, scrambled after them.

"We'll be comfortable in the kitchen," Charo said.

Tom Mitchell and Judge Cabello led the way. "My son always wanted a big family because he was an only child. He would be happy to see that all of us can sit around this table that he and I built." Tom patted the wooden top. "So, why are we sitting around this table?"

Aimee Louise shuddered, and Stuart put his arm around her chair.

She's anxious about the big group. How can I help?

Stuart took Aimee Louise's hand and cleared his throat. "While Red made sure it was safe for us to approach Nate's house, Aimee Louise made her way through the brush to the back section of the property."

"I came out at the Mitchells' back yard, and two men were hauling out broken furniture," Aimee Louise said. "One man complained about cleaning up someone else's mess, and the other one told him they had an hour to get the house in shape for the chief's southwest Georgia headquarters."

"What do we do?" Judge asked. "How do we take back Tom's house before they make it their headquarters?"

"We wait," Aimee Louise said.

"That's a terrible idea," Nate said. "We let them take over and use—"

"No." Charo interrupted. "We don't let them take over southwest Georgia. We trap them and stop them."

Nate growled, "That's too risky."

"I agree with Nate," David said. "I won't allow you to endanger our children."

Rosalie stared at Aimee Louise then smiled. "They go to the Newtons'."

Peyton rose and paced to the back door and peered outside. "Four children and the puppies? And our older folks? They can't make the walk to the Newtons' farm."

Judge Cabello snorted. "I've walked ten miles a day my entire life."

"Lela and I won't slow anybody down. Of course, I might not be as spry and braggy tomorrow," Tom chuckled.

"So, who's going to take them? What about all the kids' stuff?" Nate asked.

"Every child can wear a backpack, and we'll rig carriers for the two puppies. I'll take them to the Newtons'," Charo said.

Nate crossed his arms. "You can't go by yourself."

"Of course, she can't," the judge said. "Tom, Lela, and I will go along too."

"That's not what I meant, Dad." Nate pushed away from the table and knocked his chair over when he stood.

Charo raised one eyebrow and glared at him, and Nate carefully righted his chair. "Sorry, honey," he said.

"I'll show you the way," Aimee Louise said.

No. Absolutely not. Stuart wanted to slam his chair to the floor just like Nate did but exhaled loudly instead.

Rosalie continued, "And I'll go along because Aimee Louise will want to come back here."

"How fast will you be ready?" Tom asked.

"Sounds like we've got less than an hour." Charo headed toward the living room.

Peyton followed her. "I'll do whatever I can to help."

"I'll talk to the children, and we'll start packing their backpacks if you'll talk to Ms. Lela and put the game away."

"Do you have anything for us before we help everyone pack?" Rosalie asked.

"Go ahead," Stuart said, and Rosalie and Aimee Louise rushed to help Charo.

Stuart started to speak but noticed Tom and the judge glance at each other and nod.

Now what?

"Tom and I are not leaving," the judge said. "We are two extra pairs of eyes and both of us are fairly good shots. As long as you don't expect us to chase after any bad guys, we'll be more useful here."

Stuart glanced at Nate, who shrugged.

Stuart bit his lip to hold back his smirk. *Not going to argue with two determined old guys?*

"It's unanimous. We think it's a rotten idea and you're a couple of hardheaded hombres, but we can't beat your argument," David said.

"So, if we're ready to toss around ideas, do we have any idea of how many men there are, and do they have any vehicles?" Nate asked.

"I'll take notes," the judge said. "Be right back." When he returned with a drawing pad and a blue art pencil, he sat at the table and jotted down Nate's questions.

"Nate's right," Stuart said. "We need more information about the men at the roadblock. Aimee Louise is our best stalker, but she scares me to death."

"I stalk poachers," David said. "That makes me a professional stalker."

"I'll go with you," Andy said. "I'm not a professional stalker but darn near close. I am world-renowned for catching smokers in the boys' bathroom."

"Well, there we go then. What else?" the judge asked.

"There used to be barbed wire fences along the east and north sides of my property," Tom said. "They'd be overrun with brush, but it might be useful to know if they're still intact."

"Same at Dad's farm. It's hard to find if it's down," Stuart said.

"We could go near the state road from this property to see if we can spot any vehicles then return here. If you could take us to the north end of Nate's property, could you help us find the fence?" David asked.

"Do you happen to have any alcohol at your house, Tom?" Nate asked.

"I've got whiskey and rum, but it's locked in a closet," Tom said. "I'm sure they'll bust into it eventually."

"I doubt if whoever finds it will share, so we'll listen for rowdiness, especially in the evenings," Stuart said.

"How do we take advantage of that?" Tom asked.

"I'm not sure, but I do know my former partner has remarkable knife skills if we want to disappear a couple of guys," Nate said. "Peyton and I worked undercover together for a while and spent a lot of time on stakeouts even before we became partners. We can keep an eye on the guys at the Mitchells' house. We're a good team."

"No surprise, but I didn't know about that," David said.

"It wasn't common knowledge, even in the Agency."

"I know Peyton was always reluctant to share much of anything about her work even with coworkers," David said. "It used to frustrate me how closed-mouthed she was, but I think it saved her life and Brandon's more than once."

Nate nodded.

"Angel, Red, and I are a good team," Stuart said. "While they're gone, I'd like to check out our perimeter for vulnerable areas if we're attacked, so we can discuss ways to make our defense stronger. When Angel and Red return, I'd like to scout out some good placements for our eventual ambush. I have some ideas, but Angel sees things the rest of us miss."

"Tom and I will take a good inventory of what's in the house, particularly guns, ammunition, and food that doesn't require a lot of cooking. We'll take over the meals and clean up," the judge said.

Peyton strolled into the kitchen. "They're ready to go. Come get your kisses and hugs."

They walked into the living room, and after everyone said good-bye with hugs and kisses, Rosalie opened the front door then said, "If y'all don't mind leaving the room, we need to go over our travel instructions."

Aimee Louise pointed to the hallway, and the adults stepped out of the children's sight and listened.

* * *

After the adults left, Aimee Louise said, "Rosalie will give us our traveling instructions. She'll be the only one speaking. The rest of us will remain very quiet while we pay attention."

Rosalie said, "This is very serious, and we have to be extremely quiet to keep everyone safe. We follow Aimee Louise. No one gets in front of her, not even me. If Aimee Louise crouches, we all crouch, even Grandma Lela and Mommy Charo. No talking, whispering, giggling, falling, screaming, kicking leaves with our feet, or any other noisemaking. Not even by accident. If we have to sneeze, we stifle it to keep it quiet. Show me how to stifle my sneeze."

Rosalie paused before she spoke again.

She nodded. "That's exactly right. We grab our long-sleeved shirts and hold them over our nose to sneeze. Aimee Louise has a soft bag and will pass it around. Pretend that you're dropping any sounds or noises into it. She'll take good care of them, but no noises until she dumps out the sack at Mama Sandra's house. If you need to warn me about a terrible danger, hold up your hand, and everyone stop. If anyone in front of you does not stop, don't worry about it. Aimee Louise will stop them soon. I'll be behind everybody. Everyone understand?"

Aimee Louise waited for Rosalie's signal while Rosalie watched Lela, Charo, and each child as they nodded. After Rosalie pointed to her, Aimee Louise held the sack in front of the two women and each child. Aimee Louise silently folded the cloth bag and placed it into her backpack before she motioned for everyone to move forward.

* * *

After their travelers left, Peyton looked at the motionless men in the hallway and mouthed, "Can we talk?"

"I'm afraid to," Tom whispered. "Those two are formidable, aren't they?"

Stuart exhaled then peeked around the corner. "They're gone. That was absolutely mesmerizing. I knew Aimee Louise and Rosalie worked with the children at Major's farm, but I didn't realize how almost magical the two of them are. How are they carrying the puppies?"

Peyton tiptoed to the front door and closed it quietly. "We're safe. Charo and I rigged a front puppy carrier so they could see her. When she tried it out, they fell asleep. We're hoping the walking motion will keep them quiet and maybe asleep. What are we doing again?"

The judge chuckled as everyone moved back to the kitchen. "Let's just drink warm beer and let those two tell the bad guys to leave."

"Best plan I've heard all day," Tom said. "Meanwhile, we're supposed to inventory this house, Rodney. Let's start with the master bedroom."

"Peyton, we're supposed to stakeout the Mitchell's house. Before we go, I'll catch you up on our plans so far." Nate and Peyton filled their canteens then went out the back door.

David and Andy filled their canteens then headed toward the front door while Stuart began his perimeter walk.

* * *

Aimee Louise selected a path through the thick brush with the least amount of blackberry bushes. She maintained a slow but steady pace and signaled for frequent halts. When she reached the hunters' path, she stopped the group and crouched after Rosalie stepped through the brush. Rosalie moved to a point where she could see all the faces then waved Aimee Louise forward. When Angel stood, everyone else did too, and she motioned for the group to follow her.

I'm glad Rosalie and I have a safety check in place. No one is overheated.

When they had only a fourth of their total distance to the state road left to go, Aimee Louise stopped then sat near the brush. *The birds quit singing.*

After everyone else sat near the brush where they had stopped, she rose to her feet; when Dolly began to rise, Aimee Louise shook her head and motioned for Dolly to sit. Aimee Louise pointed to the treetops then tapped her ear, and Rosalie shook her head.

Aimee Louise slipped into the brush across from where she had taken her seat on the ground; she listened and waited. *Still no birds.*

She slipped closer to the state road then crouched when she heard men's voices near the entrance to the hunters' path.

A man shouted, "You're only half done. Get that second roadblock set up now!"

We have to go back.

Aimee Louise traced her steps back to the group. When she reached them, she saw the concern in Rosalie's cloud. Aimee Louise waved her hand to indicate movement away from the state road. Rosalie nodded, and Aimee Louise motioned for everyone to rise then turn around, and Rosalie led the group to the end of the hunters' path. When Aimee Louise saw Rosalie waiting at the end of the path, she motioned for Rosalie to continue through the brush. When Rosalie neared the Cabellos' property, she hooted their barred owl cry, and Stuart answered. After Aimee Louise cleared the brush, Rosalie led the group to the back door, and Stuart stepped into line next to Aimee Louise. When they reached the back door, Aimee Louise indicated they would go inside. When everyone was inside, Aimee Louise pulled out the cloth bag and shook it upside down.

"Thank you, Angel," Lela said. "I'm going to sit while you tell us what happened."

Charo released the puppies from their carrier. "Dolly and Brandon, give your puppies some water then take them outside for their potty break. Stay very close to the back door and come back inside after they've peed." Charo sat next to Lela.

"The bad guys are setting up a second roadblock near the entrance to the hunters' path. We couldn't continue," Aimee Louise said.

"Should we stay packed?" Charo asked.

"For now, yes, but everyone can put their backpacks in their rooms."

When Dolly and Brandon returned, Lela said, "Girls, put your backpacks in the girls' bedroom. Sam, show Brandon where the guest bedroom is. We'll put him, his mom, and his dad in there. After you put down your backpacks, meet me in the living room. You all owe me a rematch."

"I'll bring snacks," Charo said.

"What do we do now?" Rosalie asked after everyone had left the room for the bedrooms or the living room.

"We need to find another way to get them to the farm, but we don't want to take them across the road between the two roadblocks," Aimee Louise said. "We need to go exploring."

Tom and the judge came into the kitchen from the bedrooms.

"Cami Sue told us you had to turn back because the bad guys were in the way," Tom said.

After Stuart explained what Aimee Louise had discovered, the judge asked, "Is there an alternative route, Tom?"

Tom lowered himself onto a chair at the table. "Can't think on my feet; they're hurting."

Judge Rodney sat next to him.

Stuart pulled out the map his dad had drawn. "This is how we got here. The deer trail is just across the road from Dad's property line."

"That's right." He traced the curve on the hand-drawn map. "See how it curves the other way? It continues parallel to the state road and goes to the county road."

"Wow," Stuart said. "All the way to the county road. That's too far for the children to walk. How do we find a way to the Websters'?"

"Is there a county map here, Tom?" Judge Rodney asked.

Tom rose and opened a kitchen drawer then pulled out a county map. After he spread it on the table, Rodney traced a creek that meandered through the woods then went underground near the state road. "Where is that?"

"It's near the middle of the Websters' property," Tom said.

Aimee Louise left the kitchen then returned with Charo.

"Aimee Louise and I want to see the maps again," Charo said.

Tom used a pencil to trace the approximate location of the deer trail on the county map. "It comes out of the brush onto the county line road about here."

"The county line road is too far away to walk back to the Newtons'," Aimee Louise said.

Tom pointed with the pencil. "This creek crosses the deer trail then goes underground not far from the state road. This point is about the middle of the Websters' farm."

"A more doable hike for the children. Aimee Louise thinks we should eat lunch then leave while the bad guys are busy with their roadblock," Charo said.

"It may be too much for Ms. Lela," Aimee Louise added. "Charo will talk to her."

After Charo left the room, Tom said, "Can't you give her another day to recover?"

"We don't think we have the luxury of time, Mr. Mitchell," Rosalie said.

Lela came into the kitchen with Charo behind her, and she sat at the kitchen table next to her husband.

"The children are finishing up their game," Lela said. "Show me the alternate route to the Websters' farm on the map, Tom."

He used the pencil to point out the deer trail, where it crossed the creek, and the point where the creek ended near the state road. "The Websters' farm is on the other side."

"It's a longer walk," she said, "and it's through brush almost the same distance that we walked the deer trail earlier." She patted Tom's hand. "I'm still weaker than I thought from that beating."

"What if you had a day to recover?" Tom asked. "I think you should go."

"I understand, and I can go whenever Aimee Louise says, but right now, I don't want to endanger the children. Charo and I will pull together a snack for our hikers to eat before they leave."

"I'll bring the children to the kitchen for their snack," Charo said.

"Two days then," Tom said.

"Tom Mitchell, you'll just have to put up with me. Now, did you and Rodney finish your inventory?"

"Almost," Tom said as Judge Rodney grabbed his clipboard before the two men left the kitchen.

"All of us will need to carry water. Do we have enough containers?" Aimee Louise asked.

"I'll find some," Rosalie said.

Aimee Louise glanced at Stuart. "Did you want to talk to me?"

"Let's go out back," he said.

* * *

When they sat in the shade on the porch, Stuart said, "Tell me everything you saw and heard."

Aimee Louise told him the details of their hike, and Stuart listened intently.

"You knew the men were at the state road before you heard them because the birds stopped singing? You're really remarkable." Stuart put his arm around her. "Why didn't you try to find a way around them? Why did you bring everybody back?"

"I didn't know how long it would take me to find a new route; I was worried the children would become restless waiting for me, and I knew Ms. Lela was in a lot of pain."

"Her cloud?"

"Yes, but she doesn't want anyone to know how much the pain bothers her."

When Rosalie joined them on the porch, Aimee Louise shifted closer to Stuart to make room for Rosalie to sit next to her.

"I have the water bottles, and lunch is almost ready." Rosalie tilted her head and peered at Aimee Louise. "What are we talking about? What's wrong?"

Stuart stared over Angel's head. *I wish I could see her cloud.*

"You think we have to adjust our plan, don't you?" he asked.

"All the farms—Mitchell, Cabello, Webster, and Newton—are trapped inside the two roadblocks but split by the state road," Aimee Louise said. "We should consider consolidating. Also, after we take the children to your folks' farm, their parents will want to leave here."

Stuart rubbed the back of his neck. "What if you and I take the children, Charo, Nate, Peyton, and David to the Websters' then return for the rest of the group?"

"Nope," Rosalie said. "You don't have time to learn all the signals that Angel and I have developed over the years."

"Red and I could take Charo and the children to your folks' farm and return for a second trip before dark, but Ms. Lela will need help to travel through the brush, and there's a possibility that we'd be traveling in the dark," Aimee Louise said.

"Andy and I could help Lela," Stuart said. "We have to discuss our latest idea with her and at least Peyton or David, if not the entire group."

"Let's start with Ms. Lela," Aimee Louise said.

"I'll talk to her then gather as many of the group as I can find," Rosalie said.

Stuart nodded. "We'll be inside in a few minutes."

"Now, you have something more," Aimee Louise said.

"I want to go with you and Red," Stuart said. "The three of us are a strong team."

Aimee Louise asked, "What if everyone wants to go in one trip?"

"That could be an option, and I think Rosalie could train them to be quiet and follow your directions just like she trained the children," Stuart said.

Rosalie came out of the house. "I talked to Ms. Lela. She's going to sit down and put her feet up, so she'll be ready whenever we tell her she's leaving. She's determined to go. Mr. Tom announced he's going with her, and the judge said he was too. What do you think about a large group going?"

Stuart chuckled. "It has real possibilities."

When the three of them went into the house, Peyton and Nate were inside.

"We heard your barred owl call, Red," Peyton said. "We thought you were trying to get our attention."

"You were right," she said. "How did you know it was me?"

"You're the only barred owl I know who calls with musical tones." Peyton snickered.

"The children's lunch is ready. Shall we have them come to the kitchen and eat? I don't need to be included in the discussion," Lela said. "I vote however Red votes."

"That's a good idea," Stuart said. "We can go to the living room."

While the children sat at the table for lunch, and the adults gathered in the living room, Andy and David came inside.

"Thought I heard your owl call." Andy squeezed into the overstuffed chair with Rosalie and put his arm around her.

Stuart gave the group a quick summary of Aimee Louise's discovery and her decision to return. "It originally made sense for us to have our team in two locations, but now we're all in between the two roadblocks but cut off from each other."

Andy nodded. "From a defense standpoint, it's logical for all of us to be centrally located."

"Exactly," Charo said. "If a team of bad guys attacked the Newton farm right now, we may not know, and even if we did, we couldn't rush to their aid. The same is true if we're attacked."

Stuart explained the new plan to avoid both roadblocks.

"Can I see those maps?" David asked.

When David rose to accept the maps that Stuart handed to him, Nate and Andy stood next to David.

"I know this creek," Andy said. "It's across the road from Uncle Leo's farm. The brush next to it isn't very thick, and there are some good fishing spots along the way. It's not a bad trail at all. As far as anyone near the second roadblock seeing us cross the road, I think there's a slight curve and a rise in the road somewhere between the Smith farm and the creek. We could easily find the best place to cross."

"That really changes our possibilities, doesn't it?" Tom asked.

While Aimee Louise gazed above each person's head, Stuart examined their faces as he asked, "Does anyone have any objections if we all leave for the Websters' farm after lunch?"

When no one spoke, Stuart asked, "Are we all in agreement, Angel?"

"Yes, we are."

"What about Ms. Lela?" Charo asked.

"She's determined to go," Tom said, "and I was worried about her until Andy mentioned how easy it is to walk alongside the creek. I'd forgotten that my son and I sometimes took the little girls fishing there. It's not a bad walk at all, especially compared to trying to push through some of the thickets around here."

"We'll carry what we can, but our shooters must have their hands free," Stuart said. "We could consider hiding any critical items in the woods, but we don't want to spend a lot of time here."

"Rodney and I will fix lunch if the rest of you want to pack and gather what we should take," Tom said. "If you put the items for us to carry in the living room, we can divide the load up and decide what we leave here."

"I have dibs on the puppies," Charo said.

"You already had your turn; it's my turn." Peyton grumbled.

"I called it first." Charo giggled as Peyton lightly punched her arm in jest.

"Do you happen to have an old duffle bag that can be worn on the back?" David asked Tom.

"I do somewhere; in fact, I think I have two or three. Lela will know where they are."

"My things are still packed—I'll check with Lela," David said.

"I don't have anything to pack. If I could see your inventory sheet, Judge, maybe I can gather items that could go into a duffle bag," Andy said.

After fifteen minutes, Rosalie called out, "Lunch is ready. Come eat!"

Rosalie, Aimee Louise, and Stuart were already in the kitchen when everyone came to the table.

"My helpers loaded up some food items that I selected for us to take. We'll see if I can pull a rolling suitcase. If I can't, I'll hand it off to Tom." Lela smiled.

While everyone ate canned chicken on crackers and a side of canned peaches, Peyton said, "You sure have the strong voice of command when you want to blast it out, girlfriend. Does that come from being a singer?"

Rosalie snickered. "I don't know; my mother had a beautiful singing voice, but she told me that nobody in the world could outshout me, even when I was three."

Andy snorted. "Can you imagine the formidable Red at three?"

When Rosalie glared at him, he winked at her, and she laughed. "No fair making me laugh," she grumbled.

"How's progress? What do we need to do before we can leave?" Stuart asked.

Lela said, "Check the living room for items to select to go into the duffle bags. I suggest whoever is going to wear them fill the bag then walk around the house outside to see if they need to adjust the weight, shift any items for comfort, or remove any noisy items."

"I'll take one," Stuart said. "How many are there?"

"Three," Andy said from the living room. "I've picked out mine."

"I'll take the third one." Nate hurried to the living room.

"So what does that leave for me to do?" Nate asked when he returned to the kitchen.

"You may be my personal escort," Lela said.

"I have the best job of all," Nate said, and Lela beamed.

Charo and Peyton came out of the bedrooms, and the four children followed them. "We liked your idea, Grandma Lela," Charo said. "We're going to do the same thing."

After everyone had walked around the house, and Nate retrieved Lela's walking stick, they congregated in the living room.

"I know everyone knows the rules because you heard them this morning, but Red's going to give us all a refresher," Stuart said.

Rosalie stood where everyone could see her and went through the hiking rules while everyone listened intently. Before she declared it was time for Aimee Louise's cloth bag, Rosalie said, "Everyone load up, and we'll meet in the front yard."

Nate had moved all of the items from Lela's rolling suitcase to his duffle bag; he offered Lela his arm as she descended the steps, and everyone lined up.

"Follow the person in front of you," Rosalie continued after everyone was in place. "Don't get in front of them. If they're too slow, slow yourself down. If they stop, you stop. You might not always be able to see Angel, but you can see the person in front of you. Ready to give your noises to Angel for safekeeping?"

Everyone nodded, and Aimee Louise went from person to person with her cloth sack to collect their noises. She and Stuart went to the head of the line, and she waved her hand high as she pointed forward; the group followed her in single file.

After everyone reached the deer trail, Aimee Louise and Stuart continued to the right, and the group followed along. After a short while, Aimee Louise signaled a halt then crouched on the side of the trail, and one by one, everyone else crouched on the same side of the trail. When Aimee Louise rose, Dolly, who was first in line behind her, remained in place. Peyton started to rise and was almost on her feet, but when she realized the children in front of her hadn't moved, she eased back to the ground. Peyton rolled her eyes at Stuart, and he smiled.

Aimee Louise raced ahead, and Stuart listened. *Birds are singing. Thank you, birds.*

After Aimee Louise returned, she raised her hands with her palms up, and Dolly rose to her feet. After all the rest of the travelers followed the action of the person in front of them, Aimee Louise continued on the deer path.

When they reached the creek, Stuart raised his eyebrows at the sight of the green, wide path alongside the creek. The gurgling creek tumbled over rocks and slapped against the side of the bank while a fish jumped and splashed back into the creek.

Stuart bit his lip. *I wonder who else wanted to shush that fish.*

He glanced back at Dolly, and her eyes twinkled as she put her finger up to her lips, and he smiled. *Can't beat that—a five-year-old understands me.*

Aimee Louise held up her hand and remained standing then slowly lowered to a sitting position, and one by one, everyone sat down.

Stuart scanned the trees. *I don't hear any birds.*

When Aimee Louise bent at her waist to lower her head, everyone copied her, and Stuart felt a wave of dread. He slowly moved his hand toward his rifle as the terrifying sound of someone crashing through the brush toward them intensified. He glanced at Dolly, and her face showed the horror he felt.

CHAPTER SIX

A doe and a yearling burst out of the brush and onto the bank then jumped across the creek and leapt into the brush on the other side. When Stuart glanced at Dolly, she pretended to bite her fingernails, and he smiled and nodded. *Five-year-old girls are awfully smart these days.*

After Aimee Louise rose and rolled her shoulders then shook her hands to relax her muscle tension, she nodded at Dolly. Dolly copied her, and so did everyone else down the line.

Stuart narrowed his eyes as he examined the brush where the deer had emerged. *Something spooked them.* He tapped Angel's arm; when she looked at him, he pointed to a narrow point in the creek ahead of them then the brush on the other side, and she nodded.

Angel motioned for the group to follow. Dolly repeated Angel's motion, and each hiker copied the person in front of them. Angel walked to the narrow point and stepped across the bubbling creek while Stuart stood in the shallow water and held Dolly's hand while she jumped to the other side. Stuart remained in the creek and gave a hand to each person as they crossed. When Lela reached the water, Nate and Stuart put their arms around her waist and lifted her over.

She continued moving along the bank as she followed Charo, who was in front of her.

Aimee Louise disappeared into the brush, and Dolly followed her. Each person pushed through the brush at Angel's entry point. Stuart followed Red into the thicket. When Red crouched, Stuart hunkered down and listened.

"Did you see those deer?" a man asked. "That's what we've been tracking. Deer."

"Yeah, let's get back to the road before we get snake bit," a second man said. "I heard all the snakes around here are poisonous. One bite, and you're dead in minutes. Quit scratching your arms; you're making me nervous."

"I think I got poison ivy," the first man said.

"Geez, get away from me."

As the sound of footsteps crashing through the thickets became more muffled then finally disappeared, Stuart tapped Rosalie's shoulder then when she turned to look at him, he held a thumb up before he pointed at Brandon, who was in front of Rosalie and Andy. Rosalie tapped Brandon's shoulder then when he turned his head, she copied Stuart's movements. The tap, thumbs up, and pass it on routine continued up the line while Stuart motioned to Rosalie that he was going to join Aimee Louise at the front; Rosalie nodded.

When Brandon rose and resumed going through the brush, Rosalie and Andy followed him as Stuart slipped into the brush toward the creek. After Stuart hurried along the creek bank to the state road, he stayed hidden behind the trees while he listened. *Just birds. That's good.*

He strode back and eased into the brush where he guessed that Aimee Louise would soon reach then hooted the barred owl call. When he heard the hoot in reply, he waited for her.

Aimee Louise stopped next to Stuart and pointed straight ahead then to the creek, and Stuart pointed to the creek. Aimee Louise led the hikers across the creek and along the bank as Stuart stayed in the shallow water to help everyone across. After Rosalie and Andy crossed, Aimee Louise and everyone else stopped. Stuart motioned for Andy to follow him, and they joined Aimee Louise at the front of the line.

When Stuart saw the state road in front of them, he motioned for Aimee Louise to wait then he and Andy crept to the road. While Stuart stood watch, Andy crossed the road and took his position behind a tree then Stuart returned to Aimee Louise and took her hand, and when she nodded, he released her hand. Aimee Louise took Dolly's hand, Charo took the judge's hand, and the rest of the line paired off. When Stuart motioned for Aimee Louise to take Dolly across the road, Aimee Louise handed Dolly's hand to Charo, and Aimee Louise led the three Cabellos across the road. Stuart held his breath, and his heart pounded. *Was this a mistake?*

Stuart nodded when Tom switched hands with Sam so that he would be closer to the roadblock then Tom strode and Sam skipped across the road and vanished into the trees. Peyton followed Tom's example and switched hands with Cami Sue. Not to be outdone,

Cami Sue skipped across the road like her sister did, and Peyton hurried to keep up with her.

After they disappeared into the trees on the other side of the road, he exhaled and motioned to Nate and Lela to cross, and Stuart wiped away the beads of sweat on his forehead as the two of them walked at Lela's pace across the road. *I worry about every single crossing, but this one worries me the most.*

Stuart motioned for David and Brandon to cross, and he and Rosalie followed closely behind them. Stuart rushed to catch up with Aimee Louise, and Andy brought up the rear with Rosalie as Aimee Louise led the hikers through the trees then the tall grass in the field before they came to the northern edge of the Websters' homestead.

Aimee Louise and Stuart stopped the group, and Andy raced ahead to the farmhouse. After he said, "Okay, Angel, bring your band," Aimee and Stuart led the group to the house. Jennie stood at the front door. "Come in. I've got water, snacks, and chairs."

When Aimee Louise reached the steps, she faced the group and shook her cloth bag upside down, and the air exploded with cheers and laughter as everyone went inside, except Andy, Rosalie, Aimee Louise, and Stuart.

The four of them sat on the edge of the porch. "I don't think I could ever do that again," Stuart said.

David came outside with the two puppies who scrambled down the steps before they investigated the grass then peed.

"You all are an amazing team. Thank you for keeping this crowd safe." David swooped up the puppies then took them inside.

"We need to let your folks know we're here," Aimee Louise said. "Rosalie and I can run tell them."

"Red goes, I go," Andy said, and Stuart nodded.

"I'll go with you, Angel. Mom might want to come here, so Jennie doesn't hog all the company at her house," Stuart said.

"Aunt Jennie would do it too," Andy said.

"Water first?" Aimee Louise asked.

"We can get water at Mom's," Stuart said.

"We might still be on the porch when you get back. Angel released every bit of noise they had in them." Andy chuckled as he put his arm around Rosalie, and she scooted closer to him.

Aimee Louise raced ahead, and Stuart ran behind her. *She'll wait at the Smith barn.*

* * *

As they walked toward the Newtons' home after they left the barn, Aimee Louise said, "It would be nice if Brandon and Henry were together."

"I agree, but if they want to keep the three little girls together, the Websters' would have a lot of people at their house."

Aimee Louise nodded. "There will be a lot at your folks' farm too. I suspect Dr. Larkin and the Hendersons will stay with your folks for a while, at least."

"The good news is that you, Henry, Brody, and I will stay together," Stuart said.

"Always," Aimee Louise added. When Stuart grabbed her into a hug, she wrapped her arms around him.

"I am so glad we're together," he whispered. "I couldn't imagine dealing with any of this without you."

Aimee Louise held onto him then raised her head to gaze at his cloud, and he kissed her. After a long, sweet kiss, she sighed as they held hands and headed toward the house.

"That was nice," she said.

"It sure was, babe."

After they were close to the house, Stuart said, "You know what I wish?"

"Actually, I don't," she said.

Stuart chuckled. *My literal sweetheart.* "I wish that we could have one calm, normal day that we felt safe enough to take Henry and Brody on a picnic."

"I like that wish. Do you know what's funny?"

Stuart raised his eyebrows. "No, I don't."

"I thought of a joke."

"Really?" Stuart asked as he opened the back door to his parents' house.

"Oh my goodness. Scott, come see who's here. How did you two get here?" Sandra asked.

"Ready?" Aimee Louise whispered.

"Yeah," Stuart said.

"We walked," Aimee Louise said, and Stuart guffawed as his mother snort-laughed.

Scott walked into the kitchen, and asked, "What's so funny?"

Sandra wiped her eyes. "Angel told a joke."

Henry rushed to hug Angel. "You told a joke, Mama Angel? That's awesome. I'm glad you're home."

Brody whimpered, and Stuart stooped down and stroked the puppy's face and neck. Stuart smiled when Brody flopped down and rolled over for a belly rub. Stuart obliged and rubbed the puppy's belly.

Sandra poured tea into two glasses and set them on the kitchen counter. "It's more lukewarm than iced, but it's wet. I'll pull together a little snack for you."

Stuart winked at Henry, and Henry covered his mouth to keep from laughing out loud. Henry sat at the table with the adults to wait for the snack.

"There are two roadblocks now, and our four farms are in between them," Stuart said.

"Our?" Sandra placed a plate of biscuits on the table and a platter of scrambled eggs. Aimee Louise jumped up to grab plates and handed Henry the silverware when he joined her.

Stuart nodded. "Mitchells, Cabellos, us, and the Websters."

Sandra joined them at the table, and they passed the food around. "Eat first then I want to hear everything."

"Didn't realize how hungry I was." Stuart cleaned his plate. "After they put up the second roadblock, we realized that we were cut off from you and the Websters' by the state road and decided all of us needed to be together. "

"All of us? All the kids and the Mitchells?" Sandra asked. "Where is everybody?"

"At the Websters'," Stuart said.

"How did you get all those people to the Websters?" Scott asked.

Everyone stared at Scott then Henry asked, "Can I say?"

Stuart smiled and nodded.

"They walked." Henry grinned, and everyone laughed.

"I want all the details later." Sandra wiped her eyes with her apron.

Blanche came into the kitchen. "I thought I heard a party in progress." She set a plate and silverware on the table then sat as Sandra smiled and passed her the biscuits and scrambled eggs.

Sandra told Blanche the news.

"Cal and the doc will be thrilled to hear everyone's okay. We've been worried."

"How's Mr. Henderson doing?" Stuart asked.

"Thanks to Dr. Larkin, he's going to be fine," Blanche said. "Right now, both of them are sleeping, and I'm relieved because it's been exhausting for everyone."

"So, what's the plan?" Scott asked.

"I'm not sure, but I think our first priority is to have somewhere for everyone to sleep," Stuart said.

Sandra narrowed her eyes. "And they're all at Jennie's? I need to get there now." She rose and hurried to the back door.

"Just a second, Mom. We'll go with you," Stuart said as he and Aimee Louise joined her.

"I'm not a runner, but let's hurry," Sandra said.

"That Jennie will have everyone tucked into bed if I don't get there in time," Sandra mumbled and set a walking pace to the shortcut with a speed that made Stuart raise his eyebrows as he and Aimee Louise hurried to catch up with her.

Sandra didn't slow down until they approached the Websters' house. She leaned against a tree to catch her breath. "Don't ever let me walk that fast again."

"Okay, Mama Sandra," Aimee Louise said.

Sandra chuckled. "Let's do this."

She sauntered to the kitchen door and tapped on it before she opened the door.

Aimee Louise and Stuart followed her into the kitchen. All the hikers sat at the table, and she smiled. "Stuart told me that you all walked here. I'm so glad that everyone is okay."

"Come sit with us, Mama Sandra." Brandon scooted his chair closer to his mother as David moved a chair next to Brandon for Sandra.

Tracker had been sleeping at Brandon's feet, and woke when Brandon moved his chair. Brandon reached down and rubbed Tracker's back, and the puppy resumed sleeping.

"How is Cal?" Mr. Mitchell asked.

"Thanks to Dr. Larkin, he's recovering and doing much better," Sandra said.

Stuart and Aimee Louise stood near the wall, and Andy and Rosalie joined them to make more room at the table.

Andy raised his eyebrows at Stuart; when Stuart shrugged, Rosalie rolled her eyes.

"It's nice to see you, Sandra," Jennie said. "We don't visit often enough."

Sandra nodded. "So, what's the plan?"

"Well, everyone here is exhausted. I'll make up beds for them, so they don't have to do any more walking today." Jennie smiled.

"I was thinking of something a little longer term than a snack and a quick nap." Sandra returned her smile.

Stuart glanced at Andy. "Warmup," he whispered, and Andy nodded.

"I don't think Brandon would be too tired to see his friend, Henry," David said.

Stuart raised his eyebrows. *Is David taking sides, or is he an innocent bystander? Hope he doesn't get caught in the crossfire.*

"I'll bet Henry is worried about me," Brandon said. "That little guy is very serious. Have you noticed? He worries a lot."

"I'd like to keep the little girls together for homeschooling," Charo said. "We'll be fine wherever we are, but that means the Cabellos and the Mitchells would be a package deal."

Lela smiled. "Thank you, Charo; we're a regular traveling circus, aren't we?"

Sandra furrowed her brow. "If I count right, you all would need four more bedrooms, right?"

Jennie waved her hand in a motion of dismissal. "That's easy. We can figure it out."

"Red and I can move to the Newtons'," Andy said. "That frees up two bedrooms."

Sandra nodded. "We have the space for you two. Red and Angel can share a bedroom, and Andy can bunk in with Stuart."

Jennie's face reddened, and Stuart glanced at his mom's poker face.

I don't think this is going the way Jennie had planned.

"Doesn't that leave us short on security?" Nate asked.

"Not really," Rosalie said, "Andy and I go with Angel and Stuart any time they leave the farms."

"That's true," Leo said, "and Angel and Red are here every morning for the radio. Our sleeping arrangements don't necessarily reflect our day-to-day activities."

Sandra nodded. "The path between the two farmhouses has become well-worn."

Jennie sighed. "What are we going to do about the cows?"

Sigh of defeat? Stuart caught his mother's fleeting smile of victory.

"The cows are already here; Grandma Lela will teach me to care for them, and the Hendersons are close, so we can tap into their knowledge too. The girls and I will enjoy our animal husbandry lessons. Absolutely perfect." Charo beamed.

"I wouldn't mind learning myself," the judge said.

"I think you have your answer, Sandra. Andy, Red, and Brandon and his folks go with you." Jennie grinned. "I get the traveling circus."

Tom chuckled. "Everybody's a winner."

"Let's grab our stuff, family. We've got a shorter walk this time," David said.

"I'll wait outside, unless anyone needs my help," Sandra said.

"Red and I will be along later," Andy said. "We'll gather our things and help move beds around before we leave."

Stuart followed his mother outside.

"Are you okay with the arrangements, Mom?" he asked.

"I think they're perfect. I love that the families jumped in and spoke their minds. Jennie and I would have slugged it out, otherwise. Glad I didn't have to throw her to the ground." Sandra snickered.

"We forgot to mention that we gave away Red's bed." Stuart smiled at Aimee Louise, who had joined them outside.

"Isn't that something? Didn't cross my mind." Sandra snickered as Peyton, David, and Brandon came out of the house.

Aimee Louise led the way, and David, Brandon, and Tracker joined her. The three of them and the puppy moved quickly on the path and were soon out of sight. Stuart walked behind his mother and Peyton.

"Thank you, Sandra, for taking us in," Peyton said. "Brandon will enjoy being with his friend, Henry. When it comes to sleeping arrangements, you can put David and me together, if that helps."

"Oh, really? That's great news, Peyton."

"It is, isn't it? I asked him if it was okay before we left the Websters'. He told me he's been waiting eleven years for me to say something. I thought I was being impulsive." Peyton shook her head.

How could she not see it? Stuart raised his eyebrows. *Wait a minute. Didn't Mom and Dad say something similar to me?*

"The good news is that all our older folks who are better off on the main floor have a place to sleep," Sandra said. "Dr. Larkin showed up with so much stuff that we put him in the living room, but we can move him into the judge's small bedroom after he sorts through his things. I suspect a lot of his stuff can go into the attic. You and David can have your old room, and Brandon will be back with Henry in their boys' room."

"When do you expect our young couples to consolidate themselves?" Peyton asked.

Sandra shook her head. "When those young men get up enough nerve to bring up the subject; although I suspect Red will orchestrate it all."

Peyton giggled. "You know that Red speaks for Angel, right? It will be Angel's idea because it will be logical."

Sandra snorted. "You're right about that. Now, I wonder if David and Angel had a conversation before they even reached Jennie's house."

"I hadn't thought about that. Angel would definitely be looking out for Henry's interest, wouldn't she?"

"It's only logical," Sandra said, and Peyton playfully poked her arm.

Stuart felt his face warm. *Do you two know I can hear you? Maybe I should talk to Angel.*

Stuart stopped when he heard a rustling sound in the Smith field. When he heard the rustling again, he stepped quietly into the field and toward the sound. When a quail flew up in front of him, he jumped back in surprise as it flew away in a ragged pattern. He smiled. *You're luring me away from your nest with the old injured wing trick. Well played, quail.*

Stuart quietly made his way back to the path then strode quickly to catch up with his mother and Peyton, who were still in deep conversation.

"I've spent my entire life keeping my mouth shut," Peyton continued. "It's been very difficult to learn to trust people. I really appreciate that I can talk to you."

Sandra nodded. "I spend most of my time alone, and I've always enjoyed it. I never thought I'd enjoy being around people and having conversations that were more than what's for dinner or what pests there are in the garden now."

Peyton snorted. "I'm looking forward to both of those conversations. I'm really glad we didn't end up with the cows though."

"You and me both, girlfriend," Sandra chuckled.

Mom and Peyton are perfect for each other.

Stuart dropped back a little more then strode not-so-quietly to join the women.

"Where did you go, Stuart?" Sandra asked.

"I thought I heard something and flushed a quail," he said. "I guess right now, I'm suspicious of everything."

His mother nodded. "You're on high alert."

"It won't be much longer until Tracker and Brody will help you flush those fields," Peyton said.

When Sandra, Peyton, and Stuart reached the farmhouse, Tracker and Brody were yipping and puppy-wrestling in the grass while Brandon and Henry laughed.

"This is what a home is supposed to sound like," Sandra said.

Peyton grinned as she clapped her hands. "Let's get everyone set up. If you boys take the puppies to the backyard behind the kitchen, we can watch you from the window, and you won't have to come inside."

David picked up Brandon's backpack. "I'll carry your things inside."

The boys ran toward the backyard, and the puppies chased after them.

"What's the plan?" Scott asked when the adults came inside.

"We might need to shift some beds around. I'm not sure because I'm officially confused since we've moved beds so many times." Sandra chuckled. "We need a second bed in the Hendersons' room for Blanche, preferably a twin bed. Peyton and David will be staying in Charo and Nate's room and will need a double bed."

"We only have queen-sized and twin beds," Scott said.

"Told you I was confused. I do mean queen. We need two twins in Henry's room. That's our easiest one." Sandra chuckled. "Then we need a queen and a twin in both Angel's and Stuart's rooms."

When Scott raised his eyebrows, she said, "I'm afraid we might be running low on beds. I should do a quick inventory, but I have to get busy on supper first. I'll bet everyone's starving."

"I'll help, Dad. Where do you want to start?" Stuart asked.

"Let's start with the main floor."

While Scott and Stuart moved beds from one room to another to accommodate the shift in the household, Peyton and Aimee Louise followed them to strip then remake the beds with clean sheets.

After they finished their work on the first floor, Stuart asked, "Do I take this extra twin bed from Charo's old room upstairs?"

"Wait; I'll ask Sandra." Scott hurried to the kitchen.

Wonder if Mom feels like she could have done all this a lot quicker without all the help. Stuart snickered.

When Scott returned, he said, "Your mom said to take it upstairs. She may have a master plan in mind, but I was afraid to ask for details."

"

"If this has anything to do with plans for a sleepover for Dolly and the twins, Henry and I are going camping that weekend." Stuart picked up the box springs to haul upstairs.

"I'm going along with you." Scott picked up the bedframe before he followed Stuart, and Peyton and Aimee Louise picked up the mattress.

When they reached Stuart's room, Scott said, "Your mother wants a queen-sized bed in your room, and that's what's there. We've got a win."

"The boys room has the two twin beds for Henry and Brandon," Stuart said.

"Aimee Louise's room," Scott said as he rounded the corner to the other side of the stairs. "Bummer. Your mother wants a queen-sized bed in here. Looks like we'll need to do an attic hunt for a queen-sized bed."

"Let's do it now," Stuart said. "I hate trying to remember to do something later."

"Your mom wouldn't let us forget," Scott mumbled as Stuart pulled down the folding stairs.

"I'll go up, Dad," Stuart said.

"One second." Scott left then returned from downstairs. "Here's a flashlight if the bulb is out."

Stuart rolled his eyes. "Very funny, Dad. I forgot about a flashlight, thanks."

Stuart scoured the attic and found a queen-sized mattress in plastic on top of the box springs, also in plastic.

Stuart came to the opening. "Found it. I'll hand down the bedframe first. Do you want Peyton and Aimee Louise to help you?"

"My ego says no, but my back says I better take advantage of your good sense."

"We're right here, Scott," Peyton said. "How can we help?"

"Stuart's going to hand down a bedframe, box springs, and a mattress that we'll set up in Angel's room," Scott said. "I don't want to hurt my back again because I couldn't take the nagging for not asking for help. So, that's my sad tale; let's do this."

After Stuart handed down the mattress, frame, and bedsprings, Scott said, "Well done, team. It all goes to Angel's room."

After Peyton and Angel had moved the bed into the room, Peyton said, "I will personally tell Mama Sandra there is no way any queen-sized bed will ever go into the attic again."

Scott chuckled. "You're my hero, Peyton."

Stuart climbed down out of the attic then lifted up the attic stairs.

"I think you all can take it from here. I'll get out of your way," Scott said.

"We'll put the bed together and make beds," Peyton said. "Do you know where the sheets are, Angel?"

"Be right back," she said.

"I'll stay out of the way." Stuart grinned and headed down the stairs to find his dad. When he walked into the kitchen, his dad and mom were having a quiet conversation.

Scott said, "Stuart, we were just talking about distributing some of the work that your mother does."

"I don't want to give up any of the cooking, and Peyton said she'd take on the laundry, bless her heart. We decided it was worth running the generator for a day to wash all those sheets and catch up on all the clothes, but it still will be a lot of work to carry out the laundry, hang it up, bring it in, and fold it."

"We think the boys and David will be willing to take over the garden, and David and Peyton can oversee the boys' bath time—that's a big help, but Mom needs someone to take care of the chickens and someone to manage the homeschooling for the boys. All of us can pitch in with different lessons, but we need someone to coordinate to keep us from overlapping too much."

"I'll also need help with the housework. I noticed today how much dirt gets tracked in. I do appreciate that everyone's been good about taking turns to wash dishes after meals," Sandra said.

"We think we should have a farm meeting tomorrow. Everyone's too tired tonight."

"I agree, Dad. Maybe we can give everyone a heads up at breakfast, so they'll have a chance to think about how they can pitch in."

Sandra nodded. "Let's get our hungry folks inside. Supper's ready."

CHAPTER SEVEN

After everyone was eating, David said, "Mama Sandra, the boys and I were talking, and we'd like to take over the garden and chickens, if you don't mind. We might have to ask you for advice, but we like getting our hands dirty."

"That would be a great help," Sandra said, and Scott winked at Stuart.

"Can you believe how much time we spent rearranging beds?" Scott asked.

"I don't ever remember doing all this shifting before." Stuart reached for another biscuit.

Peyton sipped her water then asked, "What made this time different?"

Sandra sighed. "I think I panicked. For some reason, it seemed more permanent—not just travelers passing through like the other times. It occurred to me that everyone needed a spot to call their own."

"It got done," Scott said.

Andy and Rosalie carried their duffle bags and backpacks as they rushed inside then dropped their bags on the floor near the back door.

"Sorry we're late," Andy said, "but Aunt Jennie had a long list of things she needed for us to do."

"I was surprised at how much stuff I'd taken to the Websters' house. I thought I could pack in a couple of minutes," Rosalie said.

"Didn't happen." Andy grinned.

"Wash your hands and grab a couple of plates," Sandra said.

While they washed, Peyton said, "Mama Sandra, their empty chairs are across the table from each other. Shall we scoot around?"

"No, don't do that. Everybody eat," Rosalie said.

"They can gaze into each other's eyes while they eat," Scott said, and Peyton snorted.

Andy and Rosalie dug into their food and finished at the same time as everyone else.

"I was starved," Rosalie said. "Andy, after we carry our things upstairs, we can wash dishes."

"Andy, you have a bed in Stuart's bedroom," Sandra said.

"I'll take a plate to Ms. Blanche," Aimee Louise said. "She told me she wanted to sit with Mr. Cal."

"I'll go along with you. I'd like to check on Cal," Dr. Larkin said.

"Let's go outside for a little fresh air then it'll be bath time," David said, and Brandon and Henry dashed to the door.

"I'm coming too," Peyton said as the two boys, David, and the three dogs went outside.

Andy and Rosalie carried their bags upstairs, and Aimee Louise and Doc went to the Hendersons' room.

"Listen," Sandra said, "it's almost quiet in here."

"More coffee, Mom?" Stuart refilled their cups.

Andy came down the stairs and joined the Newtons' at the table. "I'm glad we have a minute to talk. Rosalie and I are engaged. We told Uncle Leo and Aunt Jennie before we left, and they were happy for us, of course. Uncle Leo has a friend on the ham radio who is a pastor. Uncle Leo's going to talk to him tomorrow about a marriage ceremony for us—hopefully, over the radio. Rosalie and I prefer the radio because we think it's too dangerous to travel, but we'll see what he says."

"Congratulations, Andy," Stuart said.

Scott nodded. "Congratulations to you both."

The three men rose to shake hands, and Scott clapped Andy on the back.

"Well, that's exciting news. Why didn't you say anything when you came in?" Sandra asked.

"We'd like to keep it a little quiet, at least until we hear more from the pastor then we'll break out the streamers."

"I hope we hear by tomorrow; otherwise, I'll bust." Sandra smiled.

Rosalie bounded down the stairs. "I didn't finish unpacking, but I heard you down here, Andy; let's get busy with those dishes."

"How about an evening stroll, my dear?" Scott asked.

"Sounds nice," Sandra said as the two of them left by the back door.

When Aimee Louise returned to the kitchen, she carried Blanche's plate of food. Blanche followed her then sat at the table, and Aimee Louise sat with her.

"Thank you, Angel," Blanche said before she started eating.

"Dr. Larkin told Ms. Blanche she could eat in the kitchen because Mr. Cal is doing much better," Aimee Louise said.

Blanche nodded her head. "Cal woke up when the doctor came into our room. I'll dish up a little broth for him after I eat."

"I can do that," Rosalie ladled broth from the soup pot into a bowl. "Won't hurt for it to cool a little."

When Blanche rose from the table, Rosalie cleared and washed the remaining dishes while Andy carried the bowl of soup and followed Blanche to her bedroom.

"Ready for a perimeter walk, honey?" Stuart asked; Aimee Louise headed to the back door.

When they stepped outside, Stuart glanced up. "The sky's clear, and the moon is bright. Not a good night for anyone to try to sneak up on us."

As they walked up the driveway, Aimee Louise asked, "Did Andy say anything yet?"

"Yes, he told Dad, Mom, and me."

"Good, Rosalie and Andy were worried about what people might think."

"Why?" Stuart asked.

"I don't understand that part. She told me some things, but they didn't make sense to me. It would be like if you told me what Peyton's face looked like when she was angry at me. I wouldn't have understood your words."

They walked in silence then Aimee Louise said, "If I told you that I feel joy and a strong bond with you when I look at your cloud, would you understand?"

"That I would understand because that's how I feel when I look at you, and that's why I kiss you."

"That's interesting," she said.

"And convenient," Stuart added.

They continued to the road and listened. *The southwest wind is stronger when we're away from the trees.*

"I want to check something," Aimee Louise said. "Be right back."

Absolutely not. Take me with you. Stuart sighed. *Glad I got that off my chest. Better yet, I'm lucky she sees clouds and can't read my mind.*

Stuart waited and listened. When he scanned the surroundings and the horizon, he frowned. *What is that glow in the northeast?* He inhaled. *I don't smell smoke, but I wouldn't with the wind at my back.*

Aimee Louise appeared next to him. "Come with me," she whispered. "A car is on fire."

Aimee Louise led him south away from the state road, so they could walk faster through the field toward the car fire without being seen. When they neared the fire, they crept closer to the road then dropped to a belly-crawl through the field until they reached the ditch. The acrid odor of burning plastic burned Stuart's nose and throat. Stuart pointed to his eyes then the road, and Aimee Louise nodded.

Stuart raised his head slightly and narrowed his eyes at the five men who watched a still-burning car. There was enough light from the moon and the fire for him to see a gas can on its side in the road, the burned grass on the other side of the ditch, the scorched field, and the fire in the treetops to the north-northeast. The five men passed around a large bottle, and each man took a big swig before the next man grabbed it away. One man shouted as he raised the bottle, and the others laughed until another man yelled at them, and they all quieted down.

After Stuart lowered his head, they crawled backwards then when they were far enough away from the road, they crept back to the Newtons' driveway.

As they strode back to the house, Stuart asked, "It couldn't be the same car that you saw yesterday, could it?"

"No, they were two different types of cars. What do you think about the fire?"

"There was a gas can on its side near the road, which seems to suggest arson, or maybe they moved it away from the car. If they used gas to fuel the fire, what a waste." Stuart shook his head. "The car fire caught the grass on fire, and the wind fanned it until it got to the trees, and now it's a full-blown forest fire. I don't see any risk for us, and I think it missed the Cabellos' and Mitchells' houses. Best case is that the fire will be stopped by the interstate. I want to talk to Dad about a firebreak around our house and the Websters'."

When they reached the farmhouse, Scott and Sandra were walking to the house from the barn.

"Got a minute, Dad?" Stuart asked.

"Sure," Scott said.

"If you don't need me, I'm going inside. The mosquitos have found me." Sandra hurried to the house.

"Aimee Louise and I saw a car fire on the road near the Mitchells' property, and it had set fire to the surrounding grass. The fire spread to the north-northeast, and now the trees are on fire."

"As long as the wind holds, we'll be okay, but that's not what you wanted to tell me, was it?" Scott asked.

"No, there were some men standing around the car, and they were passing a bottle around. I'm not sure what to make of that, but seeing the forest fire reminded me that we need to think about a fire break around the house. The old guidance was thirty feet. The last I heard, it was fifty feet, but what makes sense for fires that are racing through the tree tops? Wouldn't the heat from them be more intense?" Stuart asked.

Scott frowned. "Those are good questions. Who do we know that we could ask?"

"David," Aimee Louise said.

"We can talk to him first thing in the morning," Stuart said. "Dad, if Rosalie and Andy go with Aimee Louise to the Websters', you and I can talk with David."

"That works." Scott sauntered to the house.

"Let's finish our perimeter check then go inside," Stuart said.

When they rounded the final corner of their uneventful walk, Stuart stopped and peered at Aimee Louise's face. "Do you ever think about being married?"

"Of course." She put her arms around him.

"Really?" he asked.

She leaned against him.

"To me?"

"Of course."

Stuart held her at arms' length and stared above her head. "I still can't see your cloud."

"Yours is brilliant, like stars."

Stuart kissed her with all the love in his heart, and she returned his kiss with passion.

When he released her, he said, "I'll be very interested to hear what the pastor says tomorrow."

"Okay," she said as they went inside the house.

"Good night, sweetheart," Aimee Louise said.

Stuart stared as she tiptoed up the stairs so she wouldn't disturb anyone.

"Well?" Scott sat in the dark at the kitchen table.

"I didn't see you, Dad." Stuart joined him.

"Well? What did she say?" Scott asked.

"She said, of course."

Scott chuckled. "That's nice. What was the question?"

Stuart shook his head. "I think I'm in shock. I asked her if she ever thought about being married, and she said, of course. So, I asked her if she thought about being married to me, and she said, of course."

"Of course," Scott said. "That's so Aimee Louise."

"It sure is," Stuart said. "I was mesmerized the first time I saw her; when Major had a get-together at his farm with the sheriff and his family, he invited all four of us deputies. After we feasted on a potluck supper, the two deputies' wives wanted to see the garden, and Aimee Louise and Rosalie offered to show it to them. I announced that I was interested in gardening too, and the other single deputy, Jim, busted my chops for a week." Stuart chuckled. "It was worth it. The next time I was around her, she had saved the sheriff's life after Jim was ambushed and shot. She saw a danger cloud on a woman who planned to shoot the sheriff as soon as he got close enough to help Jim. The more I was around her, the more I understood and admired how complex she was, and when I realized she trusted me, that was it. I felt like I'd reached superstar status in her eyes."

Scott smiled. "I understand what you're saying. I'm in awe that your mom still sees me as a superstar." He shook his head. "It took me a while to accept it."

"Right. That's it. I'm still learning to accept it."

Scott headed to his bedroom. "Good night. See you in the morning."

Stuart carried his boots in his hand as he tiptoed up the stairs.

After he eased into bed, Andy asked, "So what did she say?"

Was the entire household hanging out the windows and listening?

"Who?" Stuart asked.

Andy chuckled. "That's funny. What did she say?"

Stuart sighed. "I think we're engaged too."

"Hard to tell with Angel, but you are."

Andy rolled over, and Stuart closed his eyes. *No way will I sleep tonight.*

* * *

Stuart woke to a quiet voice wafting from the kitchen. *Who is Mom talking to?* He dressed and quietly made his way down the stairs.

"Here's your coffee." Sandra pointed to the table. "Angel and I were going over a few plans. Well, I was. Angel's a good listener."

I'm not even going to ask.

"Of course, it all depends on what you learn at Leo's this morning, but if there is a wedding over the radio, I suppose it will have to be at Jennie's house, so we'll have the reception here. I was originally thinking we'd have an outdoor reception, so we don't disturb Cal too much, but if it's raining, the barn makes more sense."

Of course. Stuart smiled and strode to kiss Aimee Louise on the forehead, but as he bent down, she kissed him.

"Good morning," she said.

Sure is.

Sandra continued, "Thank goodness we don't have any bridezillas to deal with; that's what they're called, right?"

"That's what they're called." Scott sauntered into the kitchen. "Do I get any coffee this morning?"

"On the table." Sandra pointed. "I knew you'd roll out of bed when Stuart came downstairs. What's the plan for today?"

"I want to check the burned car again," Aimee Louise said.

Stuart tossed down his coffee. "You'll tell me why on the way up, right?"

"Yes." Aimee Louise threw on her light jacket and picked up her backpack as Stuart grabbed his rifle, backpack, and jacket.

As they strode to the driveway, Aimee Louise said, "As far as I know, there have never been two roadblocks so close together. This feels more like a trap than two roadblocks to ambush travelers, and if you look at who is in the trap, it's us."

Aimee Louise picked up their walking pace and continued, "If the car was one that a traveler drove to go somewhere, how did it get past the roadblock?"

"We could tell by examining the car. If there is no evidence of any belongings around the car then it was a trap."

"Right, even if they stripped it, they wouldn't have carried away any items they couldn't use, and we'd see evidence of human remains in the fire or alongside the road unless they kidnapped the occupants," Aimee Louise said.

"They might have taken any children for trafficking, but at least so far, there hasn't been any evidence of abducting adults."

When Aimee Louise stopped near the end of the driveway, Stuart said, "Before we crawl closer, we'll leave our backpacks in the field."

"Yes." She led the way along a route similar to the one they took the previous night. After they were close to the state road, she crouched and removed her backpack. Stuart set his next to hers, and they belly-crawled together toward the state road.

Aimee Louise stopped, and Stuart raised his head and scanned the area around the burned car. *No activity.*

As he watched and waited for any movement, Aimee Louise crawled away in the direction of the roadblock. Stuart maintained his position; when his leg cramped, he didn't move. When she returned, she had weeds and grass in her hair. *She's my Angel warrior.*

Stuart lowered his head and stretched his leg to relieve the cramp as she put her mouth close to his ear and whispered. "Two men with rifles at the roadblock; not very attentive; looked bored, and they were talking smack, if that's the right word."

He nodded, and she laid her chin on his shoulder. He kissed her ear then whispered, "Nothing. No movement."

She nodded then showed him the large rock she'd brought back.

He whispered, "We both go; you at the back; me at the front; you'll throw the rock if you see anything, and we run for cover. I'll shoot if I need to. Agree?"

She nodded, and as she prepared to rise, he did the same, He crossed the road as casually as he could then caught a glimpse of her in his peripheral vision. He kept the car between him and the other side of the road. He glanced into the car, and there was no sign of any human remains, clothing, or other items. An empty liquor bottle was on the shoulder in front of the car. As he backed away, he noted that she backed away with him. After they were back in the field across from the car, they lay prone in the grass and listened.

When Stuart was sure there was no activity across from him, he turned then Aimee Louise crawled past him, and he followed her and smiled. *I stick with you, babe.*

They rose when they reached their backpacks then walked to the driveway. As they headed toward the house, Stuart said, "I'm certain the roadblocks are a way to contain us in some type of trap, but burning the car was clumsy."

"Yes."

"I think the target is one person, not the entire group; let's talk to Dad."

"Yes."

When they went inside, Andy and Rosalie were eating breakfast.

"Your dad's already eaten," Sandra said. "Sit and eat before you leave. Your breakfasts are ready."

Sandra set a plate of hot biscuits and sausage on the table and gave them their plates and silverware before she set a jar of blackberry jam and a bowl of gravy in front of them. "Serve yourself."

She refilled coffee cups while Rosalie handed Aimee Louise a glass of water.

"I'd ask you where you've been, but we can talk later." Rosalie finished her biscuit then reached for another.

Aimee Louise cut a biscuit in half then put a generous portion of jam on each side while Stuart tore open two biscuits and ladled gravy over them.

The four of them ate quickly then grabbed their gear and headed to the Websters'. Aimee Louise and Rosalie ran ahead. When Stuart and Andy reached the barn, the two young women weren't there.

"Guess I should have expected they'd go straight to Uncle Leo's," Andy said as they continued past the barn.

"Yep."

When they rushed inside the farmhouse, Jennie said, "They're in the radio room."

"Do we lurk?" Andy asked.

"As usual," Stuart said.

Leo and two other hams discussed the weather then Leo asked, "Pastor Phillips, are you on this morning?"

A man with a deep bass voice answered. "Right here. Listening in as always. Whatcha got?"

"Just wondering, with the times like they are, have you considered performing any marriage ceremonies on the radio?" Leo asked.

"You know, nobody's brought that up before this. I don't know how the state will feel about it, but I know for a fact The Man would approve. You got something in mind?"

"We've got some folks here who would really appreciate a nice ceremony, but we don't want you traveling in these dangerous times."

"Tell me when and give me the names, so I can record them in my Bible, and we'll get it done."

Pastor Phillips was interrupted by applause from the other hams, and Rosalie giggled.

"If we can connect tomorrow morning, and the weather sounds like we can, let's have the ceremony then. Angel will give you the names."

Leo slid over, and Aimee Louise replaced him at the microphone and read from a slip of paper that Rosalie gave her. "Rosalie Jolene Elliott and Andrew Ian Webster."

"Give me a minute to write that down," Pastor Phillips said. "Okay, I got it."

"Two more names. Is that okay?" Aimee Louise asked; Andy elbowed Stuart, who beamed.

"Shoot. Not literally, right, Angel?" Pastor guffawed a booming, infectious laugh, and Leo and Andy chuckled while Rosalie giggled, and Stuart smiled.

"Yes, sir. Aimee Louise Elliott and Stuart Connor Newton."

"Let me spell what I wrote." He spelled each name then asked, "Am I right?"

"Yes, you are," Aimee Louise replied.

"It's been a while since I've performed any marriage ceremonies, and two sisters marrying their sweethearts at the same time is a blessing. As soon as we get off the radio, I'm going to record these names, so there will be no doubt that we're official."

Before Leo took over the microphone, he said, "Don't run off, Angel and Red. I'll see if I can bring up Major on the radio. I know you want to talk to him too."

"Yes," Aimee Louise said.

"I want to check out the cows," Andy said.

"I'll come with you," Stuart said.

When they went outside, Nate and the judge were adding a wire roof over the chicken run. Stuart and Andy strode to join them.

Nate was on top of a ladder and was attaching wire to the frame they had built. "We've heard too many hawks around here. We needed a little extra security, so the chickens can be out in their run during the day."

While the judge held onto the ladder to stabilize it, he asked, "Did Leo get in touch with his pastor friend?"

Nate snickered. Stuart stared at the judge then at Andy.

"Everyone knew; why didn't we?" Stuart whispered.

Andy shrugged. "Uncle Leo talked to Pastor Phillips, and he'll be available tomorrow morning, assuming the weather and our signals hold."

The judge nodded. "I can offer a contingency. I performed many a wedding ceremony over the years as part of my duties as a judge in Miami. I don't have any legal authority in Georgia, but if things fall through, I could certainly perform the nuptials."

"As far as legal authority, the pastor told us he would record our names today, so there wouldn't be anything to slow us down in the morning. I think that takes care of the legal side, but I'd still feel better with a contingency because none of us is prepared for a postponement." Stuart sighed in relief. "That really eases my mind."

"Mine too," Andy added.

"Thought it would," the judge said.

"Were you on your way to the barn? Lela, Charo, the intrepid trio, Pixie, and Holly have been there since early this morning," Nate said. "With all the females we have around here, I fully expect the old cow barn to be stylishly decorated by next week."

When Andy's eyes widened, Stuart said, "We probably need to get back to the house. Leo's trying to get in contact with Major, and I'd like to be there."

"Makes sense to me." Nate turned to his dad. "I need more staples for the wire."

As Stuart and Andy strode to the house, Stuart said, "Any bets on whether Major already knew about the weddings tomorrow?"

"How could he?" Andy asked. "Angel and Red haven't talked to him since…oh, Rosalie talked to him yesterday."

After they reached the doorway of the radio room, Rosalie leaned over and spoke into the microphone. "They're here now."

"I'd like to talk to Stuart," Major said.

"Do we need to leave the room, Pops?" Aimee Louise asked.

"Yes, please."

Aimee Louise and Rosalie rose from their seats, and Leo waved for Stuart to sit in front of the microphone. Andy hung back until Rosalie pushed him toward the radio as she and Aimee Louise left the room. Leo rose to leave too, and Andy sat in the chair next to Stuart.

"Andy and I are here, Major." Stuart glanced back, and Aimee Louise and Rosalie were technically in the hall as they stood in the doorway.

"Are my granddaughters out of the room?"

"Yes, sir." Stuart shrugged when Andy raised his eyebrows.

"Good. I have a question for you. Are you being railroaded?"

Stuart snorted. "Maybe, but I don't care."

Major laughed. "I know just what you're saying. How's everything there?"

"Not good. Nate and all his family and Peyton and her family had moved to other farmhouses, but when the attacks around here escalated, they all returned yesterday. Nate and his family and an older couple and their twin granddaughters will stay at the Websters'. Andy, Rosalie, Peyton, David, Brandon, a local doctor, and another older couple will stay with us at my folks' farm. The two farms are next to each other, so we're in a much more defensible position."

"Sounds smart. Brad and Wally will move their families here tomorrow. We're just too far apart. Kris had a scare today when a couple of thugs tried to snatch the babies. Jim will help then move to Pastor John's then he'll come here."

Mr. Young broke in. "Annie and Molly said I should tell you they wish they were there, and so do all the rest of us."

"I know I can speak for Aimee Louise and Rosalie, at least this once…"

When Mr. Young laughed, Stuart smirked before he continued, "We miss everyone too."

"You've got an adventure ahead of you," Mr. Young said.

"That's the truth. Major, do you want to talk to Aimee Louise and Red?"

"All the time, but all of us have work to do," Major said. "Hug and kiss my sweet girls for me."

Major signed off then Leo took over the mic to talk to Mr. Young while Stuart and Andy left the radio room.

After the four of them were outside, Aimee Louise said, "We need to talk to Papa Scott."

Aimee Louise and Rosalie raced to the driveway then disappeared.

"Shall we catch up with them?" Andy asked.

"We've got our entire lifetimes to catch up with them, and I'm not sure we ever will. Let's walk," Stuart said. "I'd like your opinion."

Stuart told Andy about the theory that the attacks were targeting a single person in their group, but they didn't know who.

When Aimee Louise and Rosalie ran back and joined them, Aimee Louise said, "We needed the run, honey, thanks. What are we talking about?"

"Our target theory," Stuart said.

"What's that?" Rosalie asked.

Andy chuckled. "My turn." Andy explained the target theory.

"I have more, but I don't know if it helps," Aimee Louise said. "While Stuart watched the men stand around the fire and pass around the bottle, one man shouted, 'Here's to misery.'"

"That's strange," Stuart said. "That must have been what the man who lifted the bottle said then they all laughed. I heard them yelling, but I wasn't paying attention to what they were saying."

Aimee Louise continued, "After everybody laughed, another man asked them if they'd forgotten what happened to the last man who said that."

"Is that when they all got quiet?" Stuart asked. "I thought he'd yelled because they were making too much noise."

"What does that mean?" Rosalie asked.

Stuart frowned. "We don't know."

"Yet," Andy said as they reached the Newtons' farmhouse.

CHAPTER EIGHT

After the man rescued the old desk from the pile of broken furniture that the home invasion team of thugs had tossed into the backyard, he repaired the leg with glue that he found in a kitchen drawer and carried the desk back into the large office. *Decoratin' ain't my best skill. Hope Miz R don't expect fancy.*

He searched the house for a good desk chair then limped to the pile in the back. *My arthritis in my knee says it's going to storm.* He scanned the sky. *Still clear. May not be until tonight.*

When he found a leather desk chair that looked perfectly fine to him, he grumbled, "Them bums slashed the seat."

He rolled it into the house and rummaged through a drawer that was next to the back door and found pink duct tape. He frowned then searched the rest of the house and the shed outside but didn't find any black or brown tape. *I have a feelin' Miz R don't like pink.*

He returned to the pile and removed a dark brown seat pad for a kitchen chair. *We got us a slasher.* He took the pad inside and placed it cut side down on the chair then rubbed the chair with his shirttail.

He frowned at the chair and table then lumbered to the kitchen to search for cleaning supplies. After he opened a few drawers and the pantry, he sighed. *Where do ladies keep cleaning stuff?*

He opened cabinet after cabinet beginning with the upper cabinets as he went around the room then moaned as he opened lower cabinets. *I'm getting too old to bend over like this.*

When he opened the cabinet under the sink, he pounced on the bottle of kitchen cleaner and a cloth and hurried to the office. After he sprayed then wiped down the table and the chair, he inspected his work. *A little streaked, but good enough.*

He set the bottle and the wet rag on the floor and sat at the desk. *Lookin' good.*

When the front door opened, he pushed himself to his feet, and his old pal, Mick, called out. "Hey, ya in here?"

He sunk back into the chair. "Back here in the office. I been settin' it up."

Mick strode down the hall; when he reached the door, he frowned. "You asking for trouble? You know what Miz R would do if she catches you in that chair, Gus?"

Gus rose and sighed. "Miz-er-ee, for sure."

Mick narrowed his eyes and glanced around nervously as he hissed, "Keep your mouth shut. Didn't you hear what happened last week? Geez, Gus. You got a death wish or something? Come on. We're supposed to take over at the roadblock down the road."

As they trudged down the driveway, Gus asked, "Down the road? Do you know how far that is? It's going to storm. I'm too old to be out in a bad downpour. What if it hails? Those drunken yahoos burned the car. How we supposed to get there?"

"Zip it; Miz R don't like no whining. There's a car to take us and pick up the others."

"I hope it runs better than the last one they stole."

CHAPTER NINE

As he headed to the back door, Stuart said, "I'll tell Mom what Pastor Phillips said."

"We'll go with you," Aimee Louise said, and Rosalie nodded as Andy grabbed her hand and grinned.

Sandra looked up as the four of them came into the house. "I'm working on a list, so I can feel less scattered. So far, it's not working because I still don't feel organized." She chuckled. "Come sit with me; I'm ready to hear some good news, and I have a feeling you have some for me from the looks of your faces.."

"You're right.. Leo contacted his friend, Pastor Phillips, and the pastor agreed to perform a double wedding ceremony over the radio tomorrow morning," Stuart said.

"That's wonderful news," Sandra said. "Do we know what time?"

"Not exactly," Rosalie said. "It'll be early; it depends on the weather and how long it takes for Uncle Leo to get the pastor on the radio."

"We have a contingency, though, if the weather's bad," Andy said. "Judge Cabello offered to perform the wedding ceremony. Pastor Phillips said he was recording our names today. I think that satisfies his church requirements as far as a legal record is concerned."

"Of course, the judge. That's a relief that we don't have to rely on our weather and a perfect alignment of the radio waves, or whatever it's called, and our plans to hold the reception here are still a go." Sandra said. "Definitely good news. Now I can work on my list for tomorrow's reception."

"We'll find Dad and tell him," Stuart said.

Sandra waved and turned over her sheet of paper to start a new list as they rose from the table and headed out the door.

"Your mom's excited," Aimee Louise said.

"She certainly is," Stuart said.

"Did she have an excited cloud?" Andy asked.

Stuart raised his eyebrows, and Andy shrugged. "Just asking."

"Yes, she did," Aimee Louise said. "It was excited and happy."

Andy nodded. "I'm starting to see why you say the clouds are fascinating, Red. I thought Mama Sandra was excited because I saw it in her face; however, I didn't notice she was happy too until Angel described her cloud."

"You're learning." Rosalie scanned the yard then pointed. "Papa Scott's down by the garden."

"Peyton must be at the coop," Aimee Louise said.

"We'll find her." Rosalie walked alongside Aimee Louise.

Stuart and Andy strolled toward Scott and David, who sat on the bench that Scott had built for the judge when he and Dolly first came to the farm. Henry, Brandon, and their puppies were playing in the grass.

Scott waved. "I found some old tennis balls, and the puppies haven't torn them up yet."

"We're trying to teach them to fetch," Brandon said, and Henry nodded.

"The current game is a little different, though," David said. "One of the boys rolls a ball then a puppy runs with it while the other boy chases the puppy. It's more of a catch the puppy game."

Stuart told them about Pastor Phillips and the judge's offer to cover the wedding, if needed.

Scott shook his head. "We're great at thinking outside the box, but sometimes there's also an answer inside the box that we overlook."

Stuart and Andy stared at Scott.

"Dang, Scott," Nate said. "That's downright genius."

"Maybe my new daughter-in-law is starting to rub off on me," Scott said. "She's our genius."

"I don't think you'll get an argument from any of us who have been around Angel. She amazes me all the time." David watched the boys and dogs play. "Did Henry name his puppy? Brody is an unusual name for a six-year-old boy to think of."

"It is, isn't it?" Scott said. "You know how he came up with it, Stuart?"

Stuart shook his head.

"I knew a man named Brody," David said. "He was a cop near Miami. Smart and brave. Not many people knew his full name was Broderick, and he hated it." David furrowed his brow. "Do we know Henry's last name? Wouldn't be Morrison by any chance, would it?"

"Yes." Stuart knees buckled, and he grabbed onto the back of the bench as Andy caught him and helped him sit down.

"Head between your knees, Stuart," Andy said.

After a few minutes, Stuart took in a big breath then exhaled. "Lot going on lately, and this caught me off guard."

David nodded. "Brody Morrison. He was a good man. He and his wife were murdered, but we never knew what happened to his boy. I never knew his son's name. We didn't know if the boy had been murdered or abducted. We never knew for sure about Brandon either, except Peyton insisted that Brandon was alive."

"I suggest we don't say anything for a while," Scott said. "Let's take one big event at a time."

"Aimee Louise promised Henry that he'd always be with her," Stuart said.

Dr. Larkin and his old dog, Ethel, strolled to the garden to join the men. Ethel flopped down in the grass and watched the puppies.

"Feels great to be outside. Cal's doing fine. He doesn't need me to hover over him anymore. I can't tell you how much that satisfies my old heart. What's on the agenda for today?"

Scott told him about the plans for two weddings. "We should probably gather everyone for a farm meeting. Sandra's feeling overwhelmed, so it would help if everyone had specific areas of responsibility."

"No time like the present." Dr. Larkin headed toward the house as Stuart and Andy hurried to tell the folks gathered at the chicken coop.

"I need to warn Sandra," Scott said as he hurried to catch up with Dr. Larkin.

"Boys, we're going to have a farm meeting. We need to organize, so Mama Sandra doesn't have to do everything. You can play outside if you stay close to the kitchen window where we can see you," David said.

"We need to help Mama Sandra too," Brandon said. "Don't we, Henry?"

"Yes, we don't want Mama Sandra to do everything. She'll get too tired, and that's not fair," Henry said.

Stuart, Henry, Andy, David, and Brandon strolled to the house with all the dogs following them.

After everyone had gathered in the kitchen except for Cal, Scott whistled, and the room was quiet. "There's lots of us, aren't there?" Scott smiled as he looked around the room. "That's good because we've got a lot of work to do. I think Mama Sandra might have a list of things that she's willing to hand off to someone else."

"I'd like to help with the cooking," Blanche said. "My sister and I always use to work together in the kitchen."

"We can take over clean-up after meals," Rosalie said, and Aimee Louise nodded.

"I can clear the table," Henry said.

"I'll help Henry," Brandon added.

"My specialty is laundry," Peyton said. "What else is on your list, Mama Sandra?"

"My biggest worry is the home schooling," she said. "We have talented people in different areas, but we need someone to manage the homeschooling and develop a plan for us to follow. A teacher down the road gave me some lesson plans a while ago for the children, but we've been through all of them, and I'm not sure what to do next."

"That's me," Andy said. "I've been thinking about how to bring up the subject of homeschooling myself. In fact, if Brandon, Henry, and I can have a room for a classroom, we could set it up to suit ourselves when we can't have our lessons outside. Aunt Jennie saved all my school books; we could bring the elementary books here.

"We don't use the office much these days," Scott said. "What do you think, Sandra?"

"It's a perfect opportunity to clear that room out."

"If you'll point at what you want done, the rest of us can help," Peyton said. "Andy, I want you to know how much we appreciate you."

When Andy's cheeks reddened, Red poked him, and he said, "Thank you."

"What else has been bothering you, Sandra?" David asked.

"I'd say the garden and the chickens, but you and the boys have already jumped in," she said.

"I miss my garden," Dr. Larkin said. "Can I help out in the garden too?"

"Yes, sir, Dr. Larkin," Brandon said. "Dad's good at building and taking care of chickens, but we don't know much about gardening expect squashing bugs. Isn't that right, Henry?"

"Yes, and we can invite Dolly over sometimes too. She likes to weed," Henry said.

"What else?" Scott asked.

"We need to talk about defending the farm," Stuart said.

Scott nodded. "Sandra, do you have anything else?"

She smiled. "Blanche and I will cover the kitchen, and if everyone takes care of keeping their rooms clean then we'll be fine. While you defense people get together, the rest can stay here for a snack."

"If you have an assignment for me, Stuart, I'll help however I can," Doc said, "but I think I belong in the snack crowd."

Stuart smiled. "Let's meet on the front porch."

Aimee Louise, Rosalie, Andy, Peyton, David, and Scott followed him outside.

As everyone found a seat or a place to stand, Peyton said, "I hope you can appreciate how dedicated we all are, Stuart, because we gave up a snack time to be here."

Scott chuckled. "It was a hard choice for me too. Where do we start?"

"We're all trained on what to do when someone calls out 'Inside' except for our new people," Stuart said.

"I'll explain it to Dr. Larkin and Blanche," David said. "I saw firsthand how effective it was at Major's farm. Dr. Larkin and I may need to come up with an alternative for him because of his difficulty walking sometimes."

"Let us know what you two decide, so we'll know where he'll be," Scott said. "Do we want to assign positions if we're under attack?"

"The last time we were attacked, we had assignments, and when you called out that we were under attack, we all ran to our positions," Peyton said. "Why don't we go over them to see if we want to make any adjustments?"

"We've got seven shooters, maybe eight," Scott said.

"Are you sure?" David asked. "There are six of us here; I'm not counting Angel."

"Right, but Sandra has her shotgun and will take the kitchen window, and doc might be able to take another window on the back. I'll talk to Blanche then Cal after he's well enough."

"I've been thinking about the boys," Andy said. "The safest rooms we have are the downstairs bathroom and the doc's bedroom. They should have a place to go when someone calls inside or an attack."

"I'd recommend the bathroom," David said. "I'll tell them."

"The last time that we were attacked we assigned our primary shooters to the second floor to take advantage of a wider sight range," Scott said. "I was downstairs in the living room, Sandra was in the kitchen, and Charo was in her wheelchair and took her position at her bedroom window. Stuart went outside to take a sniper's position in a tree," Scott said.

"That was Angel's idea. I originally thought I'd flank them," Stuart added.

"It was an excellent recommendation. Basically, we can have four shooters upstairs, I'll be downstairs with our available first floor shooters, and Stuart will go where Angel says." Scott grinned.

Peyton smiled. "Red, Andy, David, and I are upstairs then. That helps. Two on the front, and one on each side, right?"

Scott nodded. "Of course, it's just a plan. Anyone can call for reinforcements at their particular position."

"Angel and I will continue our perimeter checks before bed every night," Stuart said. "We can do additional checks, if you think we should, Dad."

"I think we've got a good enough plan for now. I suspect Sandra has a snack for us. Shall we adjourn?"

Scott grinned as the porch cleared except for Stuart and Angel.

"What do you think, Stuart?"

"We have the advantage of knowing the capabilities of our shooters. I'm kind of sad that Nate, Charo, and the rest of their family are separated from us."

Scott rolled his eyes. "Don't let your mother hear you say that because she'll have us set up beds for them. Let's get inside before your mother gives our snack away. That David always looks hungry to me. Have you noticed that?"

When they went into the kitchen, the rest of the defense group had already finished their snacks and left except for Red and Andy.

"We waited for you," Red said.

While the five of them ate their biscuits sprinkled with sugar, Andy said, "I'd like to go to Uncle Leo's for books. I thought it would be easier if I used a utility wagon."

"Sure would," Stuart said. "I'll have to go with you because Angel and Red will want to run."

Andy nodded. "Every time. Can you think of anything else we could bring back with us?"

Sandra's eyes twinkled, and Scott said, "You shouldn't have asked her. I already know what she's going to say."

Sandra glared at him. "The Cabellos are always more than welcome. I thought about having you ask Jennie if she has a lacy tablecloth that we can use for the reception tomorrow, but now that I think about it, don't. She might get the idea that I can't host a proper reception."

Blanche nodded. "Jennie would definitely go there. I might have something."

After they'd eaten, the four of them grabbed their backpacks, and the two young men and Rosalie picked up their rifles before they headed out.

Rosalie said, "Let's go," and she and Aimee Louise raced to the path that led to the Smith barn.

"I planned to hurry to the shed for the wagon, but we can take our time," Stuart said.

On the way to the shed, Stuart said, "I don't remember my mom and your aunt being so competitive when I was growing up."

"They weren't. I think it's their new hobby. It certainly keeps Uncle Leo and your dad entertained."

"Oops. I left the chicken feed in the small wagon," Stuart said.

"I hoped we could take the larger one, anyway. I've got a lot of books and wasn't interested in making the trip twice."

As Stuart pulled the wagon, Andy cleared the downed limbs on the path. "We're only noticing these because of the wagon," Andy said.

"Different perspective helps."

After they reached the Smith barn, Stuart said, "When you mentioned different perspectives, I wondered what Dad's farm looks like from the south side. We've focused our attention on the north side because we've assumed that's where any attack would come from."

"Sounds like a little hike after lunch might be something we should do," Andy said.

"I agree. We certainly don't want to put it off."

Before they reached the Websters' farm, Aimee Louise and Rosalie ran to meet them on the path.

"Are you okay? Both of you look like you're out of breath," Stuart said.

"Hyperventilation does that; at least, that's what we practically did when Dolly told us. We had to run find Charo, and it's true," Rosalie said.

"What is it?" Andy asked.

"Three more adults and three children at Jennie's house," Aimee Louise said.

Rosalie added, "Aunt Jennie's best friend from high school, Ms. Myrtle, brought her oldest son, Junior, except he wants to be called JR, and his family to live with Jennie and Leo because her husband died six months ago, and they ran out of food. They lived in a small town south of here and had a small garden, but it wasn't enough to feed them."

"How did they get past the roadblock?" Andy asked.

"They hiked through the woods from the south. They were never anywhere near the state road. Aunt Jennie said they used to use their old path all the time, but it's grown over. She couldn't believe they made it through in only one day," Rosalie said.

"What does that mean for Charo and Nate?" Stuart asked.

Rosalie rolled her eyes. "Aunt Jennie said they could double up. Charo's in tears, and I think Nate is kind of mad. He's packed up all their stuff."

"I'm afraid we're heading into a hornet's nest," Andy said.

"No kidding. We ran away when Charo started yelling at Nate in Spanish," Rosalie said.

"Ready to be the bad guy?" Stuart asked.

"Bad guy with you? You don't know how to be a bad guy," Aimee Louise said.

Stuart smacked his forehead. "It was a bad joke. We need to tell Ms. Jennie that the Cabellos are moving back to Mom and Dad's place because Charo was insulted that Ms. Jennie said to double up. I'm afraid I'll hurt Ms. Jennie's feelings, and I don't want to do that, but I don't want to make Charo any madder than she is, so I'm feeling like a bad guy."

"So, this calls for finesse, right?" Aimee Louise asked.

"Yes, that's right," Stuart said.

Rosalie snorted. "Angel's best skill is not finesse."

Stuart exhaled. "It's up to me to be the bad guy then."

"I'll go along if I can hide behind you," Andy chuckled.

"Yes," Rosalie snickered. "We've got your back."

"Gee, thanks," Stuart said.

"That was sarcasm, Angel," Andy said.

"Thanks, Andy. I was wondering," Aimee Louise said.

As they walked toward the farmhouse, Stuart said, "Andy, grab the most important books because we may have bags and boxes in the utility wagon."

"Wait a second. What about the other wagon?" Rosalie asked.

"It has a bag of chicken feed in it," Andy said.

"Good. We'll move it and be there as fast as we can."

Aimee Louise waved as she and Rosalie raced to the Newtons' farm.

"Do you feel abandoned?" Andy asked.

"If it was anyone else, I would, but those two are always thinking," Stuart said as they continued to the Websters' farm.

When they reached the farmhouse, Dolly, Sam, and Cami Sue were playing outside with two boys and another girl while Lela and a wiry woman with gray hair watched them. Lela waved, and Stuart and Andy returned her wave.

"Did Rosalie and Aimee Louise tell you our news?" Lela asked.

Stuart nodded. "We crossed paths on the short cut."

Lela introduced Stuart and Andy to Jennie's friend, Myrtle. "You'll learn the children's names later. It's really sweet seeing how quickly they get along."

She whispered, "Except we've already been told that Sam and Dolly are bossy."

Stuart snickered. "Everyone else inside?"

Lela nodded then when the other woman turned her attention to the children, Lela rolled her eyes and mouthed, "Caution. Firestorm."

"Thanks, Andy's here to pick out a few books for the boys."

As he opened the kitchen door, Andy said in a clear voice, "It won't take me long to pick out a few books for the boys."

Stuart followed him inside, and Andy left the kitchen to gather books. Jennie stood at the sink. When she turned, her eyes were red rimmed.

"Allergies," she said.

"Andy, is that you?" Nate called from the back bedroom.

Andy answered from upstairs. "Sure is, and Stuart."

Stuart strode to meet Nate as he came out of the bedroom. "I need to talk to Jennie; come with me."

Stuart followed Nate back to the kitchen. *I think I'm about to see FBI negotiation skills in action.*

"Jennie, are you okay?" Nate asked after he went into the kitchen. "I'd like to talk to you a minute."

"I know. Charo hates me."

"Not at all. She's more surprised than anything else. Both of us are impressed that you have such a spirit of hospitality that your best friend knew she and her family would be welcome here."

Jennie nodded. "And I haven't seen her in over thirty years."

"It's really tragic that she lost her husband." Nate pulled out a chair and sat at the table, and Jennie joined him.

"It really is. He had cancer and three months later, he was gone." Jennie snuffled then cleared her throat. "I can't let her see me all weepy."

"What can we do for you?" Nate put his hand on hers.

She straightened her back. "I have everything under control. Except…"

Her shoulders slumped. "Never mind; it's not your worry."

Nate kept his hand on hers then lifted his eyebrows slightly in encouragement.

"I have too many queen-sized beds." Her chuckle was hollow. "I need another twin bed in the little girls' room because a bigger bed wouldn't fit in there. The only extra bed I have is a queen-sized one that I bought right before the grid went down. It's brand new and still wrapped in plastic. Because I didn't have anywhere to store it, I leaned the mattress and box springs against my bedroom wall."

She shook her head.

Nate rubbed his chin. "You know, just thinking off the top of my head, if I take my family to Scott's house, that frees up two twin beds for you, right?"

Jennie furrowed her brow. "Dolly's bed would free up. I wouldn't have to move a fourth bed in there. There's already a twin bed in Andy's bedroom, so we could put the judge's twin bed in Andy's bedroom for the boys' bedroom. You are absolutely brilliant,

Nate. Now, are you sure Charo won't feel like I'm throwing her out of the house?"

"Charo's amazing. She's happy wherever her family is. You know," Nate lowered his voice, "I think Dolly misses Henry."

"I think you're right. Dolly talks about him all the time like he's her brother."

"I just thought of something." Nate smacked his forehead with his palm. "That new bed you have would make a perfect wedding present for Andy and Red."

"It would, wouldn't it?" Jennie rose. "You talk to Charo. Make sure she knows that I'm not trying to push her out because you all are more than welcome to stay, and I'll talk to Andy about the wedding present."

Jennie hurried up the stairs to find Andy.

As Nate strolled past Stuart, Stuart whispered, "That was so smooth. I was all geared up to make a clumsy mess of everything."

Nate bowed, and Stuart snickered. "We may have to make more than one trip unless the Websters' have a wagon or two that we could borrow."

"Actually, we can carry what we brought. Mama Sandra talked Charo into leaving most of our things with her until we had more time to move them."

"I guess I shouldn't be surprised, but I know they aren't in the attic because I didn't put them there."

Nate frowned. "Where is Mama Sandra going to put this brand-new bed we got for her?"

"Don't go all weak-kneed on me now, Nate. We'll put it wherever she wants."

Nate snorted. "Thanks, Stuart." He started to walk down the hall then stopped. "That was the most critical negotiation I think I've ever done."

"I couldn't have done it," Stuart said. "I'll find the judge and fill him in."

"His room is upstairs. He may already be packed because Charo told him to get ready to leave." Nate chuckled.

Stuart heard Andy, Jennie, and the judge talking in a room at the end of the short hallway.

Do I join in? Stuart shrugged, strode down the hallway, and walked into the room.

"Oh, good, you're here, Stuart," Jennie said. "The Cabellos are moving back to your dad's farm. The judge didn't have much to bring, so he's ready to go. Andy will need help with the new bed I'm giving him for a wedding present. He picked out a few books to get the boys started; he can get more later. Andy thinks the two of you can manage it with the wagon."

"I'm sure we can. Ready, Andy?" Stuart asked.

"Yep."

"I'll check on Charo." Judge picked up his backpack and headed down the stairs. Jennie hummed as she stripped the bed, and Stuart and Andy hurried to follow the judge.

Andy and Stuart stared at the large mattress and box springs.

"You ready?" Stuart asked.

"It will never fit on that wagon," Andy said.

"I know," Stuart said. "Let's do it."

Andy laughed. "Let's start with the mattress."

They carried out the mattress to the utility cart and laughed as they balanced the short side on the wagon with one corner in the wagon and the other corner hanging off.

"I'll see if Uncle Leo has any straps." Andy hurried to the house then returned. "I need to look in the barn."

He returned with two webbed straps with ratchet closures.

"Those are perfect. If we put the mattress flat and the box springs on top of it then the frame on top of that, we can creep to Dad's farm," Stuart said. "In fact, we can put small items underneath it."

"I'll be right back." Andy hurried to the house then returned with an armload of books. "I'm wearing myself out running around." He set the books in the wagon.

The judge trudged from the house before he dropped his backpack and a large duffle bag onto the ground and watched them balance the bed on the wagon. "I don't have a small item, but I'm happy to offer up this illegally overstuffed duffle bag." Judge breathed out in relief, and Stuart and Andy laughed.

Judge shook his head. "I think Charo managed to stuff everything she brought to the Webster homestead into this one, groaning bag, or maybe the groaning was me."

Stuart tipped the mattress away from the wagon, and Andy heaved the duffle bag into the wagon.

"Okay, Stuart. Set 'er down," Andy said.

After they centered the mattress on top of the duffle bag in the wagon, Andy held onto the mattress and box springs while Stuart strapped them down.

"It's solid, Stuart," Andy said.

"I'll check inside to see what's left to go then we can pull our wagon to Dad's," Stuart said.

"I still need the rest of my books," Andy said.

Stuart moaned. "I'd forgotten because I was so focused on this mattress."

"Okay if Dolly and I go along with you? We aren't the fastest walkers, but we won't slow you down," the judge said.

"That'll be fine," Stuart said. "We'll wait."

Dolly wore her backpack as she skipped out of the house. Pixie danced alongside her, and the judge brought up the rear.

"I'm ready to go back to my own bedroom," Dolly said.

"That's how I felt too," Andy said.

Stuart smiled. *I understand. Home for me is wherever Aimee Louise is.*

Dolly and Pixie danced along behind the wagon as Andy pulled it up the driveway to the shortcut. Stuart kept a hand on the mattress to be sure it didn't shift, and the judge brought up the rear.

When they met Aimee Louise and Rosalie coming from the Newtons', Rosalie laughed. "How on earth are we going to get past you?"

"Wide load," Dolly shouted.

"Where'd you learn that?" Judge asked.

"Daddy was driving one time, and Mama yelled a lot of words in Spanish. When I hollered what she said as loud as I could, she told me to yell 'wide load' when something big was in front of us because it was quicker."

Andy chuckled. "I'll pick up your wagon and move it for you, but you'll have to step off the path, so we can get by."

"We'll move it," Rosalie said as she and Aimee Louise lifted their empty wagon into the brush between two small trees.

"Wide load coming through," Rosalie said in her command voice as Andy pulled the mattress wagon past them.

"It's supposed to be just wide load because it's quicker, but you said it nice and loud." Dolly pirouetted then Red held out her hand.

"Good job." Dolly smacked Red's hand in a high five, and Red snickered.

When they reached the house, Scott and Doc were sitting on the front porch.

"Mama Sandra went into high gear after we heard about the new bed then Doc asked if we had a wheelchair that Cal could use to sit in the kitchen for a few minutes," Scott said. "Peyton, Doc, and I hustled to implement her new master plan for sleeping arrangements and shifted furniture and beds around before you got back. Unfortunately, we gave up the classroom in the shuffle, Andy, but you and the boys can claim a spot in the living room."

"That'll work," Andy said.

"Peyton has a surprise for Charo," Doc said, "but she wants to tell Charo herself."

Henry opened the front door. "Dolly, hurry. Lunch is ready."

Dolly and Pixie ran inside with Henry, and Scott chuckled. "If we're going to put the bed together before lunch, you might as well bring it in the front door and carry it straight to the bedroom, so you don't get trampled in the kitchen by the lunch crowd."

After they carried all the pieces of the queen size bed into the bedroom, Peyton carefully removed the plastic from the mattress to keep it in one piece then folded it. While she took the plastic to the storage closet and looked for pillows and queen size sheets for the bed, Stuart and Andy had the bed put together. After Peyton returned with the sheets, she quickly made the bed.

When the three of them strolled into the kitchen, the children and David and Doc were finishing their lunch while Sandra put a batch of biscuits in the oven, and Blanche made a salad of wild greens and thinly sliced radishes.

Doc grinned. "Mama Sandra said the kids eat first, and when I asked her when old people eat, she told me I could be a big kid like David."

Dolly nodded. "We were polite and didn't tell them that they are too big to be kids."

Sandra chuckled. "I actually told Doc he could join David and the children for lunch then David said only if he went outside with them after lunch. We should name this household Rules on the Fly."

After they had finished eating and cleared their dishes, Sandra said, "We're ready for our next group."

"Take a cookie for the road." Blanche gave each one a cookie as they went out the door.

"Mommy's here," Dolly said before she closed the door.

When Charo came into the house, her face was red, and she fanned herself. "I think yesterday's walk wore me out. I was sorry the wagon was so full. I considered asking for a ride."

"I have a surprise to show you after lunch. Sit at the table and cool down then we'll eat," Peyton said.

"Here's some water." Blanche set a glass in front of Charo.

Stuart strode to the door and said, "Come on in for lunch. We can unload the wagon after we eat."

Aimee Louise, Rosalie, and Nate came inside.

"Are you feeling okay, Charo? Your face is beet-red," Rosalie said.

"I'm fine." Charo felt her face and chuckled. "My face must be embarrassed because I'm so out of shape. I may have to start running with you and Angel to get back into shape."

"Sounds extreme to me," Peyton said.

After everyone sat, Sandra dished up soup while Blanche served the salads.

Charo ate half of her soup then slid the bowl and her salad to Nate who dumped the soup into his bowl and the salad on top of his.

"What's on the agenda for this afternoon?" Charo asked. "If no one minds, I think I'll spend the rest of the day unpacking."

"That's great," Sandra said. "Let me know if you need anything put in a storage closet or the attic."

"Not the attic," Peyton said. "It's more accessible in a storage closet."

Scott nodded. "You're right about that."

"Andy and I had planned to hike through the woods south of the house sometime, but after we heard that Ms. Jennie's friend and her family, including the kids, walked to the Websters' farm from the south, it became higher on my list of priorities," Stuart said.

"I agree," Andy said. "It was disconcerting that their hike was so easy because we have focused on attacks from the north and ignored the south."

We're going too," Aimee Louise said.

"I'll grab my backpack and rifle." Peyton rose from the table.

"Wait, Peyton," Nate said. "I want to go too, but we need shooters at the farmhouse."

Peyton dropped into her chair. "I hate it when you're right."

Charo patted Peyton's hand. "So do I. We're officially angry at you, Nate, for being a spoilsport and a party pooper."

Nate grinned and shrugged, and Peyton laughed.

"Now that was just mean, honey. You made her laugh." Charo tightened her lips to keep from laughing too.

"I'll help you unpack, Charo, but first, I want to show you your surprise," Peyton said.

Charo and Peyton strolled to the hall.

"What is it? You need to tell me now because I waited all through lunch and didn't say anything."

Charo squealed. "This is a wonderful surprise."

Nate hurried down the hallway to join them.

"What's the surprise?" Judge asked.

"Peyton and David moved their things out of Charo's old room and set it up for Charo and Nate," Sandra said.

"Let's move all the things inside before we leave," Stuart said. "It won't take us long at all."

When Stuart carried boxes into the room, he was surprised to see Charo sobbing as she sat on the bed. Peyton sat next to her and was hugging Charo.

"What's wrong?" Stuart set the boxes down on the floor.

"I was just so overcome with how sweet it was for Peyton to give me back my old room," Charo sniffled. "It feels like home. Sounds silly, doesn't it?"

"Not really. When Dolly left the Websters', she told us that she was ready to go back to her own room, and Andy told her that was how he felt too. You're in good company, Charo," Stuart said.

Peyton nodded. "Stuart, Nate and I can bring in everything else. There isn't much."

"We'll stack what we've already unloaded in the hall," Stuart said.

Stuart caught Andy before he reached Charo's room. "Stack that against the wall between Peyton's and Charo's bedrooms. Peyton and Nate will get the rest after Charo unpacks what's in her room already."

Stuart repeated his message to Aimee Louise and Rosalie when they came in with suitcases. The judge carried his things to the bachelors' room.

"What do we take with us?" Rosalie asked.

"Go-bag, backpack, water, and your rifle," Stuart said.

"I packed each of you a snack and a little something for your supper," Sandra said, and Blanche snickered.

The four of them collected their gear and put on long-sleeved shirts then made room for their heavy lunch sacks in their backpacks.

Before Stuart closed the door as they were leaving, Blanche said, "Their little suppers will each feed an army."

"I know, but I worry about them. If I can't go along, I can at least make sure they don't starve," his mom said.

Stuart shook his head. *No one would ever starve around Mom as long as she had a skillet and a fire.*

"I talked to your dad earlier, Stuart, and he told me there might still be an old barbed wire fence at the end of his property," Andy said. "It would be an interesting landmark if we can find it."

"Speaking from experience, if the barbed wire is down, the best way to find it is to be barefoot," Stuart said.

Andy groaned. "I remember those days."

"I'm not sure how much good it will do us, but I picked up the machete in the equipment shed earlier," Stuart said.

"Your dad gave me a small hand saw. He told me it could take down limbs and small trees but not anything bigger, and it won't cut them very quickly," Andy said.

"Aimee Louise wants to lead. Andy and I can bring up the rear," Rosalie said.

Stuart quickened his pace then strode along beside Aimee Louise while Rosalie joined Andy behind them.

Andy and I are lucky this isn't a running path.

Aimee Louise jogged when the path was relatively clear, and Stuart stayed alongside her when there was room.

He watched her intently when she slowed then shifted direction to the right or left to a previously invisible path that was clear enough for them to walk single file.

I would never have gotten this far so quickly by myself.

Aimee Louise disappeared in a slight curve that Stuart hadn't seen until she rounded it. After he made the turn, he couldn't see her.

Stuart fumed. *She did that on purpose.*

When Rosalie and Andy made the turn, he held up his hand, and they stopped. After Rosalie then Andy crouched down to wait, Stuart sighed then crouched too.

CHAPTER TEN

When Stuart got a leg cramp, he rose to extend the muscle and ease the pain. He glanced back, and Andy raised his eyebrows. Stuart shook his head then stretched out the cramp in his leg. He listened to the birds sing and smiled as a mockingbird ran through its repertoire of songs it had copied from other birds. Stuart was startled when the bird suddenly mimicked the jingle of keys and dropped back into his crouch. He peered at Andy and Rosalie; Andy's brow was furrowed, and Rosalie had eased herself onto one knee with her back to Andy for a good shooting position.

Stuart assumed the same knee shooting position as Rosalie, and the mockingbird continued through its songs.

When Stuart heard the barred owl call, he returned the call and rose to a position that still gave him the option to shoot. Rosalie and Andy copied his stance, and Rosalie remained facing away from Andy.

Rosalie is a natural. Sheriff would have recruited her, if times were different.

When Aimee Louise appeared next to Stuart, she motioned for Rosalie and Andy to join them, and they crept until they were close.

Aimee Louise pointed to Stuart's right at the one o'clock position then held up three fingers before she mouthed, "Large tent."

The mockingbird continued its song; when it sang the jingling keys tune, one man laughed, and Stuart narrowed his eyes and tensed his muscles as he readied to shoot. He scanned the area as Aimee Louise headed away from the men then pointed to her right as she glanced over her shoulder at Stuart and held up two fingers.

Stuart smiled. *Dang, she's cute.*

She continued straight ahead for a few feet then took a new path toward the Newtons' farmhouse. When Stuart followed her, Rosalie and Andy stayed close behind Stuart.

She moved quickly from one small opening to another, and Stuart focused on keeping up with her. When she finally stopped, she pointed to her ear, and Stuart listened as the hair on the back of his neck rose. *Dolly.*

The path widened, and Stuart kept pace with Aimee Louise as she broke into a run to the farmhouse. While they were still in the trees and brush, she stopped, and so did Stuart, Rosalie, and Andy.

Stuart hugged her and spoke quietly in her ear. "We need to talk and include Dad, Peyton, Nate, Charo, and David."

"Not Charo; not now," she whispered.

Stuart frowned. "Okay."

He turned to Rosalie and Andy and whispered, "Meet with Dad, Peyton, Nate, and David in the barn. No one else."

Rosalie and Andy nodded.

After they reached the yard, Andy stopped to talk to David while he put the finishing touches on an all-terrain rolling walker he and Brandon built for Doc. Rosalie and Aimee Louise met Scott on the tractor as he parked it behind the shed. Stuart went inside the house.

"Y'all are back earlier than I expected, Stuart." Sandra glanced at him as he strolled into the kitchen.

"Aimee Louise led our expedition, and she moves fast." Stuart chuckled along with his mom and Blanche.

"Have you seen Peyton and Nate?" he asked.

"I think they decided to walk the path to the Smith farm and back. Peyton said she wanted to be more familiar with it, and Nate offered to accompany her," Sandra said.

"That was after Mama Sandra cleared her throat, by the way." Blanche tittered.

"I'm not surprised." Stuart smiled and waved as he headed out the door.

As he strolled the path to the Smith barn, Stuart listened to the birds and scanned the surrounding areas for anything out of the ordinary. *I don't see how Aimee Louise does it. She's on high alert all the time.*

Before he reached the Smith barn, he met Nate and Peyton as they returned from the Smith farm.

"We're having a quick meeting in the barn. We're keeping it quiet and down to only a few people, mostly our shooters."

"Should I grab Charo when we get back?" Nate asked.

"No, everybody we need will be waiting for us in the barn," Stuart said.

"I'm glad you didn't send Angel and Red for us," Peyton said as the three of them hurried along the path to the Newtons' farm. "I wouldn't want to see Nate embarrassed by his inability to keep up."

"Me?" Nate sneered. "I might be trailing behind those two, but so will you, Ms. Slow Motion."

"Actually, we can brag all we want as long as we don't challenge those two speed demons to a race," Peyton said, and Nate and Stuart chuckled.

When the three of them reached the barn, Aimee Louise, Rosalie, Scott, and David were waiting for them.

Stuart described what they saw and heard when they scouted south of the farm. When he told the group about hearing Dolly while they were within earshot of the two men that Aimee Louise saw, he added, "I was shocked by how far voices, especially Dolly's, carried from the farm."

Nate's, David's, and Scott's faces reddened, and Peyton tightened her hold on her rifle.

"What do we do?" Peyton hissed.

Stuart glanced above their heads. I'll bet all their clouds changed drastically.

"That's why we're meeting. We've focused on our defenses on the north side of the property. We need to expand our plans," Stuart said.

"What do you suggest?" Nate asked.

"I suggest we eat lunch then get back together. Is there a reason we didn't include any of the others?" Scott asked.

"Yes, we should have a plan that we can share with them because there's no sense in scaring the entire household. If we can't come up with a plan then we might want to include others in our brainstorming," Stuart said.

"Did you find the barbed wire?" Scott asked.

"Yes, but they are camped on this side of the fence," Aimee Louise said, and Stuart stared at her.

"I'm officially scared because that means they are camped on our property. That's too close for me." Scott growled.

"I'm officially scared because you went past them to find the barbed wire, Aimee Louise," Stuart growled.

"She might be Angel, but she moves like a ghost. Let's have lunch." Peyton rose, and she and David left to gather the children, Judge, and Doc to go inside to eat.

After Rosalie and Andy followed Nate to the house, Scott said, "What have you been thinking as far as defense for the south?"

"I'd rather go on the offense," Stuart said. "I don't suppose we have any dynamite around here, do we?"

"I wish, but now that you say that, I like the idea of being proactive. We could do a controlled burn, and David might have some ideas on the best way to do it too," Scott said.

"I feel better having a viable idea for consideration," Stuart said. "Let's eat."

When they walked into the kitchen, Peyton grabbed Stuart's arm and whispered, "You came up with an idea, didn't you? I can see it on your dad's face, and yours too. Whatever it is, I'm in, no matter what."

Angel reads clouds, and Peyton reads faces. The rest of us don't stand a chance.

After lunch, Charo said, "I'll do the lunch dishes; it's too hot for me out there."

"Let's take over the living room for one of our games. I wouldn't mind staying out of the hot sun myself," Judge said.

"Is there a table we can set up for them?" Blanche asked.

"I've got a folding card table in the storage closet," Sandra said. "Charo, I'll show Blanche where it is then come help you. I'd enjoy the company in the kitchen."

Before Sandra and Blanche left the kitchen, Blanche said, "Cal would enjoy watching the children play their game, Doc."

"Be good for him," Doc said. "I'll help him into his wheelchair, and we'll meet you in the living room."

Stuart and Aimee Louise cleared the dishes and stacked them near the sink while everyone else left. Charo hummed as she slipped the dishes into the soapy water, and Aimee Louise and Stuart went to the barn.

"Charo seemed happier than the last time I saw her," Stuart said. He glanced at Aimee Louise, and she put her arm around his waist.

Did she just tell me to mind my own business?

Stuart shrugged then wrapped his arm around her shoulder. *Don't care.*

"Anybody come up with anything?" Stuart asked after he and Aimee Louise entered the barn.

"Not really," Andy said, "but this is a perfect opportunity for us to be proactive rather than wait for them to attack us."

"Good idea," Nate said. "What makes you teachers so smart?"

Andy snorted. "Teachers read, and I minored in Military History in college."

David stared at Andy. "What do you think about a prescribed burn?"

Andy raised his eyebrows. "I think it's brilliant, it could definitely work for us, and you're the expert."

"What's a prescribed burn?" Peyton asked. "How is it different from a controlled burn, and how could it work for us?"

"Prescribed is another word for a controlled burn. It would drive them away from us. We could put in a fire break far enough away from the house to leave a good cover of woods then drive the fire south; the fire will burn until it reaches the river. The next decent firebreak after that is a county road," Scott said.

"Our prevailing wind right now is from the southwest which will help us because the fire won't move too fast," David said.

"It's genius because it won't look like we're attacking them," Nate said. "What's the weather like for the next few days, Red? Any rain?"

"No rain systems or hurricanes headed our way, at least for the next two days. The wind will be predominantly from the south today but should change to a west wind by tomorrow morning. We may see rain the day after tomorrow, especially if the wind shifts to the northwest."

"What do we need to do next?" Nate asked.

"I need to see a map then I'll need to walk the area," David said. "Sounds like I'll need Aimee Louise for a guide, and I'd like Andy along to help plan. I don't suppose we have a couple of bulldozers around."

"No, but I've got two tractors, and I think Leo has at least two, and one of his is larger than either of mine," Scott said. "Stuart and I can drive tractors. Who else?"

"Aimee Louise and Andy," Red said.

"I can too, so that gives us five drivers," David said. "What about backhoes?"

"Uncle Leo's large tractor has a backhoe attachment," Andy said.

"What's a backhoe do?" Peyton asked. "This is very interesting."

"It digs," Rosalie said. "You'll understand better when you see it."

Scott nodded. "Exactly. Anything else we need to cover?"

"Peyton and I can complete our survey of our security gaps on the north side," Nate said. "We'll have a report for you all this evening. We have a few ideas, but so far, we haven't found anything major."

""Stuart, could you get my maps?" Scott asked. "You may have to ask your mom where they are because she moved almost everything out of the office."

While Stuart strode to the house for the maps, Peyton and Nate continued to the driveway. When Stuart returned, Scott asked, "Any trouble?"

Stuart chuckled. "Mom wanted to know what you're up to, and when I told her you were showing David our property and the surrounding area, she asked Charo if she'd unpacked everything she wanted."

"Charo will keep her busy," Rosalie said.

Scott unfolded the large map on the makeshift table of two sawhorses and a piece of plywood that Andy and David had put together before Stuart returned. Scott showed the group the approximate locations of his farmhouse, the Smith barn, and the Websters' farmhouse.

"Is it okay to write on the map?" David asked. After Scott nodded, David pulled out a thick carpenter's pencil from his back pocket, and Scott marked the three buildings.

"Our property ends about here." Scott pointed on the map with the pencil. "The Smith property makes an upside down 'T' behind our property and Leo's, which is one of the reasons I think that Mr. Smith deeded it to me. He always told me that Stuart would be back to take over my farm."

Stuart shook his head. "I knew I'd visit you and Mom, but I never thought I'd live here."

"We're staying, right?" Aimee Louise asked.

"If that's what you want, we will," Stuart said.

"Good."

"So, if we cut a wide swath of firebreak along the cross bar of that T, we'll still be on your property, right?" David asked.

"Yes," Scott said.

"Who owns the additional property behind you to the river?" David asked.

"I might own that whole stretch from the east side of my property line to the west side of the Webster property line then to the river. I don't have any papers, but the farmer who owned it told me it was mine before he left for Alabama. He used it for hunting and had a camping trailer on it, but he took the trailer with him. There aren't any structures or utilities on the property," Scott said.

"Perfect for a prescribed burn," David said.

"When do we start?" Peyton asked.

"We can start the fire early tomorrow morning if we get everything done today," David said. "Everyone at the farm, including the children, will need to understand what we are doing. Andy and Rosalie, could you explain to Jennie and Leo, so Jennie can tell her new household? I'd like to talk to Brandon."

Andy and Rosalie nodded.

"I'll talk to Charo," Aimee Louise said.

"You and I should tell Henry, Angel," Stuart said.

"I'd like to tell Dolly and my dad," Nate said. "I could probably tell Doc at the same time."

"I'll talk to Mama Sandra and Ms. Blanche," Peyton said. "Who have we left out?"

"I'll go with you, Peyton then they won't outnumber you," Scott said. "

"We skipped Cal," Stuart said. "I'll talk to him while Aimee Louise is with Charo."

"What do we do while we wait for you all to complete your survey?" Scott asked.

"The tractors need to be ready to roll tomorrow morning," David said.

"Got it," Scott said. "We'll need to see how many we have that are operational and what equipment we have on hand that will help us."

"I'll check the tractors at Uncle Leo's while I'm there," Andy said.

"Make sure they're diesel, Andy," Scott said. "We're short on gasoline, but we've got plenty of diesel thanks to the fuel cans of diesel that the guys who snatched Cami Sue and Sam had in the back of their truck."

"Let's get busy." Aimee Louise strode to the door then everyone else was in motion too.

* * *

Aimee Louise hurried to the house, and Scott and Peyton followed her. Aimee Louise went inside and waved at Sandra and Blanche.

"Got a few minutes, Sandra? Peyton has a few things to tell you and Blanche," Scott said.

"Oh, really? Peyton, did you know he was going to throw you under the bus like that?" Sandra laughed as Aimee Louise continued down the hall.

When Aimee Louise reached Charo's room, Charo had a shirt in her lap as she sat on the floor in front of a backpack.

Aimee Louise peered into the backpack then sat on the floor across from Charo. "It's empty. Were you looking for something?"

"Not really; maybe," Charo said. "I don't know."

Aimee Louise nodded. "Have you told Nate?"

"What?"

Charo picked up the shirt, held it close to her face, and inhaled deeply then sighed.

"How did you know?" Charo asked as she folded the shirt then twisted her neck to look over her head. "My cloud, right?"

"Yes, it is amazing. Fireworks coming out of cotton candy."

"That sounds awesome," Charo said. "I wish I could see it."

"You feel it. That's even more awesome," Aimee Louise said.

"You're so right." Charo rose then gathered up the rest of the clothes from the floor and dumped all the clothes onto the bed to fold. "My shirt's been in my backpack since I left Miami and still has the haunting fragrance of the wild jasmine blossoms outside our bedroom window when Dolly was a baby. I sound sappy, don't I?"

Charo picked up her shirt again and cuddled it against her cheek. "To answer your question, I haven't told Nate. It's been hard because I can't think of anything else; I was afraid to get his hopes up, but you've kind of confirmed it, haven't you? So, why did you come to talk to me? Other than to tell me that I'm pregnant, of course."

Aimee Louise told her about the plan to defend the south side of the farm. "You should be careful to stay away from the smoke. The wind will be blowing from the south."

"Good point. The children and I will do artwork in the living room, and they can play in the front yard, at least for a while."

Before Aimee Louise headed to the hallway, tears slid down Charo's cheeks. "Thanks again, Angel. At least now I can be weepy with a clear conscience." She sniffed back her tears. "I just realized Mama Sandra and Ms. Blanche will hover and smother, won't they?"

Aimee Louise stopped at the doorway. "Yes, they will. You'll have to tell them and everyone else yourself."

"I knew you wouldn't say anything." Charo hugged Aimee Louise.

When Aimee Louise passed the Henderson bedroom, Cal sat in his wheelchair near the window while he and Stuart talked. She passed Scott, Peyton, Sandra, and Blanche, who were in deep conversation in the kitchen, and hurried outside.

Henry ran to her. "Hi, Mama Angel. Brandon and his dad went for a walk, and Mr. Nate is talking to Dolly and the judge, so I was looking for you and Big Bear. Want to go see the chickens with me?"

"That is a great idea."

As they strolled hand in hand to the coop, Henry said, "We're going to do something important, aren't we?"

"We sure are. Remember when we checked the front field to see if anyone would notice the house from the road?"

"Yes, and I saw the lights. Big Bear didn't see them until he scrunched down," Henry said.

"That's true. Big Bear and I checked the back field and woods to see if anyone would notice the house, and we heard Dolly."

"Maybe I could notice something different. Can you show me?" Henry asked.

"You would have to be very quiet," she said.

Henry nodded, and they strolled to the west side of the backyard then he followed her into the south woods.

Aimee Louise crept into the woods then crouched; Henry was a few feet behind her and did the same. When she rose and crept toward the east end of the property, he followed her. Every few yards, Aimee Louise stopped and scanned to her right then to her left. When they were not quite midway to the east property line, Aimee Louise paused, and Henry raised his hand then pointed to his left. Aimee Louise gazed toward the house then heard the chickens. After she crouched closer to Henry's eye level, she saw the lower part of the chicken coop.

We didn't check this far west.

She held up her thumb then continued, and Henry followed her. Before they reached the property line, Stuart called out, "Has anyone seen Angel and Henry?"

She glanced at Henry, and he had his hand over his mouth to keep from making a sound, and she nodded. They continued to the property line then returned to the backyard.

"We can talk now," Aimee Louise whispered, and Henry nodded then raced to Stuart.

* * *

When Stuart saw Henry and Aimee Louise, he sighed in relief then narrowed his eyes. *What were they doing in the woods?*

Henry waved then ran to Stuart. "Hi, Big Bear, Mama Angel and I went on a special mission. She can tell you better than me."

Of course, they did. Stuart shook his head.

When Aimee Louise joined them, she told him about the chicken coop and hearing his voice.

"How deep were you in the woods?" he asked.

"About the same as when we heard Dolly's voice," Aimee Louise said.

As the three of them strolled to the barn, Stuart asked, "Do you think the plan to put the firebreak at Dad's property line is far enough away?"

"Yes, but we can check it, if you like," she said.

Stuart swallowed before he spoke, so he wouldn't yell. "There's no need to check; I agree with you."

When Henry snickered, Stuart asked, "What?"

"I thought you were going to holler, but you didn't." Henry skipped ahead when he saw Brandon and Dolly near the barn.

"I did too," Aimee Louise said.

"You and Henry know me only too well." Stuart rolled his eyes. "So, you couldn't see the house or the barn?"

"I couldn't see any structures, and I didn't hear the chickens until Henry pointed toward the house; I think I was more focused on what was visible through the trees while Henry was focused on his special mission." Aimee Louise listened to a soft roar. "Do you hear a tractor?"

Stuart and Aimee Louise rushed to the northwest corner of the backyard as Andy drove a large tractor. Rosalie jogged along behind him. After Andy parked, Aimee Louise and Stuart raced to the tractor, and Stuart said, "Looks like it went well with Jennie and Leo."

Rosalie and Andy side-glanced each other then Rosalie said, "Let's talk here, so I can catch my breath."

"So, what's up?" Stuart asked.

"When we got to the farm, the three kids met us in the yard," Andy said. "You know how popular Red is with kids, right? They were happy to see Red and gave us the inside scoop on the latest. A woman showed up on the farm earlier today and claimed she went to school with their grandma, Aunt Jennie's friend, but their grandma couldn't remember her. Grandma told the kids not to worry about it because it's important to feed people who are hungry and give them a place to stay," Andy said.

"Apparently, this supposed friend had a long, involved story about being chased away from her house by robbers and having a difficult time getting to Aunt Jennie's farm," Rosalie said. "The kids were pretty vague about the details, probably because the friend was. When the kids asked their mama about the friend that their grandma didn't know, she laughed and told them their grandma was getting forgetful. The kids didn't like the friend, especially after she told them to call her 'Auntie Connie.' They said there was something mean about her, like a bad witch or a troll. They didn't think their grandma liked her either, but they were afraid to tell their mama because she'd get angry at them for being rude and spreading tales. Aunt Jennie told me that she was nervous about having a complete stranger in their house, and if times were different, she would have sent Connie on her way after a nice dinner and an overnight stay."

"After the kids ran to the chicken coop to watch the chickens, Red and I decided we didn't know any of the people at Aunt Jennie's house," Andy said.

"When we went inside, Andy took the lead, and I'm glad he did because his new story was great," Rosalie said.

"Thanks, babe. I told Aunt Jennie that Scott sent us over because the creek behind the house had dried up and he was worried about how dry the woods were. I told her we were keeping an eye on the woods in case there was a fire, and we wanted to put in a firebreak this evening. Aunt Jennie asked about our defense plan in case of an attack, and I told her we were keeping our eyes open, but we were more concerned about a fire."

"While Andy and Aunt Jennie talked more about the fire, and Aunt Jennie told him about all the fires this season and the past twenty years, I went to the radio room and talked to Uncle Leo. I told him about the fire situation and asked if we could borrow his large tractor. He agreed, of course, and told me to take a can of diesel to refuel his tractor, and his torch and small bottle of propane if we need to start any back fires. I told him we might not be able to make it back in the morning for the wedding. We agreed that if we weren't here by the regular time, we wouldn't be coming later, so he wouldn't have to try to get in contact with Pastor Phillips if the pastor wasn't on the air. Uncle Leo agreed that it's the dry season right now, and Papa Scott was smart."

"When Red and I were leaving, Connie showed up, and it's a good thing the kids warned us because I think Red would have shot her on the spot. I could see the hairs on the back of Red's neck go up when Connie smiled as we were introduced to her and she said, 'Just call me Aunt Connie.' Her smile was like staring at an open-mouthed diamond back rattler ready to strike."

"I didn't shoot her because it would have been rude," Rosalie said.

"I think your decision was solid, and congratulations for coming up with a cover story so quickly," Stuart said.

"It was an excellent story, wasn't it? On the way to Uncle Leo's barn, I asked Andy what Papa Scott was going to do about the creek that had gone dry, and he told me he didn't know," Rosalie said. "I was really worried about it until I remembered Andy had made it all up."

Andy chuckled. "I was believing it myself for a while too. So, how did it go here?"

"Let's see who's at the barn," Stuart said. On the way, Stuart continued. "As far as I've heard, everyone is fine with the plan. How did it go with Charo, Angel?" Stuart asked. "Is she okay with our plan?"

"Yes. She plans to keep the children busy with games in the front yard or occupied with art in the living room if it's smoky."

"Cal told me he's a big fan of burning thick, old brush to promote new growth for food for the wildlife and to clear the area, so they can move through the woods." Stuart said. "He's hunted since he was a kid and has a rifle that he can use to cover his bedroom window."

When they reached the barn, Aimee Louise said, "Nate, you might check in with Charo."

"Okay, I'll won't be long; she told me she might have some questions when she sorted through my old clothes."

"Dolly, would you like to go to the garden?" Judge asked. "The boys are ready to squash bugs, and Henry said nobody can weed like you do."

"Wait up, Henry," Dolly called as she ran out of the barn, and the judge rushed to catch up with her.

David strode into the barn. "The judge has taken over kid duty. Where's Nate?"

"He went inside to talk to Charo," Stuart said. "Do we need to rescue Dad and Peyton, Aimee Louise?"

"Good idea. I'll be right back," she said.

Aimee Louise went into the house then returned almost immediately with Scott and Peyton.

"How did she do that?" David asked.

"Magic, is my best guess." Stuart snickered.

"We can start now," Scott said. "Aimee Louise said you all were waiting for us."

"Sure were, and Nate too," Stuart said.

"Nate may be a while," Aimee Louise said.

Not asking.

"Andy, would you give the group a quick recap of what you and Rosalie did?" Stuart asked.

After Andy explained what he said, and why, Stuart asked, "Anyone have any questions?"

"That was fast thinking, and I'm surprised the new friend is still standing," David said.

Scott snorted. "That's the truth. Did anyone have concerns? Sandra and Blanche agreed with our plan for the south woods."

Peyton added, "I'm going to talk to them more later about our plans to defend the house from any attacks."

Stuart told the others what Henry and Aimee Louise found. David stared at Aimee Louise while Stuart spoke, and Peyton grinned.

"After Aimee Louise, Stuart, Andy, and I mark the area to determine where we'll start fires, we'll get back together to see if we can get our firebreak in place before supper."

"And me," Rosalie said, and Andy nodded.

"I'll warn Sandra to plan to feed the kids because we may not be ready to eat until close to dark," Scott said.

"We'll be as fast as we can. Are the tractors ready?" David asked.

"Sure are, and here's the surveyor tape you asked for." Scott handed David the roll before the three of them headed to the south woods.

"Wait a minute," Peyton said. "What about the wedding tomorrow morning?"

"I guess it'll be a little earlier than we planned," Stuart hugged Aimee Louise. "Wedding, breakfast, bonfire to celebrate. How does that sound?"

"I love it," Andy said as he kissed Rosalie when she opened her mouth to speak.

Peyton laughed. "I'll let the judge know, so he can prepare."

"I'll tell Sandra, but this is giving her and Blanche too much notice. Eat light tonight because we'll have a breakfast feast in the morning." Scott smiled.

"Let's start at the east side of the Newton property line to mark our fire line," David said.

Stuart, Andy, Rosalie, and David followed Aimee Louise to the southeast corner of Scott's property. When they were midway, Stuart said, "I'll get Dad's large tractor and begin plowing at the east edge."

* * *

Aimee Louise walked the line as David continued to mark it. After they reached the far west side of their fire line, Andy said, "We'll get Uncle Leo's tractor and start here."

"When you meet up with Stuart, go north of his line to make the break larger," David said.

After Andy and Rosalie left, Aimee Louise asked David, "What are you going to do next?"

"Join Stuart, so he has a shooter along with him."

"I'll see you there, unless you have something else for me," Aimee Louise said.

"That's fine. Go."

Aimee Louise raced through the woods along their firebreak line to join Stuart as the tractor roared and plowed along the planned path. She waved when he came into sight and waited while he drove toward her.

She scanned the plowed row behind the large tractor. *David was right. A second row will be a good firebreak.*

CHAPTER ELEVEN

When Stuart saw Aimee Louise racing through the woods toward him, he smiled. *I'll never get tired of seeing her running to me.*

After Aimee Louise came close to the tractor, Stuart handed her the ear protection muffs that he'd brought for her.

"Thank you," she shouted as she donned the muffs. Stuart smiled and nodded. *I think the tractor's loud. It must be excruciating for her.*

Aimee Louise ran alongside, behind, and in front of the tractor as Stuart turned over the ground into a fire break. *I can focus on moving as quickly and efficiently as possible with my Angel guarding me.*

After David joined them, he and Aimee Louise talked then David ran ahead of the tractor.

"Where'd he go?" Stuart shouted over the engine noise of the tractor then realized Aimee Louise couldn't hear him. He pointed to David and did an exaggerated shrug.

"Check on Andy," Aimee Louise shouted.

Stuart nodded and returned his attention to driving the tractor and turning over the ground to expose dirt in his wake.

When Stuart saw Andy ahead, he moved to his right then continued the second row next to Andy's plowed ground. After Stuart and Aimee Louise reached the west side of the Websters' property line, Stuart drove the tractor back to his dad's barn, and Aimee Louise ran alongside.

Stuart turned off the engine, and Aimee Louise removed the ear protection.

"Thanks," she said.

As they strolled to the house, Stuart said, "I thought it would be easier for you." When they went inside, Sandra and Blanche were in the kitchen.

"Your dad's in the living room," Sandra said, and Stuart hurried to talk to his dad.

* * *

"We'll have supper ready for the grown-ups in a few minutes, Angel," Sandra said. "We were waiting to hear you all return before we got too serious about it."

"Did you know Ms. Jennie's friend, Myrtle, from high school?"

Sandra shook her head, but Blanche said, "I did. They weren't close friends or anything and didn't run with the same crowds, but Myrtle considered everybody her friend."

"Did Myrtle have a friend named Connie?"

"I don't remember anyone named Connie, but they were two grades ahead of me," Blanche said. "Why?"

"Ms. Connie showed up at Ms. Jennie's this afternoon. Ms. Myrtle's grandchildren didn't like Ms. Connie, and they said their grandma didn't remember Connie. They told me their mama said that Grandma Myrtle was forgetful. Is she?"

Blanche snorted. "Myrtle was always dramatic and a little flighty; I can see where some might call her forgetful, and it could have worsened as she's gotten older. If Myrtle didn't like Connie, the kids wouldn't either because they idolize their grandma. They are such sweet kids."

"We understand there's a slight adjustment in our plans tomorrow," Sandra said. "Wedding, breakfast, bonfire. You know Blanche and I won't be able to sleep tonight, so I guess we'll be in the kitchen cooking all night."

"Or talking." Blanche tittered, and Sandra nodded.

"What can I do to help with supper, Mom?" Aimee Louise said.

"Oh my goodness. I was hoping you'd call me 'Mom,' but I've been afraid to ask. You have made my entire week."

Sandra hugged Aimee Louise, and Blanche blew her nose.

Sandra brushed her cheek and stepped to the stove. "Do we know how much longer Rosalie, Andy, and David are going to be?"

"I don't hear Mr. Leo's tractor yet; I thought Andy might park it here. I'll check," Aimee Louise said.

"Take Stuart with you," Sandra said. "He's a bear when he's worried about what you're doing."

"I'll bet that's how Peyton got his nickname," Blanche said. "I've wondered about that."

Aimee Louise hurried to the living room, and Stuart asked, "What?"

"Time to check on Rosalie, Andy, and David," she said.

"Let's go."

* * *

After they were outside, Stuart asked, "What's up, really?"

Aimee Louise repeated what Blanche told her about Myrtle, the kids, and Connie.

"That's really interesting. If Rosalie and Andy hadn't had the reaction to Connie that they had, I'd be inclined to believe that Ms. Myrtle exaggerated her concerns, and the kids caught her mood. Either way, it was wise for Andy and Rosalie to have taken the direction they did."

"Mama Sandra and Ms. Blanche are excited about tomorrow, and so am I. You were brilliant to announce the wedding comes first then breakfast and the bonfire," Aimee Louise said.

Stuart pulled her into a hug as he buried his face in her hair. "Henry's excited too. I asked him to be my best boy, and Dad to be my best man."

"What does the best boy do?" Aimee Louise asked.

"Dad told Henry the best boy is included in the wedding because we are a package deal," Stuart said.

"Dad is brilliant," Aimee Louise said. "It's okay if I call him 'Dad,' isn't it?"

"He'd love it," Stuart squeezed her then they continued their stroll toward the property line.

"I could call him Mr. Newton," Aimee Louise said, and Stuart burst out laughing.

Aimee Louise sighed. "Oh, good. I thought it might be a funny joke."

"It was funny, and let me be there when you do," Stuart said. "Never mind, he'll say I put you up to it."

"I called your mom, 'Mom,' and she was happy. I hear the tractor."

The two of them ran toward the Newtons' property line and met Rosalie on the way.

"Andy's done," Rosalie said. "I saw a couple of guys in the woods as they watched Andy drive along the firebreak. They didn't point any weapons at him, so I just watched them. There were wearing sneakers and shorts. If they're the guys who are in the tent, they must be miserable. I decided they were just curious about what Andy was doing. Do you think they'll run for the firebreak when we light the fire in the morning?"

"I doubt it," Stuart said, "especially if they don't know what it is. I think it's more of a natural reaction to run away from a fire rather than toward it."

"You're right," Rosalie said. "They made me more anxious than I realized."

David waited for Andy near Leo's back equipment shed. After Andy parked the tractor, he and David joined the others, and Rosalie and Aimee raced to the Newtons' while Stuart, Andy, and David jogged along behind. Stuart stopped before he reached his dad's backyard and walked back to the fire line and scanned the woods then ran to catch up with Andy and David.

Men in the woods that spy on any of us makes me anxious too.

It was after sundown when they walked into the house, and Peyton said, "Finally, you're here. I'm starving. Ms. Blanche told me the chuckwagon's closed until everybody is back at the fort."

"Gather the troops and circle the wagons, Peyton, and we'll rustle up the grub," Blanche said.

Sandra rolled her eyes. "Cowgirl Blanche read one of Andy's cowboy books to the children today."

Andy snickered. "I can't wait until she reads some of my space alien books."

"Don't tell her that, Andy," Sandra groaned.

"Too late, buckaroo. Sounds like a good one for our list," Blanche said.

"Howdy, ma'am," Henry said as he and Brandon swaggered into the kitchen, and Dolly waved with her palm pointed forward and a slow turn of her wrist as she followed them and politely nodded to her imaginary devotees.

Stuart snickered. *Proper girls in the old west must have invented the princess wave.*

"Howdy, yourself, cowpoke," Aimee Louise said, and he rushed to hug her.

"You're awesome, Mama Angel," Henry said.

"She is, and so are you, Little Bear," Stuart said. "So, Cookie Blanche, where did you find cowboy hats for these two?"

"Boss Sandra dared me to go into the attic and look. Dolly has one too, but she won't wear it because it's not pink."

"Cowgirl Blanche found me a red bandana and helped me tie it on my head." Dolly modeled her head band with the big floppy bow.

"Very stylish," Peyton said, and Dolly curtsied.

"I will never dare Blanche to do anything ever again," Sandra said. "She scared me to death climbing those steps, and I had to leave the house when she climbed down. The boys promised to come get me if she fell and broke her neck. Grab a seat. The judge, Cal, and Doc ate with the children, so don't worry about seniority. Dad will eat with Blanche and me, but he may sit with you."

After the children returned to the living room, and everyone was seated, Blanche and Sandra quickly served the plates of stewed chicken and canned sweet potatoes with sliced tomatoes on the side.

"This is delicious," Charo said.

"Glad you're enjoying it, Charo," Blanche said.

After everyone ate, Stuart went to the living room. When he sat on the sofa, Henry joined him.

"Are you ready for the wedding tomorrow?" Judge asked.

"Sure am," Stuart said.

"I'm ready too," Henry said.

"If I understand the plan, we'll have the wedding then breakfast, and you all will start the fire before daybreak," Cal said.

"That's the plan." Andy came into the living room. "Stuart, David would like to have a fire meeting in the barn."

Stuart hugged Henry before he and Andy left for the barn.

When Stuart and Andy reached the barn, Aimee Louise and Rosalie were waiting for them at the door.

"Nate and Peyton are here too," Rosalie said. "They technically aren't the fire team, but they need to know what we'll be doing, so they can tell if something's not going as planned."

"Good, we're all here," David said. "Andy, Scott has a propane torch that most farmers call a flame thrower too. That makes two torches to start fires. We'll start at both sides and move toward the middle as far as we can go. If we run low on propane, we'll go the old-fashioned way and sacrifice a little diesel. Has anyone besides me used a farmer's flamethrower?"

"I have. Uncle Leo always had me manage the burns," Andy said.

"Dad and I have too," Stuart said.

"I want to learn," Aimee Louise said, and Stuart and Scott said, "No."

"We'll ask again next time." Rosalie snickered.

"You two can light the diesel," David said. "If that doesn't give us the incentive not to waste propane, nothing will."

Stuart and Andy nodded.

"Correct me if I'm wrong, but Angel, Red, and I see the order for our priorities tomorrow as weddings, fire, and breakfast," Scott said.

David nodded as Stuart and Andy glanced at each other.

They went to Dad, and the three of them teamed up on us.

Nate said, "After my dad performs the weddings, if you start the fire then we can all enjoy breakfast together. I know the fire will need to be watched, but we could do that in shifts, right?"

David nodded. "We could take our time to enjoy the wedding breakfast and festivities. Nate, you and I could take the first shift."

"I'll stand guard for you," Peyton added.

"We can be fluid with the second shift. I wouldn't mind having a third observer outside. Blanche has already volunteered to be an observer," David said.

"Cal told me he could be a spotter from the house. I knew they had a tree farm, but I didn't realize the tree farm was over five hundred acres of slash and loblolly pine that they've been managing for over thirty years. I suspect after the fire gets going, Jennie and Leo will keep an eye on it too," Scott said.

"I need to talk to Cal. Blanche asked me about a backfire, and I'm sorry to admit that I'd forgotten about it."

"I'll go with you," Scott said. "With the wind coming from the south, seems like it wouldn't be that hard to do."

After the two men strode to the house, Peyton asked, "What was Blanche talking about, or does everybody else know but me?"

"In our context, a backfire means to burn an area between us and the larger fire to keep the big fire from coming back on us. If the wind blows the raging fire toward us, it will stop at the charred area," Stuart said. "Let's look at our firebreak."

Everyone followed Stuart and Peyton outside.

Stuart pointed. "See the firebreak? Beyond it you would see our burned area that we're calling backfire then the big fire. The combination of the backfire area and the firebreak will keep us safe."

"Thanks, Stuart. It's totally clear to me, and I even understand why David was so upset," Peyton said.

After Peyton and Nate headed inside, Andy said, "Are you thinking what I'm thinking?"

Stuart said, "Yeah."

Rosalie added, "We are too. Let's go talk to the Judge. Our choice is to postpone our weddings—"

"Or backfire." Aimee Louise finished Rosalie's sentence.

Rosalie giggled, and Andy stared as Stuart hugged Aimee Louise. "You got it, babe."

On the way to the house, Andy asked, "Do all four of us converge on the judge? Isn't that court intimidation or something?"

"We can pull everyone together and take a vote," Aimee Louise said.

"That's crazy," Rosalie said. "Are you getting cold feet, Andy? Let's do it."

"Whatever you say, sweetheart." Andy winked at Stuart.

When the four of them walked into the kitchen, Sandra eyes widened. "What on earth is going on? What are you four up to?"

"Mom," Rosalie said. "We need everybody in here."

Blanche bustled out of the kitchen and stood at the living room doorway. "Avast, ye maties. All hands on deck in the kitchen."

Blanche returned to the kitchen then stood to the side of the doorway to avoid being stampeded by the crowd. "Got 'em."

Judge pushed Cal in his wheelchair, and David and Scott followed them.

"Your show, Red," Andy grinned as he and Stuart moved the kitchen table to the corner, and Rosalie and Aimee Louise stepped closer to the kitchen sink.

After Judge smiled and made his way toward Rosalie and Aimee Louise, he stood with his back to the sink, and they turned to face him as Stuart and Andy stood by their brides' sides.

"Judge," Stuart said, "We thought it made sense for us to have the wedding now, but Angel said we should call for a vote."

"All in favor," Judge said, and everyone shouted, "Aye."

"In all fairness, opposed?"

Everyone was silent as they glanced around then the judge said, "The ayes have it. Best men, matrons of honors, best girl, and best boys, please take your places."

Charo hurried to stand behind Aimee Louise, Peyton and Dolly held hands as they took their place behind Rosalie, Scott and Henry stood next to Stuart, and Nate, David, and Brandon stood next to Andy. Sandra moved to stand with Charo, and Blanche pushed Cal's wheelchair next to Scott then remained behind Cal.

The judge raised his eyebrows at the standing crowd. "Looks like no one is missing from the wedding party." He glanced out the kitchen window. "The full moon is bright; it's a perfect night for weddings."

The crash of shattered class from the living room interrupted the judge, and Scott said, "Defense team, take your positions."

Charo gathered the children. "Let's go to the hallway near the stairs."

David put his hand on Andy's shoulder. "Let's back burn now."

Before David and Andy reached the back door, Rosalie said, "I'm going too."

"Wait, Red," Judge said. "Until we understand the extent of our current threat, you're needed more on defense. I'll back them up."

While he rushed to grab his shotgun, Sandra said, "Blanche and I will cover along with the judge."

Red dashed upstairs as Aimee Louise headed to the back door.

"I'm going with you." Stuart picked up his rifle.

"Stop the attack on the house then join me." Aimee Louise left, and Stuart grumbled under his breath as he raced to the living room.

* * *

By the time Aimee Louise reached the barn, David and Andy were striding to the firebreak with their flamethrower equipment.

"What's your plan?" she asked as she kept pace with them.

"I'm going to the west corner, and David will start here," Andy said.

"I'll start at the west side first. I won't be in your way."

The sound of two gunshots ripped through the night as Aimee Louise raced into the dark before either man had a chance to say anything.

"If it was anyone else, I'd be worried, but I believe her," David said. "She won't be in our way. Let's go."

Aimee Louise raced past the firebreak and into the woods before she turned west.

The bright moon gives me an advantage, especially if the men have been relying on night vision goggles.

She remained still as she scanned the area for any movement and listened for any unexpected sounds then continued west. When she reached the end of the firebreak she stepped to the south across the tilled dirt and waited for Andy. She listened as he hiked her way then joined her.

"Did you see anyone? Hear anything?" he whispered.

She shook her head. "Here to the midpoint."

Andy started a swath of small fires the same width as the firebreak, and after they burned until they reached the dirt, he moved to the next small section.

Aimee Louise walked slowly in the woods parallel to the firebreak and repeated her short pauses to scan and listen. When she saw the flames of a small fire ahead, she crossed the firebreak to the trees closer to Scott's farm and ran to see David's progress.

When David saw her, he waved but continued working. "Is Andy okay?" he asked.

"Yes, he's being careful. I didn't hear anything at all, but I know there are at least two camps."

"After we have the fire break in place, I need to talk to Stuart, Scott, and Cal. The wind is dying down, and I'm wondering if we should go ahead with our prescribed burn tonight instead of tomorrow."

"Rosalie would know if the wind will stay calm all night."

David nodded. "If Cal feels like coming to the barn, he has the all-terrain wheelchair."

As she headed toward the backyard, movement from the house caught her eye, and she realized Stuart was motioning for her to join him. She raced to him, and he caught her in a hug.

* * *

"How are they doing?" Stuart asked as he snuggled her.

"They'll soon have the backfire completed. They're burning an area as wide as the firebreak. They want to get all the experts together to discuss their next move. I heard two shots then nothing else, but I was at the far west end of Dad's property. What was the attack?"

"Remember the guys we saw at the burning car? From what Rosalie described, two of them decided to attack the house. One of them threw a rock through the front window then they hid in the trees next to the field. Rosalie thought their plan was to shoot us as we came outside to see who threw the rock. I'm not sure they thought about how bright the moonlight is tonight. Rosalie shot one, and when the second guy charged the house, Nate shot him. We waited, but there was no second wave, which I expected."

"Can you skip David's meeting?" she asked. "After David and Andy are away from the burn site, I'd like to see if I can hear anything back in the woods where the men were camping. I'll have to change shirts because this cream shirt that Peyton lent me is too light to wear in the dark woods."

"That shirt is cute on you, and I can skip the meeting."

Aimee Louise gazed at Stuart's cloud then hugged him, and they laughed as they awkwardly stumbled with their arms tightly wrapped around each other on the way to the house.

After they entered the house, they raced up the stairs, and Aimee Louise reached the landing three steps ahead of Stuart.

"I let you win," Stuart said.

"Ha." Aimee Louise flipped her hair and sashayed to her bedroom.

She's catching on to jokes. Stuart stared at her until she closed her bedroom door. *Dang, she's sexy.*

When Stuart turned, he bumped into Henry and caught him before Stuart knocked him down.

"Where are we going, Daddy Angel?"

When Stuart raised his eyebrows, Henry said, "You and Mama Angel are going somewhere. I've got my go-bag. Do I need a jacket?"

"You can't go this time, Henry Angel," Stuart said.

"I think I'll just call you Dad for short, and you can call me Henry. Is it because it's dangerous?"

"No, it's because it's late and after your bedtime. Did you have your bath and snack?"

Henry hung his head and nodded.

"I'll walk with you to bed, but I won't tuck you in unless you want me to," Stuart said. "Then I'll need to change my clothes before Mama leaves me because I was too slow."

"Let's go." Henry ran down the hallway to the bedroom he shared with Brandon.

Stuart hugged Henry in the hallway then kissed him on top of his head. "Sleep well."

Before Henry climbed into bed, he shook Stuart's hand. "Good night, sir."

As Stuart left the room, Brandon asked, "Why did you call your dad, sir, Henry?"

"Just something special between me and Dad," Henry said, and Stuart smiled as he hurried to change to a long-sleeved, dark shirt.

After Stuart changed, he joined Aimee Louise and Scott who were waiting in the kitchen.

"I told Dad our plans, so he wouldn't worry about where we were," she said.

Stuart's eyes widened at the holstered pistol on Aimee Louise's hip.

Scott smiled. "Aimee Louise asked for a pistol to carry in case you're trapped between the fire and the bad guys. I'll still worry, but I'm glad you have a plan."

We do?

"We'll have what we need for at least two days," Aimee Louise said. "I packed my biscuits; your extra water and biscuits are on the kitchen counter."

Stuart nodded. "A little extra ammo then we're set."

After Stuart returned to the kitchen, Scott said, "Angel told me she'll wait for you outside. When she asked for a pistol, I knew the plan was hers, and you didn't know what it was. I'm actually not worried about either of you. I know you'll fight to the death to keep her safe, and she'll have a plan in place, so you don't have to." Scott chuckled.

"You're right, Dad, and thanks for not busting me." Stuart slipped on his backpack and picked up his rifle.

Scott smiled. "Any time. I'm proud of you and Angel."

"Thanks, Dad." Stuart hurried outside and found Aimee Louise at the barn.

"We'll start on this side. The burned area is cooler."

"One second." Stuart embraced her then kissed her lightly before he teased her mouth open with his tongue, and she wrapped her arms around his neck and pulled him closer as she returned his kiss with the same intense passion he felt. After he released her, he grinned. "Let's do this."

When they were in the woods past the firebreak, Aimee Louise held up her hand for him to stop then she disappeared into the trees.

Not sure I'll ever get used to that. He scanned the area and listened.

Aimee Louise reappeared and motioned for him to follow her into the woods. He stayed close because the thick canopy of trees obscured the bright moonlight. After she stopped, she tapped his ear, and he listened.

I don't hear anything. After he slowly, silently inhaled then exhaled a breath, he heard it. *Someone snoring.*

When he nodded, Aimee Louise tapped his palm with two fingers. *Two of them.* He waited then heard a second man snort before he gasped for air. *You've got a little apnea, there, bud.*

Aimee Louise tugged on his sleeve, and they crept back toward the midline of the burned area. After she pointed to the flames in the trees east of them, they smacked an air high-five then moved deep into the next section of woods. Stuart crept behind Aimee Louise until they reached a narrow, fast-running river. She pointed in the direction of the flames they had seen earlier, but he didn't see any fire.

No one in this section. He nodded. *Possible escape route.*

She picked up a straight, thick branch then jumped over the river onto the opposite bank and moved south through the woods, and Stuart stayed close. The thick brush slowed them, but Angel poked with her stick and found paths that were invisible to Stuart, so they continued to move forward. After a long trek, she crept through the trees and pointed.

Stuart scanned the county road before Aimee Louise walked along through the trees and parallel to the shallow ditch; Stuart hurried to catch up with her, but when she stopped abruptly, he bumped into her. *What the heck.* He wrapped his arms around her and kissed the back of her neck before he peeked over her head. *Another truck.*

When Aimee Louise stepped toward the truck, Stuart grabbed her again, and she tugged on his hand to follow her.

"What are we doing?" he whispered.

"Stealing a truck," she said.

"No, we aren't," Stuart said as Aimee Louise dashed to the truck then eased the driver's door open. Stuart ran to the back of the truck, pulled back the tarp, and sighed with relief. *Empty.* He raced to jump into the passenger's seat. "Okay, we're stealing a truck. Let's go. They obviously looted a farm from the contents, but nobody's in the back."

Aimee Louise nodded as she balanced her stick against the back of the seat, turned on the engine, and accelerated east on the county road.

"What if they heard the truck?" Stuart asked.

"It will take them a while to get to the road, but when they do, they're stranded."

"What are we going to do with the truck?" he asked.

"Crash it."

Before Aimee Louise reached the frontage road that paralleled the interstate, she pulled over. "Let's check the back for anything that we can use."

Aimee Louise jumped into the back of the large truck and slid five cases of canned fruits and vegetables, a long, coiled rope, and three large tarps to the edge of the truck.

"There's a can of gasoline, a bale of hay, a shovel, and an ax. Do we want any of them?" she asked.

"The ax and the shovel."

"How do you feel about canned spinach?" she asked.

"Not my favorite," Stuart said.

"Put the two cases of canned spinach and the rope on the seat with us then we'll put the cases of canned peaches, the tarps, and the tools in the ditch across the road."

After they had moved all the items then jumped into the truck, Stuart said. "What's our crash plan?"

"We'll point the truck at the roadblock that's near the Mitchell driveway and tie the steering wheel to keep the wheels straight then jam the accelerator down with a case of spinach."

"Sounds dangerous. Wait, what about the second case of spinach?"

"We might need it to hold the first case in place, but if we don't, I don't like canned spinach either."

Stuart laughed. "I'll cut a long section of rope to save us some time. How do you come up with stuff like this?"

Aimee Louise shrugged. "It's logical. We can destroy their truck and get a psychological edge by crashing the truck into the roadblock. Stranding the two men was a bonus."

"What about the other men you saw closer to the west side?"

"They don't have a truck; if they did, we could crash into the other roadblock except we'd have lost our element of surprise by our attack on the first roadblock."

"It still sounds dangerous."

"It isn't because after I position the case on the accelerator, I'll drop it into gear then jump out of the truck, and you'll grab me and snatch me away from the truck, so I won't get hurt."

Stuart stared at her. "No, we won't do that. There has to be another way."

"How's this? I leave the truck in gear and run alongside and use my stick to push the case onto the accelerator."

"Better. Stop the truck, and let's see how fast it rolls with no pressure on the accelerator."

Aimee Louise nodded then stopped the truck. When she removed her foot, the truck inched forward slowly.

"Okay, I'll set up the cases, and you can push them over with your stick."

"I knew you'd like that plan."

Stuart rolled his eyes. *She tricked me into this, and I don't care.*

CHAPTER TWELVE

Before Aimee Louise turned from the frontage road onto the state road, she turned off the headlights then maintained a steady speed. When the roadblock came into sight in the moonlight, Stuart wiped his damp hands on his jeans and lowered the driver's visor while Aimee Louise slowly applied pressure to the brake. After the truck stopped, Stuart quickly tied the rope around the steering column and looped the rope around the visor before he threaded the two ends of the rope through the spokes then tied it with a square knot around the steering column. After he finished, he gave the steering wheel a tug, and it remained stationary.

"Hold on a minute. I want to check one more thing in the back." Stuart hurried to the back of the truck and fastened the back flap open before he removed the top from the old metal fuel can then poured gasoline on the bale of hay and moved the bale toward the back of the truck.

He climbed into the passenger's seat, and slid into the driver's seat after Aimee Louise stepped out of the truck. The truck began slowly rolling as Stuart swung his legs out of the driver's door before he balanced the first case of spinach. "Here's my rifle. Get back."

After Aimee Louise grabbed his rifle and backed away, he slid the second case to the driver's seat before he stepped onto the road. He pushed the second case onto the first, and the truck took off as Aimee Louise grabbed the back of his belt and jerked him back before she handed him the rifle. They ran behind the truck then Stuart said, "I'll meet you in the field."

He switched the magazine in his rifle to his magazine with tracer rounds. When men shouted warnings and ran from the roadblock because of the oncoming speeding truck, Stuart took aim then shot the bale of hay with a tracer bullet, and the hay caught on fire. He dashed to the field and crouched down next to Aimee Louise, who had covered her ears with her hands.

"Watch," Stuart said.

When Aimee Louise rose with Stuart, he put his hands over hers to help cover her ears. She cringed at the loud crash of metal and concrete that drowned out the men's shouts then leaned against Stuart at the sound of the explosion and squealed in delight at the sight of the rolling flames.

"I added a little to your plan." Stuart said.

"The explosion and fire on top of the crash were brilliant," she said. "Tell me how you did it."

"What do you know about tracer ammunition?"

"I know that tracer ammunition was common in wartimes when planes shot at each other because the gunner could see where the bullet went and adjust their aim. The disadvantage was that the enemy aircraft could also see the tracer bullet."

"Right, and the reason the gunner could see the bullet was because the tracer bullet was hot. It's not uncommon for a sportsman to practice with tracer ammunition from time to time. I've always carried a magazine with tracer ammunition in my go bag."

"When you shot the hay bale that you saturated with gasoline, the hay caught on fire, which ignited the gasoline fumes. Is that what the explosion was?"

"That's it. How did you know I saturated the hay with gasoline?"

"Because you smelled like gasoline after you returned from the back of the truck," she said.

"Let's get back to the farm to see how David's fire is doing. I'm sure they heard the explosion," Stuart said.

"Set the pace."

Stuart ran at his comfortable pace, and Aimee Louise ran alongside him. When they reached the Newtons' driveway, Stuart said, "Let's race," and Aimee Louise took off, Stuart ran as hard as he could. Aimee Louise waited for him at the house, and he ran past her and into the kitchen.

"I win," he said.

"What on earth are you talking about, and where have you been?" Sandra asked. "And why do you smell to high heaven of gasoline?"

"Is Stuart trying to cheat?" Scott asked as Aimee Louise came inside.

"Of course," she said, and Stuart and Scott laughed.

"You're not leaving the kitchen until you tell me where you've been. If you'll sit at the table, I'll give you a snack, but you still need to take a bath before bed because both of you stink," Sandra said.

Scott joined Stuart and Aimee Louise at the table while Sandra mixed then fried sweet potato pancakes. While Stuart told his parents about the sleeping men, the truck, the crash, explosion, and fire, Sandra joined her family at the table.

When Stuart mentioned the explosion, Scott and Sandra glanced at each other, and Scott smirked.

Sandra said, "When we heard the explosion, Dad told me that now we knew where you two were."

"When can we expect them to retaliate?" Scott asked.

"I'm not sure they will because it was one of their trucks and we approached them from the interstate side," Stuart said. "What about the fire? How's it doing?"

"David and Andy were pleased, and finally turned over the fire watch to Nate and the judge," Scott said. "Blanche and I will take the next turn. Speaking of which, our kids are home, so you can go to bed now, Sandra."

Sandra nodded. "We saved Dolly's bathwater for you; I put fresh towels in there for you, and Rosalie and Andy left you a note. Don't worry about leaving the tub dirty because Blanche is a cleaning fanatic and cleans the bathrooms every day. See you in the morning."

"I won't be able to sleep unless I check the fire," Stuart said, and Aimee Louise rose.

"Blanche and I will be out soon; I promised her I wouldn't go out without her," Scott said as Stuart and Aimee Louise headed outside.

The judge met them as they approached the fire break. "Good to see you. The explosion was you, wasn't it? Scott told us it was."

"Yep. It was Aimee Louise's idea to shake up the bad guys at the roadblock, and I saw the opportunity to add an explosion."

"I'll bet it was impressive. The fire on this side is staying strong, and our backfire and fire break are doing their jobs. Are you going to check on Nate?"

"Sure are. Your replacements will be out soon."

As Stuart and Aimee Louise walked along the fire break, they inspected the backfire area and scanned the active fire.

When they reached the Websters' property, Jennie rushed to meet him. "I'm worried sick. I haven't seen Nate since he ran after the dogs."

"What happened?" Stuart asked.

"When one of Leo's farm dogs freaked over the fire and got out of its pen then ran down the firebreak, Holly took off after it. I think she was going to bring it back home."

"We'll look for them. Dad will be along soon. Tell him to stay here," Stuart said.

"Will do. I'm about ready to throw out that conniving Connie and Myrtle's daughter-in-law. I've had my fill of complaining and sniping. I'd keep the kids though." She snickered.

Stuart and Aimee Louise ran along the fire break on the other side of the burned area as they followed Nate's and the dogs' tracks. When they neared the edge of the Websters' property, the tracks turned toward the burn area, and they examined the fire.

"There." Aimee Louise pointed to a smoldering area in the active fire a few feet past the point where the dogs and Nate had turned.

"I'll go; you stay here. If I'm not back in a half hour or so, go get Dad." Stuart dashed into the smoldering fire.

* * *

Aimee Louise ran along the firebreak until she reached a charred field with no signs of fire in the woods to the south. She raced to the trees then made her way closer to the fire on her left then stopped on the edge of the fire. She remained still and listened.

She heard a cough not far from her and called out, "I hear you."

She found a small break in the fire and ran toward the coughing then saw Nate huddled over two dogs in a charred area.

"Follow me," Aimee Louise said.

"Angel." Nate coughed. "I thought I was hallucinating. Can you carry a dog?"

After Nate rose, Aimee Louise snatched up Holly, and Nate picked up the farm dog and followed Aimee Louise to the unburned section.

Nate limped to join her as Aimee Louise gently lowered Holly to the grass. After Nate laid the farm dog next to Holly, he dropped onto the grass alongside them.

Nate coughed. "The fire scorched the dogs' paws." Nate wheezed. "Holly was wrapped around the other dog. I think she was trying to protect him. I don't know what the other dog's name is, so I called him Fire Dog. I carried Holly, and Fire Dog followed me then I couldn't tell which way to go through the thick smoke." Nate coughed again.

"Do you think you could make it to the fire break?"

Nate coughed then when he got his breath, he said, "Sure."

"No, you can't. Wait here. I'll get Jennie."

Nate coughed and nodded as Aimee Louise raced to find Jennie.

Jennie waved when she saw Aimee Louise then ran to meet her. "What happened?"

"I found Nate and the dogs. Nate inhaled a lot of smoke, and the dogs' paws are burned. Nate told me that when he found the dogs, Holly was protecting the other dog from the fire."

"Oh my goodness. Let's go. Where's Stuart?"

"I don't know. Nate and the dogs are at the far end of your property on a section that didn't burn. I think Nate can walk with help. Do you have a wagon for the dogs?"

"I had pulled my utility wagon to the firebreak with water and some crackers for the observers. It won't take me long—"

Aimee Louise interrupted her. "It won't take me long to run grab the wagon. If you'll head to Nate and the dogs, I'll catch up with you with the wagon."

Jennie nodded then ran toward the west side of her property as Aimee Louise sprinted back toward Jennie's house. When Aimee Louise reached the wagon, she removed most of the water and crackers then ran with the wagon toward Nate.

After she caught up with Jennie, she said, "Here's the wagon. I'll tell Nate you're on your way then look for Stuart."

Jennie pulled a pair of leather gloves out of her pocket. "Here are my work gloves. Maybe they'll protect your hands."

Aimee Louise pulled on the gloves before she left Jennie with the wagon and continued her run until she returned to Nate. When she reached him, Nate was draped over Holly.

"Nate, are you okay?" Aimee Louise rushed to his side.

He raised his head then sat up. "I'm fine; I think I dozed off from either relief or exhaustion."

"Jennie is on her way with a wagon for the dogs. Do you think you could walk with her help?"

"I think I could."

"I need to find Stuart."

Aimee Louise made her way through the scorched ground to the active fire then listened and scanned the fire as she walked along the fire line.

When she saw Stuart lying on the scorched ground in front of her, his cloud was bright with strong edges. She sighed with relief. *He's okay.*

"Hi, honey. How you doing?" she asked.

He pushed himself up to a sitting position. "I didn't hear you sneak up on me. I was just resting."

Of course you were. "Are you okay?" she asked.

"I'm fine now; I knew you'd come find me." He brushed his hands together. "Is Dad with you?"

"Not yet. Can you walk?"

"I'll give it a try, but I think I hurt my leg."

As she helped him up, his left leg gave out from under him when he put weight on it; he clutched her shoulder to steady himself.

"I must have landed wrong when I tripped and fell. This fire line is closing in on us from the south, and I was running away from it. Let's go. I'll move as fast as I can."

"I found Nate and the dogs," she said as he wrapped his arm around her shoulder and leaned on her. "They're fine, and Jennie has a wagon to take the dogs back to her house. Nate was exhausted and coughing from smoke inhalation."

Stuart groaned as he struggled to walk without putting weight on his left leg. "I'm glad Nate and the dogs are okay. I'll be ready for that bath when we get back to the house."

"You smell wonderful to me," Aimee Louise said. "Let's go."

With Aimee Louise's help, Stuart developed a smooth rhythm and moved as quickly as he could. When they reached the spot where Aimee Louise had left Nate, she said, "Nate and the dogs were here. Jennie may have Nate at her house; we'll have to take him home."

"I need your stick," Stuart grumbled.

"Good idea. As soon as we're at the firebreak, I'll run get you a stick and check on Nate."

"No, don't leave again," Stuart said. "There's the fire break."

When they reached the Websters' property, Scott was running toward them until he saw them then he slowed to a walk as he approached them. "Let me take that weight off you, Angel," he said.

After Stuart was leaning on his dad, Scott said, "Rodney took Nate back to the house. I told Jennifer we may see a wedding soon.

She asked if we could have the wedding at her house, and I took the liberty to speak for the group. We'll get a vote later, Aimee Louise. I told her that she, Leo, and the Mitchells were always s welcome to our home, but some of us couldn't deal with strangers right now. She assumed I meant you as the one who couldn't deal with strangers, Aimee Louise, but I meant me."

"And me," Stuart said.

Scott continued, "She told me she would send Leo and the Mitchells because she's not comfortable leaving her company alone in the house, and I told her it might be time to pull the welcome mat."

"I agree with you, Dad," Stuart said.

"How did you hurt your leg?" Scott asked.

Stuart winced as he took a misstep. "I should have told you this right away. There is a large, unburned area between us and the fire, and the wind from the south has blown the active fire to the new fuel. Now we have a raging fire coming back at us. I was running from the fire and tripped after I reached a burned area. That's where Angel found me."

"We need to get someone to replace me right away," Scott said.

"Right." Aimee Louise raced across the Websters' property. She waved to Blanche, who was walking along the fire break from the east toward the Newtons' property line and dashed into the house.

The house was quiet, and the only light was the moonlight that streamed in the windows. She breathed in the silence and smiled at the thought of knowing that everyone was asleep then sighed. *How can we stop the growing fire or at least slow it to keep everyone safe? I'll ask Blanche.*

She left without a sound then joined Blanche on her patrol and told her about the new, threatening fire. "I'm not sure what to do," Aimee Louise said.

"I have to see it, but you're right to be worried. Give me a minute to tell Cal that I'm going with you. I'm sure he's been awake while I've been outside. I'll help him into his wheelchair, and he'll watch from his window; if he sees anything, he'll wake Charo."

Blanche soon returned. "Cal's on duty. If you want to run, go ahead. I don't run, but I do speed walk, so I won't be too far behind you."

Aimee Louise raced to Stuart and Scott.

"Cal took over for Blanche and will wake Charo if he sees anything. Blanche is coming to help me assess the fire."

Stuart and Scott simultaneously said, "No."

Not unexpected, but not logical either.

She waited to give them time to think then Stuart said, "Fine, but only because Blanche will be with you, and you'll learn a lot from her. Don't run off and leave her though; remember it's your job to watch."

He said fine, and that's what I was waiting to hear.

She raced away while Stuart continued talking. When she reached the end of the Websters' property, she could see the newly fueled fire as it roared, devoured trees, and leaped toward the Websters'. She continued watching the growing fire, but it wasn't long until Blanche joined her.

Blanche stood next to Aimee Louise and watched the fire for a few minutes. "David designed our firebreak for a prescribed burn not a wildfire, which is what's staring us in the face right now; beautiful in its own way but deadly. We need a wider firebreak for a wildfire. Do we have a bulldozer handy?"

"The tractor that Andy used for the firebreak has a backhoe still attached, and it's at the Websters'," Aimee Louise said. "I'll be right back."

"I'm going to scout our backfire and the fire line," Blanche said.

When Aimee Louise returned, Blanche said, "I found an ideal spot to cut a new firebreak for the wildfire. After we finish that, we'll widen our existing firebreak and burn a new backfire. We don't have a lot of time though. Follow me."

Aimee Louise focused on the area that Blanche had selected to widen the existing firebreak. As she dug the firebreak with the backhoe, she ignored the searing heat of the fire. When an ember landed on her jeans jacket and caught fire, Aimee Louise smacked the flames with her gloved hand until she extinguished the fire. She ignored the rest of the smoldering holes in her jacket and the backs of her gloves.

"Back off," Blanche shouted. "Fire's getting too close."

Aimee Louise completed digging the row she had started then turned away from the licking flames and cut another row with her backhoe. When she started the third row, she wiped the sweat out of her eyes and smacked the burning embers until she finished the row and drove the tractor away from the fire.

Blanche motioned for Aimee Louise to turn off the tractor engine. "That was terrifying to watch, but you did it. While you cut another row beyond our backfire, I'll check the wildfire." She pointed to the next section for Aimee Louise to work on, and Aimee Louise nodded.

Blanche continued, "If my plan works, the wildfire will divert toward us, and we won't have much time to be ready for it. I'll need a flamethrower to follow you and start a new backfire. You cut; I burn."

"While you check the wildfire, I'll get the flamethrower that Andy used," Aimee Louise said.

"Even better." Blanche powerwalked toward the wildfire as Aimee Louise raced for the flamethrower.

When Aimee Louise returned, she began digging the second firebreak next to the charred sections. When Blanche returned, Aimee Louise turned off the engine.

"Thanks. The good news is that the wildfire has shifted the way I'd planned. The bad news is that the wildfire is headed our way, just like I planned. We don't have a lot of time. Dig one row fifty feet or so from here, and I'll backburn that section. I think we may have to do one more section, but that should be all if our luck holds. Fingers crossed and spit over my shoulder. Unfortunately, I don't have a lucky rubber chicken to swing over my head."

Blanche cackled then hurried to check the flame thrower while Aimee Louise completed the row, so Blanche could burn her backfire.

After Aimee Louise finished the fifty-foot row, Blanche began her burn facing the row that Aimee Louise had cut to allow the wind to push the small fire toward the firebreak. By the time Blanche had finished setting her new fires, her first fires had burned out and left a blackened barrier for any fire.

"Let's do a second firebreak just for giggles and grins," Blanche said. "Cut another fifty feet."

Aimee Louise dug the firebreak, and Blanche burned her backfire then they waited until the ground was charred from the origin of the flames to the freshly dug firebreak.

"Let's go check our wildfire," Blanche said, and the two of them hurried to the last place they'd seen the wildfire.

Aimee Louise gasped. "It's gone."

"I'm surprised too," Blanche said. "The fire behaved exactly like it should, in theory; to our credit, we performed each step with perfection. If you hadn't been determined to finish those first rows, we never would have pulled it off. Congratulations, Aimee Louise, you've earned your fire-eater badge. Now, let's check our second firebreak to see if it's been breached."

When they returned to their newest firebreak, Blanche said, "You can go to bed now. You've been up all night, and the moon is low on the horizon. Take Leo's tractor to your folks' house. One of our young men will return it to Leo. See you at lunch."

Aimee Louise started the tractor. *No sense in wasting gas.* She drove it to the Websters' farm and parked it near Leo's shed before she ran home.

When she stumbled into the kitchen, Sandra whispered, "I've been waiting for you. There's fresh warm water, a towel, and clean pajamas waiting for you in the bathroom. Leave your dirty clothes in the bathroom, and I'll toss them into the washer with the rest of the stinky clothes. Everyone else is still asleep. Is Blanche staying on the fire line?"

Aimee Louise nodded then went into the bathroom, stripped, and climbed into the tub. She scrubbed with goat milk soap and rinsed then climbed out and quickly dried herself before she changed into the wonderfully clean, fresh, soft pajamas. After she brushed her hair, she saw the open envelope addressed to her from Rosalie. "Andy and I took Stuart's room; Stuart can bunk with you."

Aimee Louise giggled. *Mom knew. Probably everyone knew except Stuart and me.* She tiptoed up the stairs and peeked into her room.

Stuart was sprawled out on top of the bedspread on his stomach with his head on one pillow and his arm wrapped around her second pillow. *He was too tired to pull down the covers.* She climbed into bed next to him and slipped away the pillow under his arm before she snuggled against him. He rolled onto his side in his sleep and draped his arm over her to pull her closer. *What a honeymoon.* She smiled as she drifted off to sleep.

* * *

Stuart woke with a start when something tickled his nose then opened his eyes and grinned. Angel was snuggled up against him, and her hair had fallen across his face. He inhaled the gardenia-scented goat milk soap. *Mom told me she was going to have a fresh bath for Angel.* He carefully untangled himself from Angel's arm and leg that she had thrown over him then carried his shoes as he limped down the stairs.

"I just poured your cup." Sandra pointed to a cup on the table.

After Stuart sipped his coffee, Sandra asked, "How's your leg?"

"Much better," he said. "If I can stay off it this morning, I think I'll be fine by this afternoon."

"That shouldn't be too hard," Scott said. "It'll be lunchtime before you know it."

Stuart's eyes widened. "Oh no, did I miss my shift?"

"No more shifts," Scott said. "The wind changed from the south to the west right after daybreak, just like Red predicted. The fire has pretty much run its course. All of our fire patrol team slept in. Andy, Rosalie, and Peyton checked the roadblock earlier and declared it a royal mess before they left to go to Leo's farm. Good job, Stuart. I'm proud of you and Angel."

When Blanche came into the kitchen, Sandra poured a cup of coffee for her. "What time did you sneak in? I tried to wait up for you, but I gave up."

Blanche sipped her coffee. "Angel is amazing." She told them about the wildfire and how she and Angel stopped it. Stuart's face paled as Blanche recounted the details of Aimee Louise digging the trench through the fire.

"Are you okay, Stuart?" Sandra asked.

Stuart shook his head. "She scares me every day."

"The good news is that you aren't alone," Scott said.

"It was awesome to see her in action," Blanche said. "I could almost see the gears whirring as she calculated her next move. She's not a daredevil at all; I don't understand what's so scary about her."

Sandra sighed. "Blanche, you and Angel obviously live in a different dimension than the rest of us."

"At least I'm in good company." Blanche cackled. "Any breakfast left?"

Sandra opened a jar of canned apples. "What about you, Stuart? Ready for a bite of brunch?"

While Sandra fried apple fritters, Aimee Louise ran down the stairs and hurried into the kitchen. She had dressed in jeans and a long-sleeved shirt over a T-shirt, but she was barefooted.

"I overslept," she said as she stopped to kiss Stuart on the cheek.

He smiled and wrapped an arm around her waist. "Do that again."

When she leaned to kiss him again, he soundly kissed her before she sat next to him. "Blanche told us about the wildfire," Stuart said.

"How many people know how to turn a wildfire? That was amazing; you're a great teacher, Blanche. Thanks," Aimee Louise said.

Blanche grinned as Sandra set plates and a platter of apple fritters in the middle of the table.

"I put your clothes in the washer, Angel," Sandra said. "Do you know how many burn holes you had in your jacket and jeans? Roll up your sleeves, so I can check your arms."

After Angel rolled up her sleeves, Sandra examined the skin then shook her head. "I was certain you had a blister or two, but your skin's only slightly reddened. You had an angel along with you last night, Angel."

Stuart stared at Aimee Louise.

"Now, don't that beat all? I was right there and could have sworn that Angel was being burned by the fire when it surrounded her," Blanche said.

"I'm going to be old before my time," Stuart mumbled as Aimee Louise rolled down her sleeves then put fritters on two plates.

While they ate, Rosalie, Andy, and Peyton came in the back door.

"Good, you're awake; we'll be right back," Rosalie said before she and Andy rushed out the door.

"Good morning, sleepyheads." Peyton peered at the platter. "Are those donuts?"

"Apple fritters," Sandra said.

Peyton grinned when David, Brandon, and Henry came inside and left the door open as Charo, Dolly, and the judge followed them. Henry hurried to Aimee Louise and Stuart and hugged them. The judge stood near the door then opened it while Nate helped Cal inside.

Leo, Tom, Lela, and the twins followed Andy and Rosalie into the house, and the judge said, "You are just in time."

"Jennie sends her regrets," Leo said.

"We're having our weddings, aren't we?" Sandra smiled.

"Yes, we are; however, we have a slight change. I understand that Andy, Rosalie, and Peyton discussed the wedding plans with Leo this morning, and he contacted the pastor on the radio," Judge said. "David, you have more to add?"

David nodded. "Peyton asked the pastor to include our names in his Bible."

When everyone applauded, David and Brandon beamed.

"Would the three couples and their best boys please come forward?"

Aimee Louise, Stuart, and Henry, Rosalie and Andy, Peyton, David, and Brandon faced the judge.

"Would the rest of the wedding party please join us?" The judge asked.

Rosalie motioned for Dolly to stand next to her, and the judge added, "And best girl." Everyone else gathered behind the brides and grooms.

Judge Rodney said, "We are here to witness the solemn vows of marriage of our friends. The pastor has recorded their names in his Bible as a record of each couple's promise to love and protect each other and to stand together in times of joy and times of sorrow."

After each couple recited their vows to each other, Judge said, "I now pronounce you bound together in holy matrimony, as long as you both shall live." The couples kissed, and everyone applauded then swamped the three couples.

Sandra and Blanche wiped away their tears as they rushed to mix and fry apple fritters.

Stuart pulled Henry and Aimee Louise close to him for a hug, and Aimee Louise said, "I love my two favorite men."

"We love you too, Mama." Henry held tightly to Stuart and Aimee Louise.

"We surely do." Stuart squeezed Aimee Louise then whispered, "I love you so much, sweetheart. Please don't scare me today."

Aimee Louise gazed at Stuart's cloud. "Honey, the center of your cloud is fire, and it's so bright that it's almost blinding." She kissed him then smiled after he returned her kiss.

Stuart chuckled when Henry and Brandon punched each other's arms then hurried to their seats after Blanche set a platter of apple fritters on the table. Dolly and the twins rushed to claim their seats, and Blanche gave each child a plate with two apple fritters.

"After your snack, Cowgirl Blanche will go outside with you, if you like," Sandra said.

"We'll have to get our hats first," Henry said with a full mouth.

Doc pushed Cal's wheelchair to the table, and the judge joined them.

When Blanche placed their plates in front of them, Judge said, "If you want to stay here with Sandra, I'm going outside too."

"Doc and I will too," Cal said.

"At least you won't be outnumbered." Blanche snickered as she served another platter of the hot pastry.

Scott hugged Aimee Louise and Stuart. "I can't tell you how proud and happy your mom and I are for you two."

Sandra handed over the frying duty to Blanche and hurried to join them. Tears flowed down her cheeks as she hugged Aimee

Louise then Stuart. She sniffled back her tears. "I am so happy for you."

Scott hurried to help Cal while Charo and Nate congratulated Stuart and Aimee Louise then Leo and the Mitchells congratulated all the newly-wed couples.

Before Leo and the Mitchells left, Leo said, "I talked to Major, and he was excited to hear that your weddings were today and sent his love. I told him you'd be on the morning call when you could."

When Stuart and Aimee Louise finally reached the other two couples, Stuart grinned at Peyton and David. "After Major heard we were planning to marry, he asked me if I was being railroaded, and I told him that I probably was but didn't care."

David burst out laughing. "I'm right there with you, Stuart."

Charo hugged Peyton while David grinned.

"Mrs. Griffin," Charo said. "How do you feel about that?"

Peyton smiled. "Like it was about dang time."

"Wasn't me dragging my feet, you know," David said.

"I was playing hard to get." Peyton flipped her hair.

David rolled his eyes. "Stuart, ready to go check our fire? We can limp along together, or we could even race, but I warn you, I have a stick."

"We'll go too," Andy said. "I'd like to know if I could have prevented the wildfire then we can go see Aunt Jennie."

As they walked along the firebreak, smoke still lingered in the air, and David inhaled then grinned. "Charred woodsmoke is one of my favorite smells because it means the fire is out. This is textbook perfect and a game warden's dream. I'd loved to have had a couple of forestry students to train here."

"We'll be right back," Aimee Louise said as she and Rosalie raced to the trees that fire had cleared of brush.

"Wait," Andy called. When they disappeared, he turned to Stuart, "Where did they go?"

"If we knew, we'd have a heart attack," Stuart said. "Although, not knowing drives me crazy."

When they reached the far west end of the burn, Aimee Louise and Rosalie raced from the south where the wildfire had burned then joined them.

"The campers didn't take their tents, but we could tell the men that had the truck made it to the county road because they tossed their empty canteens into the ditch," Aimee Louise said.

"I checked one, and it reeked of alcohol, but it was still a dumb move on their part," Rosalie said.

David snorted. "What about the other campers?"

"We could tell where they fell into the county road ditch, so they got away from the fire," Rosalie said.

"Did you find where the wildfire started?" Andy asked.

"We found a scorched metal gas can next to what looked like a campfire. We don't know if they were using the gas to start their campfire or if they left it, but I'm convinced it started a separate fire."

"Good find," Stuart said. "What else?"

"We found a notepad in the ditch where they fell." Rosalie pulled it out of the back pocket of her jeans and handed it to Stuart. "We think they used it to write notes."

Stuart thumbed through the notepad. "Not the best penmanship, is it? On the first page it says, 'miz r said no talking, but we can rite notes.' Evidently, in addition to being poor spellers, the thugs weren't experienced campers either because the next few pages are complaints about bugs, heat, cold, sleeping outside on the ground, and more misery. Where have we heard that before?"

"When the men stood around the burning car, one man raised a bottle and said, 'Here's to misery,'" Aimee Louise said.

"That's it," Stuart said, "and you told me another man asked if he remembered what happened to the last man who said that, and the revelry went from rowdy to quiet."

David frowned. "Misery? That sounds familiar, but I can't remember why. I'll ask Peyton."

"We'll see you all back at the Newtons' after we spend a little time with Aunt Jennie," Andy said. "Let's walk, Rosalie."

Rosalie smiled as he took her hand before they headed toward the Websters' while Aimee Louise strolled alongside Stuart and David as they limped toward the Newtons'.

Before they reached the Newtons' farmhouse, Stuart asked, "Did we just open up the south side for an attack on us?"

"From my point of view, we have the shooting advantage with the cover of the outbuildings on the south, and they have lost their only advantage of a surprise ambush unless they have far more men than we've seen." David furrowed his brow. "I'm sure they don't know how many competent shooters we have. I would think that is information they'd love to have."

"I think that's why strangers make me nervous." Stuart winced before he paused then put his arm around Aimee Louise's shoulders for balance. "Need to stop a second."

"You stop; we stop," David said.

Stuart chuckled. "Don't tell Mom or Doc. I don't want to spend the rest of my honeymoon with a retired Doc and an over-protective Mom."

"I have a feeling Aimee Louise won't let that happen," David said.

"You're right," Aimee Louise growled, and Stuart's eyes widened.

David smiled. "Mama Angel is a force."

And fierce. Who knew?

Stuart pointed toward the scorched area south of them. "Do we need to worry about the hotspots?"

"No, even if we have any flareups, they'll burn themselves out and be another deterrent for any attacks unless the thugs have a fire savvy leader," David said.

Stuart snorted. "Not likely."

CHAPTER THIRTEEN

As Andy and Rosalie approached the farmhouse, Leo came out of the barn with Holly and waved; Andy and Rosalie headed toward the barn.

"Glad you're here to see your Aunt Jennie. I had a long talk with Myrtle's son, JR. He's been as unhappy about the arrangements here as Jennie has been. He wants to take his family to his cousin's farm in Alabama. Do you think we could provide him with an escort for the twenty miles to the state line?"

"Give us a chance to talk about it with our team but seems like something we could do," Andy said.

"What about Connie?" Rosalie asked.

Leo snorted. "JR made it clear that Connie was not included in his plans, so I asked Jennie to tell Connie that we had more families on the way and needed her to move on."

Andy raised his eyebrows. "What did Connie say to that?"

Leo chortled. "I don't know; I left to take care of my dogs."

Andy's eyes twinkled. "Need any help?"

Rosalie punched his arm. "Not funny."

"Ow." Andy smirked. "Okay, let's go inside."

When they were in the kitchen, Andy called out, "Aunt Jennie?"

"Up here," she said.

When Andy and Rosalie raced up the stairs, Rosalie beat him by three steps, even though Andy took the stairs two at a time.

"I'll figure out a way to beat you yet, cutie," he said.

Rosalie grinned. "I'm happy you like to race."

"I'm in the kids' room," Jennie said. "We're almost finished packing. Their dad said he wanted to leave before lunch. There's lemonade in the pantry if you'd like to help yourself. I'll be down in a few minutes."

Andy and Rosalie went down the stairs and to the kitchen together.

"I'll get the pitcher," Andy said as Rosalie stood on her tiptoes to reach the glasses.

"Must be annoying to be so short," Connie said as Rosalie sat at the table while Andy poured two glasses of lemonade.

Andy froze when Rosalie smiled at Connie and raised an eyebrow as she peered at Connie's knees. "How's your bad knee?"

Andy narrowed his eyes at Connie. *Connie better quit while she's ahead. Stuart told me Red's signature shot is a shattered knee.*

Connie glared. "My knees are fine."

"Good news." Rosalie smirked then sipped her lemonade.

Connie cleared her throat as she sat at the table.

Andy coughed into his elbow to hid his smile. *Trying to hide your knees, Connie?*

"Jennie told me that two more families will be here this afternoon. That was a big surprise to me." Connie dramatically placed her hand on her chest to emphasize her surprise then side-glanced Rosalie. "There must be a lot of people at your house too."

"Why was it a surprise?" Andy asked.

Connie glared at Andy then drummed her fingers on the table. "Oh, you know. It was just so sudden."

Rosalie giggled. "Might have seemed sudden to you, but Aunt Jennie has been talking about them for a while. She's really excited to see them. We came over to help her clean the bedrooms. We'll tackle the kids' room first as soon as their packing is finished. Did you already clean yours?"

"Me? Clean a room?" Connie's eyes widened. "Of course, not. I'm a guest." She raised her chin and puffed out her chest. "So, I heard there were guests at your farm that were FBI agents. Is that true?"

Rosalie rolled her eyes then rose from the table. "No guests at our place or Aunt Jennie's. This is Aunt Jennie's home, not a hotel. There's no maid service here."

She flipped her hair before she cleared the two glasses then washed and rinsed them. After Rosalie left to go upstairs, Andy turned the chairs upside down on the table then raised an eyebrow at Connie until she rose so he could add her chair to the others. When he went into the utility room and returned to the kitchen, Connie stepped backward to the hallway.

"Did you want to sweep?" he asked.

"I don't sweep," Connie grumbled. "Allergies."

"You might want to clear the kitchen then," Andy said.

She nodded. "What about the Mitchells'?" she asked.

Andy cocked his head. "What do you mean?"

Her face reddened. "I mean when are they leaving?"

"Couldn't tell you. You'll have to ask Aunt Jennie." Andy began sweeping at the back door, and Connie huffed as she left the kitchen.

After he finished sweeping and was putting away the broom, Rosalie and the children came into the kitchen.

"Aunt Jennie sent us down for a snack. She'll be here in a minute then we can leave after we say goodbye to Uncle Leo."

Andy nodded. *I'm good to go with the flow.*

When Aunt Jennie came into the kitchen, she said, "Thanks for your help, Red. I'll see you later." She glanced at the kitchen floor. "Did you sweep, Andy? It looks nice."

"Good," Andy said as he and Rosalie left.

"What's the scoop?" he asked as they headed to the barn.

"Aunt Jennie told Connie to leave," Rosalie said.

"Connie kind of told me while she was pumping me for information, but golly gee, I didn't have any straight answers for her."

Rosalie snickered. "I thought you were pretty smooth. I promised Aunt Jennie that I'd tell Uncle Leo that Connie's leaving."

When they reached the barn, Leo and Holly were waiting for them.

"Aunt Jennie wanted you to know that Connie's leaving, so you can go into the house whenever you want," Rosalie said.

"Somebody will be back to escort JR and his family," Andy added.

"You set the pace," Rosalie said as she and Andy left the barn. "Take the shortcut; it's cooler."

Andy ran at his comfortable speed, and Rosalie ran alongside him. When they reached the Newtons' farm, Rosalie said, "You've picked up your pace."

Andy rolled his eyes. "You're being nice."

When Rosalie snorted, he chuckled. "My mistake. I know better than that. I actually thought I was running a little faster too."

She hugged him, and he brushed her hair away from her face then kissed her.

He stroked her cheek with his fingertips. "You are so beautiful."

Her eyes twinkled as she fluttered her eyelashes and gazed at his face. "You're being nice."

Andy burst out laughing. "Touché, my sassy sweetheart."

When they strolled toward the back door, Aimee Louise came outside.

"We need to talk," Rosalie said.

"You're right," Aimee Louise said. "We need to talk. Pick up a snack if you want one then come to the barn. I'll let everyone know you're here."

When they went into the kitchen, Mama Sandra said, "Did Angel see you? You can take your snack to the barn." She sliced two squares of cornbread in half then smeared blackberry jam on each half. "Here you are."

After Andy and Rosalie picked up their cornbread and jam snacks and headed to the barn, Andy said, "You must be in trouble because it couldn't be me. I have an alibi; I was with you."

Rosalie rolled her eyes. "You know that's the worst joke I've ever heard."

"Thank you, honey. I strive to excel. Are you going to eat all your snack?" Andy reached for her second half of cornbread.

Rosalie put her hand with her cornbread behind her back. "Yes, I'm going to eat it, and keep your hand away from my cornbread, or you'll draw back a stump. I need a sword."

"You think I'm giving Dead Eye Red a sword? Ha. By the way, I loved the knee reference you used with Connie. Priceless."

* * *

When they entered the barn, Stuart said, "When everyone gets here, we'll need to decide what we'll do next."

"We have a decision for the group too." Andy explained what his uncle asked them to do.

Stuart furrowed his brow. "It's twenty miles to Alabama. It would take three days to walk that with Myrtle and the three children. Do we know who is meeting them? Do we take them to Alabama and leave?"

Andy nodded. "Good questions. JR is level-headed. While having an escort on a trip like that makes sense, I wonder whose idea it was. After we've had a chance to discuss what we could reasonably offer, I'll talk to JR to see what he had in mind."

After Scott, Nate, Charo, Peyton, and David came into the barn, Scott said, "Farmer Blanche's lesson for today is part one of taking care of chickens. She told me the class includes chicken math then laughed when I asked her what it was. Does anybody know? Judge and Doc are helping Sandra with canning blackberry jam, and Cal's guarding Blanche and the kids from his window."

David smiled. "My grandma had chickens. She started with four baby chicks then a neighbor gave her four more. She soon had ten chickens because she wanted to diversify. It wasn't long until she had twenty chickens then forty. That's chicken math. Grandpa never complained because Grandma was always baking something to use up all the eggs."

Andy chuckled. "Ms. Blanche is a brilliant teacher. She told me she was including more math in her lessons."

"We have two major items to discuss," Stuart said. "I'll start with a little background for our first item." Stuart described the car fire and the word 'misery.'

"After I glanced through the notepad with complaints about miz r, which I thought was a shortcut way to spell misery, David told me it sounded vaguely familiar, and he took the notebook," Stuart said. "Peyton, you're next."

"David showed me the notebook. Miz R is my former mother-in-law. I always suspected she was the brains behind her husband's operation, and I could see her letting Troy and his brother duke it out then she'd take over, or more accurately, take away the businesses they had built up."

"So, you're her target?" Scott asked.

"Yes. I am probably the last person alive who knows how involved she's been in the family business since its inception and can identify her. Here's the kicker: her name is Consuelo Romero. The guys who hung around with Troy always called her Miz R to her face and Miz-arr-ree behind her back. Misery."

Andy and Rosalie stared at each other then Andy said, "Connie is Consuelo Romero, and you're her target. No wonder she asked about any guests here who were FBI agents. Rosalie told her there were no guests at Aunt Jennie's or here."

"What an amazing way to have answered her probe," Peyton said. "Your reply was far superior to a denial."

"We've only slowed her down for now, not stopped her," Aimee Louise said.

"Uncle Leo told her to leave. Do we want her to stay, so we can keep an eye on her?" Andy asked.

"It might work to our advantage because I don't think she expected to leave so soon. Now she has to act fast or change her plans and may make some mistakes in her haste," Nate said.

Scott asked, "Peyton, do you have any physical evidence of her involvement in her husband's business?"

"I don't know. I may still have some of Troy's papers from our safe. I'll have to look."

"Next item," Stuart said. "Myrtle's son, JR, wants to take his family to his cousin's farm in Alabama. Leo asked Andy if we could provide an escort for them to the state line. That's all the detail we have right now, but Andy is planning to talk to JR to see what his plans are."

"The state line is twenty miles away," Scott said. "At one time, that wouldn't have been a problem. How many kids are there? Three? I don't see how walking would be feasible. It would take more than two days if conditions were ideal, and if Myrtle could keep up the pace."

David rose and leaned against a stall door. "We've been using gasoline only for the tractors or very short trips. As far as I know our major source of gas has been donations from the bad guys."

"That's true, but we do seem to have a ready supply of bad guys," Aimee Louise said.

Scott laughed. "Angel's right, as usual. I think the only way for us to get them to the state line relatively safely is if we drive them."

"Not to be contrary, but isn't now a bad time to send two of our people to Alabama?" Charo asked.

"Four people," Rosalie said. "Angel is our best driver, and I go where Angel goes, and so do Stuart and Andy. We're a package deal."

"Good point," Nate said. "Dad is an outstanding driver. I'm an excellent shot. We could go."

"Not what I had in mind," Charo grumbled.

"Charo's right. Why don't I ride with the judge? I'm a good shot, and Connie certainly couldn't find me for an entire day," Peyton said.

"No," David said. "You are not spending our honeymoon away from me."

"It's settled then," Scott said. "Judge and I will go, and we might take Cowgirl Blanche to wrangle the riders."

Stuart narrowed his eyes. "Do you think Mom would approve?"

"Heck, no, but that's half the fun. Anything else to discuss?" Scott paused. "Good. I'll go talk to the judge then Andy, if Red won't make us run, I'd like to go with you to talk to JR."

"Who is going to talk to Mom?" Stuart asked.

"I will," Aimee Louise said. "I'll ask the judge to come talk to you in the barn then I'll talk to Mom.

Scott grinned.

CHAPTER FOURTEEN

After Aimee Louise, the Cabellos, and the Griffins left, Scott leaned against a stall and smiled as he glanced at Stuart, Andy, and Rosalie. *Should have known these three would wait with me.*

"Dad, are you sure it wouldn't be better for us to go?" Stuart asked.

"I'm positive. The only thing I regret is that I could use Angel. She's got a talent that no one else has, but I suppose that there's no way she could go with me because we're back to the package deal again, right?"

Scott watched his son's face.as Stuart struggled with a decision. *He knows I'm right about Angel.*

Stuart sighed. "You can ask her, Dad. I'll fully support whatever she decides."

Scott held out his hand, and the two men shook hands then Scott hugged his son. "I know that was a hard decision. Thank you. We'll see what she says. I respect her opinion. Actually, I'll ask her if I should go. She'll tell me."

"That she will, Dad." Stuart chuckled.

"When Rodney gets here, would you tell him the plan while I talk to Aimee Louise?"

Stuart nodded as Aimee Louise and the judge came into the barn together.

"Judge," Stuart said, "I've got a little background for you."

"Angel, while Stuart talks to the judge, I'd like to talk to you." Scott offered his arm, and Aimee Louise slipped hers into it.

As they strolled away from the barn together and toward the burn, Scott asked, "Angel, what do you think about the idea of the judge and me escorting the family to the state line?"

"If it was a low-risk trip, it would be perfect for you and the judge to learn to operate as a team."

Scott raised his eyebrows and stopped. "Wow. We're not a team." He scanned the burned area. *Could the judge and I have plowed the rows like David and Andy did?*

"Not yet."

He frowned. "What would it take? How long?"

"The answer is as long as it takes, and I know that isn't what you wanted to hear. No one can tell you. Rosalie and I were instantly a team. Stuart understood me before I realized I understood him, but it was a while before we were a team. Nate knew that he and Peyton weren't a team because of her distrust of anyone until Charo then Rosalie broke through to Peyton. It's all very complex."

Scott exhaled. "You're right, so how many teams do we have?"

"Peyton and Nate are a team now. The judge is a perfect support person for any team, but he hasn't been a primary team member yet."

"What about David?"

"As a game warden, he was used to working solo, and that is actually his best skill. He can work with any team, but I think right now his best position is at home defending the family."

David carries the guilt that Brandon was kidnapped. Angel's only nineteen. How can she read people so well? Through their clouds?

"I hadn't really thought about it before, but you're right because he needs to be with Brandon. So, we have two teams," Scott said.

"For high-risk tasks, yes. For slightly lower risk tasks that can be completed by two, we could mix and match; for example, Peyton and Rosalie or Stuart and David," Aimee Louise said.

"So, what are low risk tasks that the judge and I could do?" Scott asked.

"Stuart and I patrol the north perimeter every night. That's low risk."

"No one is patrolling the south perimeter. That's one. Would you help me draw up a list of low-risk tasks?" Scott turned toward the barn.

"We could do that, but better yet, you could gather the medium and low risk folks together and explain the different types of risks for their ideas."

"We'll have our defense better organized. I'm glad we talked, Angel. I have a better grasp of how we need to operate. While I'm asking, what about Jennie and Leo?"

"As a ham operator, Leo is used to working solo but can work with a team of hams. Jennie prefers to work alone."

Scott nodded. "So, how do we operate without you four?"

"You still have a strong attack team with Nate, Peyton, and David, and a strong support team."

When they reached the barn, Scott's eyes twinkled as he said, "Do you think Stuart will be surprised?"

"No."

When Scott and Aimee Louise strolled into the barn together, Rosalie asked, "Which vehicle do we take?"

Scott chuckled. "You are getting ahead of me, Red. Angel explained high, medium, and low risk tasks and matching the team to the task. Can I tell them a story, Angel."

"Please do." She sat on the barn's dirt floor.

"Once upon a time there was a beautiful young woman who was very smart, and an old man who was smart enough to listen to her. The End."

His audience laughed and applauded, and he bowed with a flourish. "Newtons and Websters, let us know what the plan is and how we can help."

"Thank you for letting me in on the planning process, and I look forward to my assignment," Judge left the barn and headed back to the house.

"Ready, Andy?" Stuart asked then the two of them left for the Websters'.

"Angel, thank you for making me look good." Scott gave her a hug then left.

* * *

"Feel like a run?" Aimee Louise asked.

"Where are we going?" Red asked.

"We need to find a truck, but I think we'll find a car."

"I've got my rifle. What about our backpacks?"

"We have to take them. I'll slip inside and grab them," Aimee Louise said.

"No, hold my rifle. You aren't sneaky enough." Rosalie ran to the house then returned with the two backpacks.

"You were fast. No one noticed?" Aimee Louise asked.

"Blanche did, but she smiled and winked at me. She's the best. Which way do we go?"

"South to the interstate then west to the county road. I'd rather find a truck, but if Connie has a car stashed, it wouldn't be too far away. I don't think she hid it on the road north of the farms, though, because she would have been caught in her own roadblocks. I'm sure she wouldn't trust her thugs, and if we move it, she'd be sure one of them stole it."

The two of them raced south then turned east and dashed to the interstate then took a water break.

"I don't think she'd hike much farther than the edge of Uncle Leo's farm. She had a fit when I asked her if she was going to clean her room. If straightening her own mess is beneath her, I can't see her walking very far. Should we be looking for a golf cart or a side by side like Number 48 at Pops' farm?" Rosalie asked.

"I like it. Let's run on both sides of the road in the trees. Do you want north or south?" Aimee Louise asked.

"I'll take south, Mrs. Newton," Rosalie said.

"You got it, Mrs. Webster," Aimee Louise said, and Rosalie giggled as they took to their sides of the road and disappeared into the woods.

When Aimee Louise reached the edge of the burned area, she sounded their signature barred owl call, and Rosalie answered. Aimee Louise dashed to the south side of the road, and Rosalie met her at the edge of the woods.

"I liked your idea of a side-by-side utility vehicle. Let's scour the woods between here and the edge of Mr. Leo's."

The two of them zig-zagged through the woods. When Aimee Louise heard the barred owl, she answered then raced to Rosalie who sat in the passenger's seat of a utility vehicle that seated four.

"The key was in the drink holder. Original, don't you think?" Rosalie snickered. "Is it car theft if we move a utility vehicle to a safer location?"

"I don't know, but we can ask the judge," Aimee Louise said.

"Where do we want to stash it?" Rosalie scanned the area.

"How about deeper in the woods behind Dad's property?"

"Drive on, driver."

After Aimee Louise drove the utility vehicle across from the Newtons' farm and parked it deeper into the woods, she stuck the key into her pocket.

"Now what?" Rosalie asked.

"Let's find a truck."

They ran on the shoulders alongside the road. After they passed the Websters' property, Aimee Louise stopped then stepped back into the shadows of the woods as Rosalie ran across the road to join her. Aimee Louise pointed ahead of them where six transport trucks with canvas covers over the back were parked on the side of the road. Men stood in the back of two of the trucks and handed rifles to other men who milled around after they received their weapons.

"They're staging for an attack," Aimee Louise said, and they whirled back and raced to the Newton farm.

When they ran toward the house, Stuart and Andy strolled out of the barn.

* * *

"We were looking for you," Stuart said. "We talked to JR, and they are ready to go. We can leave after lunch."

"Change of plans," Aimee Louise said. "We relocated Connie's side by side."

"And discovered six pickup trucks with maybe twenty or so men being handed rifles from the bed of the trucks," Rosalie added.

"Did they look ready to deploy?" Stuart asked.

"Not immediately. Not all the men had rifles, and the process didn't seem very fast," Aimee Louise said.

"Andy, go tell JR to come here to load up. Have him come the back way through the firebreak. No sense in giving away our short cut. Wait a minute, do you think they'd be safer there?"

"Might be," Andy said. "If Peyton's the target like we think then yes, but if Connie sees them as potential hostages then no."

"Let's get with Dad for his perspective," Stuart said.

On the way to the house, Stuart said, "I just realized you two were within sight of an army of thugs."

"Not really," Aimee Louise said. "We were watching for them; they weren't watching for us."

Stuart lowered his head and furrowed his brow in thought as he strode in silence the rest of the way to the house. *It's hard to be angry when I know she's right.*

Aimee Louise patted his arm. "I know you worry."

Stuart leaned down then kissed her. *I'm a lucky, worried man.*

When they walked into the kitchen, Scott asked, "What's our plan?"

Stuart poured himself a cup of coffee before he sat at the table with his dad. "We have a change. Aimee Louise and Rosalie discovered approximately twenty men with rifles on the county road to our south. We're not leaving."

"Rosalie and I need to check the state road," Aimee Louise said.

Stuart took in a breath then exhaled. "You're right."

Andy slammed the back door in his rush to hurry outside.

"He needs a private minute," Rosalie said. "We'll wait until he returns."

"Don't blame him at all," Stuart said. "Dad, we can't decide whether we should leave JR and his family at the Websters' or bring them here."

"If they come here, they've still left the Websters', so there would be no indication that our plans have changed," Scott said. "I'm confident that Jennie and Leo can take care of themselves, and maybe their neighbors, but the additional family put a strain on them." Scott frowned. "What about the Mitchells'? Isn't it time for the twins to come for a play date?"

"Good idea. Aimee Louise and I will run by to remind them. Ms. Lela will catch on right away," Rosalie said. "We'll need to warn Mama Sandra. Do we have any cots?"

Andy came back inside. "That was a shocker, Stuart. I was counting on you to put up a fight then I realized you're smart enough to pick your battles. So, what did I miss?"

"Not much, honey." Rosalie kissed him then she and Aimee Louise left.

"So, why did you really go outside, Andy?" Scott asked.

Andy chuckled. "Did you see the look on Red's face when Stuart told Aimee Louise that she was right? I think my sweet wife was all geared up for a big argument, and Stuart ruined it. Red would have been irritated if I'd laughed, so I had to escape. Did she say anything?"

"She said you needed a private minute. Have I told you how much I enjoy y'all being here?" Scott smiled.

* * *

Before Aimee Louise and Rosalie reached the end of the driveway, Aimee Louise veered into the woods, and Rosalie continued to run alongside her. When they neared the roadblock, they slipped closer to the road.

Aimee Louise scanned the area. *No one here. Did Connie pull everyone to the south? How can she issue orders from the Websters'?*

When she noticed a large truck with a canvas cover across the back of the truck bed parked in front of the Cabellos' driveway, Aimee Louise elbowed Rosalie and pointed.

Rosalie smiled as she nodded, and they dashed across the road to the truck. Aimee Louise pulled back the canvas cover while Rosalie pointed her rifle inside. After Aimee Louise peeked inside, she dropped the cover. *Gas cans and cases of food.*

Aimee Louise checked the driver's seat and found the truck keys on the floor. She dropped them into her jeans pocket then jumped over the ditch and slipped into the woods with Rosalie alongside her. They crept halfway up the driveway then returned to the truck. After Rosalie hopped into the passenger's seat, Aimee Louise started the engine then pulled onto the road. She turned at the Newtons' driveway and parked the truck in the trees close to the downed tree that blocked the driveway.

"Dad and the judge can move it closer to the house." Aimee Louise left the key in the ignition. "Let's use the shortcut to the Websters'; we can check in front of the Smith property on the way."

"I'll find Dad then meet you at the Smith barn."

After Rosalie dashed toward the house, Aimee Louise searched the front field for any hidden bad guys. *Clear. Certainly looks like Connie has pulled all her resources to attack from the south. She expects to be swift and successful.*

Rosalie caught up with Aimee Louise at the Smith barn then they raced to the state road.

While Rosalie covered her from the tree line, Aimee Louise searched both sides of the road. *Nothing. I'll bet the roadblock to the west is unstaffed too.*

They returned to the shortcut path and raced to the Websters' farmhouse.

Aimee Louise lifted her hand to knock on the back door, but Rosalie said, "I'm a niece now; we can go on in."

When they walked into the kitchen, Myrtle and Jennie sat at the kitchen table; Myrtle was sniffling, and her eyes were red-rimmed.

"I'm sorry that you missed saying good-bye to JR and the kids," Myrtle said. "I told JR to wait until morning when it would be cooler, but that wife of his threw a fit, and they left."

"They would have headed northwest from here, right?" Rosalie asked.

Myrtle sighed. "Yes. JR tried to tell me it would be cooler, but this is the south. And it's humid, hot, and buggy. His wife said I was trying to control their lives, and I told her what I thought of her opinion."

Jennie patted Myrtle's hand. "Don't get all worked up again. They need their space and so do you. I'm looking forward to your cooking, and so is Leo. It's a wonder that man stuck around with my terrible cooking."

"While we're here, I'll remind Ms. Lela about today's playdate. It's Friday, and Dolly's been looking forward to it all week." Rosalie headed toward the stairs.

Jennie motioned her hand toward the back. "They're probably with the chickens or the farm dogs."

Rosalie dashed out the door then returned with Tom, Lela, and the twins.

"We may stay for a sleep over, Jennie," Lela said. "The girls reminded me it was their turn to stay at Dolly's. We'll pack a few things for an overnight."

Tom nodded. "I'll pack for us too. I'd like to spend a little time with my old friend, Cal. Is he doing better?"

"Much better," Rosalie said.

While Lela and Tom packed, Aimee Louise asked, "Where's Connie? I'm surprised she isn't here in the kitchen."

"It is a gathering place, isn't it? Connie goes for a walk three times a day. I keep telling her I envy her devotion to exercise and to her schedule." Jennie chuckled. "I told her to be careful walking in the burned area, but she told me she enjoys the charcoal smell. She was worried about the weather, so she won't be leaving until tomorrow."

"Smelling charcoal would just make me hungry." Rosalie snickered.

"Isn't that the truth. All I'd think about would be a nice juicy steak, and I'd instantly put on five pounds." Myrtle tittered.

"She goes for a walk the same time every day? Morning, noon, and night?" Aimee Louise asked. "That's real discipline."

"Yep, about the same time every single day. I think of it as more obsessive than disciplined, but that may be my jealousy talking." Jennie laughed.

Tom waited at the bottom of the stairs for Lela and the twins. When they came downstairs, Cami Sue had her unicorn backpack, Sam carried her horse backpack, and Lela had a olive-drab duffle bag slung over her shoulder.

"Here's your backpack, honey," Tom said. "I'll take the duffle bag if you can carry this smaller one."

"We'll carry the duffle bags, Mr. Tom," Rosalie said. "Ready to go?"

Lela and the girls headed to the back door.

"We can walk along the firebreak. It's easier to get to than the road," Aimee Louise said.

After the Mitchells followed Rosalie outside, Aimee Louise said, "The burned area makes it easier to see if anyone is trying to sneak up on us."

"That's true," Myrtle said, "but at the same time, it cleared a path for an attack."

Aimee Louise nodded as she left. *Myrtle understood.*

When Aimee Louise joined the group, she took her position at the end of the line. *We're hiking under the Red rules: no talking, stay with your partner, and follow the person in front of you.*

Rosalie halted the group when they reached the Newtons' farm. Dolly saw them, and squealed, and Rosalie said, "Our silent hike is over." Cami Sue and Sam screamed as they ran to join Dolly.

Lela laughed. "We may have to have a chat to make it clear that squealing and screaming remain outside."

Tom shook his head. "Those three could shatter a city block of windows. So, what's the scoop on our sudden weekly Friday playdate and sleepover?"

Henry and Brody ran to Aimee Louise, and she stooped to hug Henry as he threw his small arms around her neck and hugged her.

"I missed you, Mama," Henry said as Brody danced around them until Aimee Louise rubbed his face.

"Farmer Blanche said I could hug you hello, but I want to go back to the garden because Farmer Blanche is telling us the names of the bugs and which ones to squish."

Aimee Louise kissed his cheek then he ran back to the garden.

"Let's take the backpacks and bags inside, and we can talk," Aimee Louise said.

"I'll check on the twins then come inside after I make sure Farmer Blanche isn't overwhelmed," Rosalie said.

"I'd forgotten that Blanche and Cal are here. She is a Peter Pan, isn't she? An absolute genius at relating to children," Lela said. "She fostered children for years and would only take kids who had been kicked out of at least one foster home. She told me once that the others didn't need her."

When they went inside the house, Sandra rushed to greet the Mitchells. "I'm so glad you're here. We've got your room all set up. Nate found a double bed in my attic after I thought I had only queen beds. Charo told me it was Cabello magic. There was a bit of a fight for your room, by the way, after Charo and Peyton discovered you had the dining room, which is also the closest room to the kitchen."

Lela laughed. "Sandra, you're the magician."

"Shall we put their bags in their bedroom?" Aimee Louise asked.

"Yes, then I think we're all supposed to go to the barn," Sandra said.

* * *

As the group came into the barn, Stuart said, "Dad, I'd like for you to keep the meeting going. I don't mind telling what I know, but you're better at running a meeting."

"Okay," Scott said. "We'll start with you. We're taking questions, right?"

"Absolutely. It's hard for me to remember to watch for people who have questions; I appreciate it."

When Blanche came into the barn, she said, "Lela told me to come to the meeting, and she'd spend time with the children. I had to pinky-swear that I would fill her in completely, or she'd pinky-swear curse me, and that's very serious, you know."

Judge came into the barn behind Blanche. "Don't get yourself put on my docket, Blanche. That's the worst possible infraction in my jurisdiction on this farm."

"Yeah, and this whole place is crawling with cops and kids of cops. I don't stand a chance around here."

Scott chuckled. "I get so caught up in your stories, Blanche, that I forget they might not be real; I was about ready to provide you with an ironclad alibi."

Nate and Cal were the last two to come to the barn.

After the judge offered up a prayer for protection and wisdom, Scott opened the meeting.

"I'd rather hear this story from Blanche, and maybe we will someday around a campfire. I can tell you that each new piece of information that we've gathered has resulted in a change of plans. We asked the Mitchells to come here under the guise of a sleepover for the girls because we believe no one is immune from being attacked, and we think the Mitchells are safer with us."

"What about the Websters and Myrtle?" Blanche asked.

"If we could think of a good way to do it, we would. We don't think they are the target, but the bad guy has a history of kidnapping children and human trafficking." Stuart said.

When Lela gasped, Tom put his arm around her. "Sorry, honey; it's a scary thought, I know, but we have good friends who have our backs and won't let the girls be hurt."

"It's just becoming a little too real. I'll be okay," Lela said.

"Ms. Myrtle knows there is an attack coming. She may come up with a way..." Aimee Louise's voice trailed off as she was lost in thought.

Scott waited then continued when Aimee Louise stayed silent. "We know an attack on the farm is imminent, the attack will come from the south, and we even know who is directing the attack. We're here so everyone has all the information to provide input into our defense plan and to probe any potential offensive actions we could take. Let's talk about the attack coming from the south and how we know. Angel? Red?"

"This morning, Angel and I saw six trucks with men handing out rifles to twenty or so men on the county road south of us," Rosalie said. "When we checked the roadblocks, no one was there. In fact, we brought home a truck that had been abandoned at the first roadblock. There were no trucks at the second roadblock."

"We also found an abandoned four-seater utility vehicle," Aimee Louise said. "We could use that to transport Ms. Myrtle, Uncle Leo, and Aunt Jennie here. But I think we need a honeypot."

"You mean like bait?" Rosalie asked.

Aimee Louise nodded. "Can we talk about who is directing the threat and why?"

"The background is that Aimee Louise heard a complaint about misery at one of the roadblocks then found a notepad that one of the bad guy campers dropped when he ran from the fire. The men used the notepad to write notes to communicate, and one complaint that showed up frequently was misery. I also found a reference to Miz R," Stuart said. "Peyton, it's your turn."

Peyton nodded. "My ex-father-in-law ran a human trafficking and drug operation in the southeast. When he was murdered, my ex-husband tried to pick up the business, and his brother tried to muscle in. Behind the scenes, my ex-mother-in-law was running the show when her husband was alive then after he died, she waited to see which of her sons survived to take over the business. Her plan was to step in and take over. We stopped both my ex-husband and his brother, so the only person alive who knows who she is and her history is me. She may think I have documentation, but I can't imagine what it might be."

Everyone in the barn was silent until Charo said, "You are the target. Your mother-in-law wants to silence you."

Peyton nodded. "My ex-mother-in-law's name is Consuelo Romero, or as the bad guys say, 'Miz R,' which is where they came up with Miz-arr-ree."

"Quite imaginative for thugs," Judge said.

"Are you saying that Connie is Consuelo Romero, aka Miz R?" Lela asked.

"Yes," Aimee Louise said. "She takes a walk three times a day and heads south of the Websters' farmhouse."

"So, she updates the men on her ambush plans then returns to the Websters'. How do you think she plans to keep from getting caught in her own trap?" David asked.

"She had a utility vehicle hidden in the woods. I think she planned to use it to get away right before the ambush begins, but I moved it," Aimee Louise said.

Scott raised his eyebrows. "So, now she's stranded but doesn't know it."

"She's not the type to go hiking through the woods looking for it either," Lela snickered.

"Not at all," Peyton said. "I don't think she's even walking to the county road. She must have a set meeting with a few of her trusted lieutenants."

"What do you think they would do if she didn't show up?" Tom asked.

"She doesn't take kindly to independent thinkers. I think they'd wait for her orders," Peyton said.

"You mentioned honeypot, Aimee Louise," Andy said. "I like the idea of tossing them a tempting lure to divert their attack to a point away from us. Red and I could visit Aunt Jennie and tell her that Peyton and her family left and are traveling north along the interstate frontage road. I would think that would entice Connie to send at least part of her team to chase down the travelers."

"We could also ask Myrtle, Aunt Jennie, and Uncle Leo to come to lunch or a post-wedding reception here," Rosalie said.

"And the dogs," Aimee Louise added.

"Baby shower." Peyton smiled as Charo blushed.

Scott nodded. "Is your utility vehicle close, Aimee Louise? If Leo and Jennie walk to the Smith barn, you could pick them up to shorten the amount of time they're in between the two farms. I'm sure the dogs will follow along."

Aimee Louise rose, but Stuart said, "Wait. I'll go with you. So, Andy and Red will drop the false information and invite the Websters' here. Aimee Louise and I will meet them at the Smith barn with the utility vehicle. David, could you and Dad plan the defense with everyone else?"

"Will do." David rose. "Let's take the children inside the farmhouse and plan there."

* * *

After they picked up their backpacks, Andy set the pace for their run to the Websters'. When they arrived at the Websters' driveway, Andy said, "You do the talking, honey."

"Why, certainly, sweetheart; whatever you say." Rosalie snickered as she fluttered her eyelashes.

Andy felt his cheeks warm. "I did ask for that one, didn't I?"

Rosalie snort-laughed. "You're fun."

When they went inside, Jennie said, "Well this is a surprise, but it's nice to see you. Can you stay for lunch?"

"We actually came to invite you, Myrtle, and Uncle Leo to a baby shower, and Angel said the dogs are invited too."

"That's exciting," Myrtle said. "I roasted a chicken and baked bread earlier this morning."

"That sounds great, and I made cookies last night," Jennie said. "I have a stash of baby gifts that I bought for showers that were canceled after the power crashed. We can take them too."

"Pack a few things, so you can make a day of it. I think Blanche is planning some games for the kids."

"That will be fun to watch," Jennie said as she hurried to her room.

"It's good to see Jennie happy again," Myrtle said quietly. "She didn't mind at all when my cranky daughter-in-law left, but she misses the kids almost as much as I do."

"Thanks for inviting us," Jennie called out from her bedroom, and Andy smiled and winked at Rosalie.

We couldn't have scripted this any better.

Rosalie answered in her loud voice. "We tried to plan it a little earlier before Peyton, David, and Brandon left, but it didn't work out."

Connie strolled into the kitchen. "Did I hear you say that Peyton left? That's too bad. I never had the chance to meet her and her family. How long ago was that?"

"Not that long ago; maybe an hour or so. Her husband has family in north Georgia. They're hiking on the frontage road along the interstate because it's the quickest way there. Why don't you come to the baby shower too?"

When Connie smiled, Andy almost shuddered.

"That is so sweet of you," Connie said, "but it sounds like a family thing, and I wouldn't want to barge in; besides, it's about time for my walk. I swear if I miss one walk, I put on fifteen pounds."

Andy raised his eyebrows at Rosalie's wicked smile.

"You would have been more than welcome, but I understand," Rosalie said. "I've heard a lot of older women say the same thing."

"Well." Connie puffed up her chest. "I'll be going."

After she stomped out of the house, Rosalie said, "Pack fast, Myrtle. We're on a tight timetable."

"You got it, Boss Lady." Myrtle chuckled as she hurried to pack.

Andy hugged Rosalie then kissed her. "You are awesome, Boss Lady. I'll grab Uncle Leo."

Within ten minutes, everyone was ready to go. Andy carried the large duffle bag of presents for the baby and more presents for all the children. Jennie, Myrtle, and Leo slid on their backpacks, and Jennie carried her rifle.

"We'll go by way of the Smith barn," Andy said.

"Just a second; I forgot something." Leo hurried to his office and returned with his handheld radio then picked up his shotgun and extra shells. "Now, I'm ready."

Andy led the way; Leo walked behind him with Holly at his side. Rosalie took her position behind Myrtle and Jennie while she carried the chicken, bread, and cookies. The farm dogs stayed close to her. When they reached the Smith barn, Aimee Louise and Stuart were waiting for them.

"Is this for us?" Myrtle asked when she saw the utility vehicle.

"Climb in," Stuart said.

After Jennie and Myrtle were seated in the back seat, and Leo, in the front, Leo said, "Here, Red. You take my seat."

"No, sir. I'm on patrol duty. I will let you hold the cookies and bread though. Call Holly. She might fit right at your feet."

After Holly jumped up with Leo, Jennie poked Leo's back. "Don't you go snooping for those cookies, old man."

Leo chuckled. "Not making any promises."

"Andy, put the duffle bag between my feet," Myrtle said.

Aimee Louise checked her passengers. "Everybody ready?"

"All set," Jennie said.

"No talking on the way," Rosalie announced in her command voice, and the passengers nodded.

Aimee Louise started the engine and followed Stuart to the Newtons' farm while Rosalie, the farm dogs, and Andy trailed along behind.

When they reached the Newtons' farm, Scott was waiting for them in the side yard.

"Here we are," Rosalie said. "I'll take the farm dogs to the barn to see what they think." Rosalie trotted to the barn, and Holly and the farm dogs followed her.

As Leo climbed out of the vehicle, he chuckled. "If this was an abduction, it was the smoothest and most enjoyable operation I've ever seen."

"We aim to please." Scott grinned. "We'll give you a rundown of events after you eat."

"Are we still having a baby shower?" Jennie asked.

"Of course," Aimee Louise said, and Stuart and Scott chuckled.

"Sandra has plans for everyone to be comfortable," Scott said as Sandra came outside.

"That's right. Jennie, you and Leo are upstairs in the boys bedroom, and Myrtle has a bed in the girls bedroom," Sandra said.

"Now, I want you to know that I had nothing to do with this next part. Blanche and the boys set up a tent in the living room for the boys' private quarters."

Leo chuckled. "Sounds like they've been waiting for the chance to sleep in a tent."

"They obviously have," Sandra snickered. "I thought we'd do lunch buffet style and let everyone fix their own plates with the adults eating in shifts. We're taking turns with guard duty. Scott will explain all that to you after you put your things away and eat."

Rosalie returned. "The dogs were ready to relax. They flopped down in a stall where it's cool."

Rosalie and Sandra helped carry bags to the house.

CHAPTER FIFTEEN

After everyone else went inside, Stuart, Andy, and Scott stood in the shade while Aimee Louise parked the utility vehicle in the trees near the equipment shed.

"How did it go, Andy?" Stuart asked.

"I was brilliant, and it went perfectly. Connie took the bait."

"Handed it off to Red, didn't you?" Scott asked.

"Sure did. I'm no dummy." The three men chuckled.

"Aimee Louise hasn't said anything, but I think she's planning to steal another truck. I'm going along," Stuart said.

"If she wants to set one or two on fire, let me know," Andy said.

"That's actually not a bad idea," Scott said. "A bit harebrained, but not bad."

After Aimee Louise joined them, they strolled to the house.

She slipped her arm through Stuart's. "Andy's idea has possibilities."

He moaned. "I knew you heard as soon as Andy said it."

"Do you think Connie will wait for the men to return from chasing Peyton?" Aimee Louise asked.

"I would think they wouldn't return until they found her. From everything I've heard, Connie's not inclined to forgive failure, but she might send her best and most trusted team."

When they went inside, Blanche greeted them in the kitchen. "Grab a plate. We set up a buffet on the kitchen table, and the party's in the living room, but we're not encroaching on the boys' private quarters. Cal's on guard in our bedroom, but I fixed him a plate, and Henry and Brandon are eating with him. Henry told me that cowboys guard their families."

When Aimee Louise put her hand over her heart and patted, Stuart hugged her. "I know, sweetheart. We've got us a great cowboy."

Aimee Louise and Stuart hurried to Cal's room. "Hey there, Henry," Stuart said.

"Dad and Mama!" Henry ran to them, and they stooped to hug him. Brody tried to wiggle in with Henry until Tracker attacked him then they rolled on the floor in a puppy wrestling match.

"Family hug." Henry giggled.

"So what have you been doing?" Stuart asked.

"Me and Brandon are eating our grub and keeping Mr. Cal company." Henry bent down to play with Brody.

"Cowgirl Blanche put us on watch duty," Cal said. "We're taking first shift because the party was too noisy."

"We might volunteer for second shift too." Brandon rolled a ball for Tracker.

"We'll grab our grub then check out the party. We'll have to stay a while because it's polite, but I might check on you in a bit," Stuart said.

"We wouldn't mind if you sneaked us a cookie or three." Cal smiled, and the two boys nodded vigorously.

Stuart grabbed a handful of cookies then hurried to Cal's room.

"Compliments of management." Stuart winked at Cal while the boys cheered then returned to the kitchen. Aimee Louise handed him the plate she had served for him, and they strolled together to the party.

After Stuart and Aimee Louise ate and listened to the chatter and the squeals, they took their dishes to the kitchen, and Scott, Rosalie, and Andy followed them.

"Uncle Leo asked for a favor," Rosalie said.

"He's worried about his ham equipment. He wanted to know if we could grab it quickly without the bad guys catching us. What do you think?" Andy asked.

"I'm very familiar with Uncle Leo's equipment," Aimee Louise said. "I could disconnect it and box up everything he will need except the antenna in just a minute or two."

"You'd have to be quick," Scott said.

Stuart frowned. "That's right; we have no idea when the attack will begin."

"Is the utility vehicle faster than running?" Andy asked.

Rosalie glanced at Aimee Louise. "Who is running?"

Stuart crossed his arms. "All four of us."

"We should take the vehicle. Rosalie, give it a name or number," Aimee Louise said.

"Number 48-4." Rosalie said.

"Good, I can remember that: Number 48, four-seater. We'll leave 48-4 at the Smith barn, so we'll be more flexible at Uncle Leo's farm to scatter then meet up at the Smith barn if something happens. Andy and I can go inside and box up the radio," Aimee Louise said.

"Be safe," Scott said.

Stuart nodded. "Rosalie and I will stay outside to watch for the beginnings of an attack."

"What if Connie's there?" Andy asked.

"You'll entertain her while I disconnect and pack the radio," Aimee Louise said.

"Okay if I pray that she'd not there?" Andy mumbled.

"I would," Stuart said.

"Ask Uncle Leo what he wants us to use to transport the radio equipment, and I'll get 48-4." Aimee Louise ran out to the equipment shed.

"I'll talk to Uncle Leo," Andy said.

"Dad, if we don't come back soon, don't send anyone for us. You'll be able to hear gunfire from the Websters' on the front porch," Stuart said.

"Aimee Louise isn't foolhardy, and she seemed confident; you'll be back." Scott grabbed a cookie and his rifle and stood at the kitchen window.

Stuart and Rosalie were waiting with the four backpacks and their rifles when Andy returned to the kitchen.

"Uncle Leo said he has an empty box that he's kept in the radio room closet specifically for the radio equipment in case they had to evacuate."

When they went outside, Aimee Louise had moved the utility vehicle to the side of the house. After they arrived at the Smith farm, Rosalie said, "I'd really like to see how many men are chasing after Peyton on the interstate, but getting Uncle Leo's equipment before an attack is more important."

Stuart rolled his eyes.

* * *

When they arrived at the Webster farmhouse, Aimee Louise and Andy ran into the house. Aimee Louise rushed to the radio room, and Andy called out, "Connie?"

After she began disassembling the radio equipment, he called out again then as she boxed up the equipment, he rushed into the radio room. "I searched the house. She's not here."

"Not good." Aimee Louise lifted the heavy box. "All packed up. Let's go."

The two of them raced to the woods, and Stuart and Rosalie joined them.

"Connie's not there." Aimee Louise said.

"I'll take the box, Angel, so you can pick us up," Andy said.

Aimee Louise and Rosalie disappeared into the woods.

* * *

Stuart followed Andy who speed-walked with the heavy box. Before they were halfway to the Smith property, Stuart said, "There's a wide spot in the path just ahead where Aimee Louise can turn 48-4 around. Let's stop there."

"Sounds good." Andy grunted as he tried to shift the weight. "This box is heavy."

When they reached the widened portion of the path, Aimee Louise and Rosalie were waiting for them, and 48-4 was pointed toward the Newtons' farm.

Andy lowered the box as gently as he could on the floor then collapsed in his seat. After Rosalie jumped into the back seat with Andy, Stuart sat next to Aimee Louise.

"Hang on," Aimee Louise said as she sped away.

Aimee Louise dropped off Andy at the back door to carry the heavy box inside. After she parked, they heard three shots from the south of the property as they ran to the house.

When Stuart slammed the door after they were inside, Scott said, "Glad you're here. Blanche has taken all the children to the closet under the stairs for story time. We have all the windows covered. Dead Eye, pick your position. If someone is there, we all have alternate positions if you show up. Stuart, replace Charo upstairs; we want her with Blanche and the children, and Andy, relieve Cal. He needs a break. Angel, I expect you to find your own assignment, and I'll help you anyway you like."

While the upstairs shooters returned fire, Rosalie dashed up the stairs, and Andy hurried to Cal's bedroom.

Aimee Louise said, "I need to check their strengths and weaknesses, so we can stop them."

"I'll go with you, but I can't run," Scott said.

"Give me Stuart, Rosalie, and Andy."

Scott's face reddened. "We don't want Charo in the line of fire; Cal needs a break; I can't give up a shooter like Red."

Aimee Louise smiled, and Stuart said quietly from the corner, "Tell me about his cloud, honey."

"It reminds me of Pops'. It's strong, intense, and protective," she said.

Scott stared at his son. "I thought you'd left, Stuart."

"I knew my Angel had something in mind. I was waiting," Stuart said.

Scott sighed. "You're right, and I have to tell you that I appreciate your strong leadership; so, now that I've got my panic attack out of the way, I can focus on our defense and let you manage your offense. Charo is a priority; I'll replace her. Don't tell Cal I said he needed a break. He's always up for a good fight, just like the rest of us."

"I'll get Andy and Red," Stuart said. "Don't leave without us, sweetheart."

"I won't."

I believe her. Stuart ran to Cal's room then upstairs and returned with Andy and Rosalie.

"What's your plan, Angel?" Stuart asked.

"I'll run to 48-4 while Andy runs to the equipment shed for the flamethrowers. We'll meet you in front of the house."

"Red and I will cover you. Dad, will you tell the defense team what our plan is? Shoot south to keep them pinned down, but we don't want anyone shooting north," Stuart said, and Scott nodded.

"Give me a minute to run back upstairs then I'll give the signal to start shooting." Rosalie dashed to the stairs while Stuart took his position at the kitchen window.

"Listen up." Scott shouted from the bottom of the stairs. "Everybody keep shooting south when Rosalie gives the signal. Repeat: South only. North shooters: Hold your fire; Do not shoot to the north. Hold your fire and watch for Angel and Andy in the front yard."

"Ready," Rosalie shouted, and Stuart said a silent prayer as the shooting began.

* * *

"I'll go first," Aimee Louise said. "After I'm drawing fire, you go."

"Got it," Andy said.

Aimee Louise zig-zagged to the equipment shed where she had parked 48-4. When she was midway to the shed, Andy dashed after her in a similar zig-zag pattern.

Aimee Louise started up 48-4 as Andy jumped into the back seat with the flame throwing equipment. Aimee Louise drove into the trees and away from the shed, and when the gunfire from the south slowed then stopped, she turned toward the house and stomped on the accelerator then stopped at the front of the house.

Stuart and Rosalie ran out the front door and hopped into 48-4; Aimee Louise accelerated to the path to the Smith barn. When she reached the barn, Aimee Louise drove along the curving driveway until 48-4 was hidden from the burned-out homestead. After she parked in the trees near the Webster property, she said, "I'll leave the key behind the driver's side back tire, so that any one of us can drive 48-4."

"What's our next step to disrupt their operation and turn their focus away from attacking the farm?" Stuart asked.

"We'll get close enough to see where the guards are for the trucks; I expect only one or two men," Aimee Louise said. "Andy will set fire to two trucks, so they'll have one to use for a getaway. We'll take the three that are parked the farthest west. Andy will drive one, and I'll drive the other; Stuart, the third truck is yours and Rosalie's. Rosalie, you're our shooter."

"Always," Rosalie said. "Stuart, I'll back up Angel until you have a truck. You keep Andy safe."

"What are we going to do with all those trucks? Stuart asked. "Never mind; sorry I asked. Okay, let's go. Andy, feel free to ditch the flamethrower if we need to leave fast."

As they strode to the south, Aimee Louise slowed her pace to walk next to Andy and spoke in a quiet voice. "After you set fire to the two trucks, run toward the trucks that you and I are taking. If I run away from the trucks, follow me. I'll move one truck away from the group then return to the second truck and wait for you."

Andy gulped. "Okay."

Aimee Louise ran past Rosalie and Stuart then slowed to a fast walk. When Aimee Louise stopped to listen, the other three stopped then Stuart crept close to Aimee Louise and tapped her arm before he pointed at his eyes with two fingers. She nodded, and he crept closer to scan the road.

Aimee Louise, Rosalie, and Andy crouched to wait for Stuart. When he returned, he held up one finger then motioned for Andy to follow him. After they were out of sight, Aimee Louise motioned for Rosalie to follow her, and they moved closer to the road.

When a truck burst into flames, the guard shouted, and two men ran from the Websters' field toward the road as the second truck flamed up. The men backed away from the two burning trucks while the canvas on the third truck smoldered. The guard ran to the third truck and moved it east and away from the burning trucks, and the other two men raced to the third truck and cut away the scorched canvas then jumped into the back of the truck as the driver honked the horn then drove the truck farther from the burning trucks and honked again.

Aimee Louise and Rosalie raced to the farthest truck, and Rosalie jumped into the passenger's seat while Aimee Louise snatched up the ignition key from the driver's seat then started the engine. She drove a hundred yards down the road then the two young women jumped out of the truck and raced back to the second truck. Aimee Louise climbed into the driver's seat and started the engine while Rosalie sprinted toward Stuart and the third truck.

When Andy jumped into the passenger's seat with his flame throwing equipment, he said, "Go. Red and Stuart have the third truck."

Aimee Louise accelerated then slowed when she reached the first truck. "Head to the Websters' driveway, but go slow enough that we can catch up with you."

After Andy jumped out and reached to open the driver's side door of the first truck, both of them instinctively cringed and ducked at the sound of an explosion behind them.

"Go," she shouted, and he jumped into the driver's seat and took off.

Aimee Louise watched the third truck speed toward her before she accelerated. Andy waved as she passed him then he closed the gap between his truck and hers when Stuart and Rosalie caught up with him.

After Aimee Louise turned right at the county line road, she slowed, and the other two stayed behind her. She pulled over onto the shoulder and parked before she reached the right turn to the state road. After Aimee Louise leapt out of her truck and raced to the state road, Rosalie caught up with her. When they were within sight of the roadblock, Rosalie said, "Stuart was having a fit."

"Not a surprise." Aimee Louise scanned the road ahead. "I still don't see anyone there. Tell him to go onto the shoulder on the right past the roadblock, and Andy and I will follow. Park in the Smith driveway where we can't be seen from the road."

"Got it."

They raced back to the trucks then after Rosalie jumped in with Stuart, he roared past Aimee Louise, and Rosalie waved.

Aimee Louise motioned for Andy to follow Stuart, and when he passed her, she accelerated to keep up with him. The three trucks sped to the roadblock and drove along the shoulder until they cleared it. When they came close to the Websters' property, two men ran from the field to the state road and aimed their pistols and shot at the first truck. Angel held her breath until both of them dropped alongside the road. A third man ran toward the trucks and raised his pistol to shoot at Andy's truck, but a shot rang out, and he collapsed on the road before he could pull the trigger.

Aimee Louise shook her head. *Bad guys should never point guns at Dead Eye Red's husband.*

Aimee Louise slowed her truck as Stuart then Andy pulled into the Smith driveway. The three trucks weaved their way across the property as they followed the winding driveway. When they were well-hidden from both the road and the homestead, all three drivers parked and turned off their engines. Andy and Aimee Louise hopped out of their trucks, and Rosalie raced to Andy and threw her arms around his waist with such force that she almost knocked him over. Stuart reached Aimee Louise and grabbed her into a tight hug.

"You scared me, but I was there," he whispered. "Thank you."

The sound of another explosion ripped through the air.

"We need to get back to the house," Stuart nuzzled Aimee Louise's neck then kissed her ear.

"Look in the back of your truck, Angel," Andy said as he dropped the canvas flap back on his truck. "I have ammunition and gas cans."

Andy and Red hurried to check Stuart's truck while Stuart and Aimee Louise strode to the back of her truck.

Stuart chuckled. "Looks like you stole the chuck wagon, Angel. Cookie Blanche will be proud of you. Canned ham, bags of potatoes, onions, and cases of canned vegetables and fruit."

Rosalie and Andy rushed to join them as Aimee Louise said, "We also have large jugs of bottled water, bags of beans, and coffee."

"Jackpot." Stuart grinned.

"Stuart, your truck has tents, cots, ammo, and gas cans. Wonder what was in the rest of them? They'd be self-sufficient with these three trucks," Andy said.

"The other three might have been transportation for their men," Stuart said. "Let's get back to the house. Grab your ignition keys; we'll leave them in 48-4. You lead, Andy."

Andy grabbed his flame thrower out of Aimee Louise's truck. "Do we just leave everything here?" he asked.

"We'll pick up the supplies after we're sure the attack is over," Stuart said.

When they reached the utility vehicle, Stuart said, "I'd like to drive."

Aimee Louise nodded. He started the ignition, and when everyone climbed on board, he headed toward their farm and frowned at the sound of continuing gunfire.

As Stuart drove toward the Smith barn, Rosalie said, "I think we've got some weather headed our way. We may have a big storm this evening. I don't like the looks of those clouds to the west. Do you suppose Uncle Leo will be able to set up his radio?"

"It wouldn't have much of a range without an antenna. I wonder if Dad has a small one that we could set up inside near a window," Aimee Louise said.

"We'll ask him, which will mean another attic trip," Stuart said.

"Do you think any of the men will head toward the farmhouse?" Rosalie asked.

"Sounds like a few stayed behind, and we'll have to watch for them, but I think most of them rushed to the truck before it headed to the interstate," Andy said. "All the supplies and ammo they'd have is what they carried with them and whatever might be in that truck. Some of them may think they can catch up with Peyton and her family and take their food and ammunition."

Rosalie tittered. "I still worry about Peyton and her family on the road."

Stuart grinned. "I agree, Rosalie. I'll be glad when Andy tells us that they turned back."

"Those are jokes?" Aimee Louise asked.

"Yes, honey, bad jokes to relieve stress," Stuart said.

Aimee Louise examined her companions' clouds. "Interesting. It seems to work."

Andy chuckled. "You don't have a chance, do you, Stuart?"

"Nope."

Aimee Louise gazed at Stuart's cloud. *Now, why would that make him happy? I'll ask him later.*

When they reached the house, Rosalie said, "Drop us off here; we need to talk to Uncle Leo and Papa Scott."

Rosalie and Aimee Louise dashed to the back door while Stuart and Andy took 48-4 and the flamethrower to the equipment shed.

When they went inside, Sandra said, "After the first explosion, men who had been shooting shouted for everyone to run to the trucks. Since the second explosion, there has been some gunfire from the south, but it seem to be slowing."

Rosalie smiled. "That's good news. Stuart and Andy will be in after they put away the equipment. We need to talk to Uncle Leo and Papa Scott."

While Rosalie looked for Leo, Scott rushed to the kitchen.

"Dad, do you have a radio antenna?" Aimee Louise asked. "Rosalie wants to check the weather."

"I noticed it was a little dark to the west too. I don't think I have anything we could use as an antenna in the barn or equipment shed, but we could look," he said.

"If we do, it would be in the attic," Sandra said as Stuart and Andy came inside.

"I knew it," Stuart grumbled. "Come on, Andy, you can help me look, but Dad, we still need to keep up our defenses. I'm not convinced that everyone made it to their last truck."

"Before you two climb up into the attic, can you give us a quick recap of what you did?" Scott asked.

"We stole three trucks and burned up two; we left one truck for the bad guys to use for their getaway," Stuart said.

"Wow. I did ask for a recap; I can't wait to hear the full story," Scott said.

"You two look flushed," Sandra said. "How about some water?"

"Sounds good, but we'll look for the antenna first, Mom," Stuart said. "Rosalie is worried about the weather."

While Stuart and Andy were in the attic, Henry and Brody came to the kitchen, and Aimee Louise hugged Henry.

"Where's Dad?" he asked. "I missed you."

"He and Uncle Andy are in the attic looking for an antenna. I missed you too."

Henry returned her hug; after he and Brody scampered back to the living room, Aimee Louise joined Rosalie and Leo in Cal's bedroom.

"Angel, I was just telling Red that I don't have any antenna wire with me, so if Scott's antenna doesn't include any wire, we might be better off to go back to my house to set up the radio. You and I can have it operational again in less than five minutes," Leo said.

"We're concerned there might be a few strays that didn't get the memo to jump onto the truck before it left," Rosalie said.

"Might be easier to defend our house from a few men before they take over the house, though," Cal said.

Rosalie frowned. "Maybe, but we'll check with Stuart. We'll have to wait to see what he and Andy find, and what Stuart thinks. I don't think they'll be long."

"If it's like our attic, it might take them a while. Jennie's got a regular department store in ours." Leo chuckled.

Henry tapped on the door, "Excuse me, Mama, but Brandon's worried. Would you come talk to him?"

"Certainly." Aimee Louise took Henry's hand, and he led her to the living room.

Brandon stood at the window. *Worried cloud.*

"What's wrong, Brandon?" Aimee Louise asked.

"Fire Dog ran to the short cut; we think he wanted to go home. Holly followed him, and Tracker followed Holly. I was afraid

Tracker would get lost because he wouldn't know the way back, but Mama ran to find him."

"Did your mama take her rifle?" Aimee Louise asked.

"No, she didn't have it with her in here. We was just talking then we saw Tracker run past the house and not come back. She went out the front door, but I don't see her. She left right after Uncle Stuart drove past the front of the house."

"I can catch up with them," Aimee Louise said.

"Yes, Mama runs fast," Henry said, and Brandon sniffled and nodded.

"Tell your dad where I went, Henry, but I'll probably be back before he is finished in the attic."

Aimee Louise grabbed her backpack and tightened her belt with her holster before she ran out the front door then raced to the path while occasional shots from the south continued. When she reached the Smith barn, she paused to listen. A squirrel jumped from one tree to another, but she didn't hear anything else other than the sound of the occasional gunfire. *Peyton and the dogs got more of a head start than I expected.*

She ran then paused to listen on her way to the Websters' farm in case Tracker veered from the path to traipse through the woods. As she approached the Websters' driveway, she heard a woman's voice and crept closer. *Connie.*

Connie was outside the house near the trees along the driveway with her back to Aimee Louise, and Peyton faced Connie. *Peyton must have found Tracker in the barn.*

Aimee Louise crept closer. *Connie is pointing a gun at Peyton.*

"So, Ms. High and Mighty," Connie said, "you probably knew I was looking for you. It was very accommodating of you to come see me. I should have known you'd never leave your precious friends."

When Connie raised her voice, it cracked, and her hand shook. "You made me send my best men to chase a ghost."

She lowered her voice to a hiss. "You're the one who destroyed all my trucks and chased off most of my men, aren't you?"

Connie's maniacal laugh at the sound of a distant shot that came from the direction of the Newton farm sent chills down the back of Aimee Louise's neck. "They didn't all abandon me though. I suppose you stole my precious four-wheeler too. You're the only piece of dirt standing between me and my new operation at my headquarters with my lovely private office that I deserve. Do you hear me? I deserve it. You must be proud of yourself, but you know what they say about pride going down in a fall? You're going down, my girl."

Aimee Louise stepped closer and pulled out her pistol from her holster, and Peyton's eyes widened.

"About time you were afraid, you stupid wench." Connie snorted. "I thought you FBI creeps were supposed to be impervious to fear." Connie cackled.

"I'm right behind you, and I have a gun pointed at your back," Aimee Louise said. "Put your gun on the ground."

Connie didn't flinch or turn. "That's a laugh, Angel. I know everything about you, and here's a news flash for you: you're terrible at bluffing. You don't even carry a gun."

Connie aimed her pistol at Peyton, and Aimee Louise aimed her gun at Connie, but before Aimee Louise pulled the trigger, a shot rang out, and Connie dropped to the ground.

"Thanks, honey." Aimee Louise holstered her pistol as Peyton ran to Connie and kicked away the pistol before she checked Connie.

"Dead," Peyton said. "Clean shot to the temple."

Stuart raced from the trees to Aimee Louise, and she clutched him in relief as he wrapped his arms around her.

"How did you know it was me?" He asked as he stroked her hair and kissed her forehead.

"I knew you'd be here as soon as you could. You certainly were quiet when you moved through the woods. I didn't hear you."

"But you would have shot Connie if I hadn't gotten here in time," he said.

"Of course."

Peyton stepped over Connie's body. "I hate that she got the drop on me; I ran out without my rifle because I was so focused on Tracker. Dang rookie mistake. How did you know where I was, Angel?"

"Henry and Brandon told me you'd gone after Tracker," she said. "I knew Fire Dog and Holly would head home."

"And Henry told me his mama went to look for Tracker and you, Peyton," Stuart said. "We've got some pretty sharp boys."

Tracker scampered to Peyton, and she picked him up then they headed to the Newtons' farmhouse with Holly and Fire Dog following them.

On the way back, Peyton asked, "Would it be okay if we took a break at the Smith barn?"

When they were inside the barn, the dogs flopped down on the cool dirt floor, and Aimee Louise handed Peyton a canteen with water.

Peyton exhaled then leaned against a stall and took a long sip. "Thanks. Connie told me she knew I was at the Newtons' because her men were watching when we moved to the Mitchells'. She sent a team for me, but we were gone. She knew we had to have gone to the Newtons'. Her men stopped Myrtle and her family when they were on their way to Jennie's and asked where they were headed. When Myrtle told them she was going to her friend Jennie's, Connie realized that would be the perfect 'in' for her to find out what was going on. Evidently, Myrtle and Jennie talked about the Newton farm people a lot."

Stuart shook his head. "So much for not telling our business to strangers."

Peyton took another long drink then said, "No kidding; I'm ready now; thanks for the water."

As they headed out of the barn, Aimee Louise asked, "Do you think it's safe to take Uncle Leo and Aunt Jennie back home? Uncle Leo would be happy to have his radio back."

"I'll be happy to see Jennie and Myrtle out of the house," Peyton said.

"Mom might agree with you there, but we'll have to send shooters to accompany them," Stuart said as more shots were exchanged at the Newton farmhouse.

"I'll volunteer. What about the Mitchells?" Peyton asked.

Stuart snorted. "I suspect Mom won't have to twist Lela's arm too much to convince her to stay. If we can chase away the last few thugs, and if the Cabello and Mitchell houses are not in bad shape, they might be able to move back, but it's a little early to decide."

"By the way, Stuart, I've never known anyone before who could be so quiet that Angel didn't hear them. You are my hero in more ways than one." Peyton smiled as Stuart's face reddened.

After they returned to the farmhouse, they went inside through the front door. Peyton gave Tracker to Brandon, and Stuart and Aimee Louise hugged Henry before they joined Scott in the kitchen while he maintained his position at the window.

Stuart wrapped an arm around Aimee Louise and held her. "Connie's dead, Dad."

"Good." Scott didn't change his focus as he scanned the yard. "The gunfire from the south has slowed, but we're staying on alert."

Aimee Louise leaned the side of her face against Stuart's chest and wrapped her arms around him then relaxed as she listened to his heart.

"We can finally begin our honeymoon, sweetheart," he said.

Aimee Louise gazed at his cloud. "Of course."

ACKNOWLEDGMENTS

Huge thanks to my husband for his patience, support, talented technical expertise, and guidance, and to my editor for her encouragement and eagle eye for a stray comma.

DANGER IN THE FIELD is Book 4 in the exciting GRID DOWN SURVIVAL Series.

Next to read: DANGER ON THE FARM, Book 5

Major's farm is no longer safe after all the neighbors flee from the vicious waves of attacks.

Major learns organized marauders are moving north toward the farm and leaving devastation behind them; time is not on his side. Major must act fast, or the family dies.

Judith's motto: *You keep reading; I'll keep writing!*

ABOUT THE AUTHOR

Judith A. Barrett is an award-winning author of thriller, mystery, crime, and survival novels with action and adventure to spark the reader's imagination. Her unusual main characters are brilliant, talented, and down-to-earth folks who solve difficult cases and stop killers. Her novels take place in small towns and rural areas in the southern states of the US.

Judith lives in rural Georgia on a small farm with her husband, dogs, and chickens. When she's not busy writing, Judith is busy with farm chores, walking with her husband and dogs, or watching the beautiful sunsets from her porch.

Website   www.judithabarrett.com

Newsletter   *Subscribe* to her eNewsletter via her Website

Let's keep in touch!